HOME
to
CEDAR
BRANCH

HOME
to
CEDAR BRANCH

BRENDA BEVAN REMMES

LAKE UNION
PUBLISHING

Text copyright © 2016 Brenda Bevan Remmes
All rights reserved.

Published by Lake Union Publishing, Seattle

www.apub.com

Amazon, the Amazon logo, and Lake Union Publishing are trademarks of Amazon.com, Inc., or its affiliates.

ISBN-13: 9781503953000
ISBN-10: 1503953009

Cover design by Laura Klynstra

Printed in the United States of America

My sister once told me that my writing was fluid. She paused and then added, "But so is diarrhea. You need more roughage." This book is dedicated to her memory.

Megan Anne Bevan

1958–2004

CHAPTER ONE
March 18, 1994

Katy never heard the little telltale creaks above. She never saw a shadow. If she had been paying attention to anything other than Doc, she might have preempted the disaster to come.

The outsized magnolia leaves over the medical office nearly hid the three boys from view, but the proximity of the tree made this secret invasion risky. Still, Todd had already discovered from previous climbs that the peril was well worth the payoff. A peek into one of Doc's exam rooms often revealed women in nothing more than a sheet. "You can see everything in there," he told his friends, and they knew he meant the chance to see naked women.

Todd wrapped his arm around the branch above him and pulled himself an additional three feet higher, pushing his white Nikes into the rough bark of the tree to gain traction. His two pals followed behind. Ten-year-old Joey was the youngest by a year and the smallest of the three. His short reach slowed him down. A branch cracked as he propelled himself up with a slight jump. He let out a cry before realizing that he had secure footing in the hook of the next fork of the trunk.

"*Shhhhhhhhh,*" Todd shushed him as he looked down over his shoulder. The enormous tree between the parking lot and the entrance of the clinic had stood for over sixty years. It reached eighty feet up the side of the building. Although an evergreen, the magnolia's wide, glossy leaves littered the ground below year round. The extraordinary large white blossoms appeared in June and made Bixby, North Carolina, famous in the eastern part of the state. Come late spring, the town would be bathed in their sweet fragrance.

The heating unit in the back of the building flipped on and began to hum. All three boys held their breath. Todd slowly began to inch out over the roof to the skylight. At first he saw nothing, but then a woman moved into view below them. She looked vaguely familiar. Katy Devine. She worked at the high school, he thought. She was curvy and cute—younger than his mother, thank goodness. He'd had a terrible premonition that they might stumble on someone's grandmother.

Todd stopped, raised his hand to halt the other two, and waited. The March air was chilly. Todd pulled his knitted Tar Heel ski cap over his ears, glad to have on his parka and gloves. Danny, the third member of the trio, climbed into view and exhaled an appreciative whistle.

Todd glared at his friend. If they got caught, he knew he'd be on bread and water for the rest of his life. His mother would never accept whatever excuse he could concoct. She'd be mortified, and the thought of having to apologize to Aunt Laura and her husband, Doc, made him start to second-guess his plan. But movement had commenced in the skylight below, and the boys stared in heart-stopping anticipation of what might happen.

Dr. Attwuld entered the room, and a rather robust-looking nurse who had not initially been in view left. Katy Devine started to cry. Doc handed her a Kleenex and gently embraced her, at first stroking her shoulders and then lightly kissing her lips. If the lovers had not been otherwise preoccupied, at least one of them would have seen the limb swaying precariously above them. But this was not their first time together, and they had never questioned the sanctity of the exam room.

Todd waved his two friends forward on the magnolia limb. He had pushed himself midway up the branch before he saw Doc unbutton Mrs. Devine's blouse and slip it off her shoulders. She unhooked her brassiere. Todd's eyes widened, and he motioned frantically for the others to move in closer. Danny scrambled as fast as he could to get within sight of the disrobing. Then he gasped. "Holy moly, Doc's taking off his pants."

Todd paled. The caper had just turned disastrous. Naked women? *Yes*. Naked Doc? *No*. His mother would skin him alive.

Joey sensed that he was missing something big and struggled to catch up with his two friends. He inched closer to Danny, and the magnolia limb creaked, but no one below looked up. Joey bounced a few times in an effort to get within viewing distance faster. Doc and Mrs. Devine fell behind the exam table, out of view.

"Move up farther." Danny nudged Todd. "Go on, quick, so we can see."

"I can't." Todd's hands felt glued to the tree as he was seized by a burst of panic. His mind raced for a way out.

"Quick, quick," Joey insisted, fearful that after all his effort he would miss the show.

In unison Joey and Danny struggled to reach the end of the branch, where they got a bird's-eye view of Doc bobbing up and down.

Joey caught his breath. "They're doing the dirty duck dive."

When Doc rolled off Katy, he left exposed a pair of magnificent bosoms. The boys gawked, thunderstruck at the sight. Todd's mood immediately shifted. The boys applauded as they unconsciously bounced one more time in unison. There was a sharp crack and a brief sensation of weightlessness before they felt the limb give way beneath them.

The leafy end of the branch hit the skylight first, raining pieces of glass down on the adulterous pair. They both instinctively rolled toward one another to cover their faces. Todd hit the edge of the roof, tried desperately to grab hold of anything as his gloves skimmed across the broken glass, and then he fell through the opening. He turned upright as he did so, and his leg slammed into the exam table. The wind was knocked out of him when he landed on the floor.

Danny fell forward on the limb, which hadn't completely detached itself from the trunk. There he held on like a monkey, finding himself precariously stranded midway between the floor and the ceiling of the exam room, staring panic stricken at Todd. Joey let out a scream before he jumped clear of the limb onto the roof and, with more agility than he'd ever shown, ran to a different branch stretching over the office and scampered down.

The nurse and the bookkeeper burst through the door. The lab tech, office manager, and receptionist followed. Several patients in different stages of undress peeked out of their rooms at the sound of the commotion. Others, still waiting, got out of their seats and stretched their heads over the reception desk to see what they could.

Doc fumbled with his pants. The nurse focused on Todd, who was struggling to regain his breath and wincing in pain. The office manager squared her shoulders and helped Danny descend to the floor. The lab tech and bookkeeper shuttled the two boys to a different exam room while the office manager called an ambulance and their mothers.

Hurriedly Katy attempted to dress. The nurse, Rosemarie, helped her grab the rest of her clothes, wrapped a sheet around her shoulders, and ushered her into the adjacent bathroom.

Katy shook uncontrollably. Rosemarie's previous temptation to lecture her suddenly turned to pity. She knew more about Katy than Katy suspected. She'd heard the rumors. She'd read the files. She knew there were signs of domestic abuse. Katy seemed small now, frail and vulnerable.

Katy looked down—ashamed, embarrassed. She turned back with frightened eyes that pleaded for help as she struggled to button her blouse. Rosemarie let out a long sigh and shook her head.

"He never was the answer, you know. He won't leave his wife."

Katy said nothing.

"Have you got someplace safe you can go?" she asked.

Katy seemed paralyzed. She shook her head no.

"I promise you this will be all over town in minutes, and you don't want to be in the house when your husband finds out."

Katy nodded and slipped her arms into her coat.

"Are the kids at home?" Rosemarie felt the need to do something to help. She knew as well as Katy did that this could turn deadly within the hour.

"I think so," Katy said, not absolutely sure.

"Your husband in town or on a run?"

"He's headed back from Atlanta," she murmured. She never scheduled her appointments with Doc when Hank was home.

"So you've got a little time?"

"A little."

"Pick up the kids. I'll see if I can find a safe house and call you," Rosemarie said as she slipped Katy out the back door. "Hurry, honey."

Doc was next on Rosemarie's agenda. He had retreated to his office, but Rosemarie had no intentions of letting him hide. She wanted to beat his head against a wall. He'd made a couple of foolish mistakes in the past, but he'd broken every rule in the book this time. She opened the door without knocking and slammed it behind her. "Well, this is a mell of a hess," she said.

"Reschedule the rest of the patients, would you please?" he said, head bowed.

"Reschedule?" she about choked. "You think you'll still have a practice this time tomorrow?"

He looked past her at the wall. "Stupid, stupid, stupid," he muttered.

"And Katy, she's going to get beat to a pulp tonight when her husband gets hold of her. Her kids. Your kids. Your wife! What in God's name were you thinking?"

Doc pinched the bridge of his nose as if to stop a headache or erase the memory. Rosemarie was the only one in the office who would get in his face and confront him, and she was right. They'd been through a lot together and weathered the storms. In many ways their relationship was more honest than the one he had with his wife.

"Get in touch with her, will you?" he asked Rosemarie, imploring her with his eyes to intercede on his behalf. "Find someplace for her until things cool down."

Rosemarie groaned. Why did she jump in to bail him out again and again? She could walk into the hospital in Edenton anytime and get a job, and yet she stayed . . . twenty-five years now. He was a charmer—no doubt about it. Every woman in town thought he was the cat's meow, the Southern gentleman doctor nursing everyone back to health through attention and reassurance. Darn it. Patients paid just to listen to him talk. His voice was hypnotic.

"The boys?" he asked.

"They'll survive. We called the ambulance. They're taking them to the hospital in Edenton. Todd Winslow broke his ankle, I think."

"Lord, Lord." Doc groaned. "Todd?"

Rosemarie nodded. "Call your wife before your sister-in-law does. One of you needs to talk to your kids. They may be in Chapel Hill and Winston-Salem, but I'll bet you a dollar to a donut they'll hear about this mess before nightfall." She wanted to add *and call your lawyer,* but that was a no-brainer. She turned to go see what help she could get for Katy Devine, and then on second thought she added, "Call your lawyer."

❧

Their double-wide sat at the edge of a small, well-kept trailer park just within the town limits. Hank Devine stood in the living room. Savannah's and Dusty's schoolbooks were scattered about on the forest-green shag rug. Pages of homework lay on both the couch and floor in various stages of completion. President Clinton flashed across the TV screen, but Hank couldn't care less.

"Katy!" he screamed. "Where the hell are you?" Slamming doors, he stalked to the bedroom. He grabbed his .357 revolver that he kept in a drawer and pulled out a box of .38 bullets. His shotgun remained in the bunk of his eighteen-wheeler. His brother, Ray, waited outside in the truck. Ray had called Hank on his CB not thirty minutes after everything happened.

"Hank, I hate to be the one to tell you," he said, "but Katy's been caught messing with Doc Attwuld. The whole town knows. Stay vertical, man. I'll be there when you get home."

Hank had kept the speedometer of his rig on eighty-five for the past two hours, driving in from Atlanta after a week on the road. Now he stormed back through the living room. A blinking light on the answering machine caught his attention. He hit the "Play" button.

"Katy, pick up if you're still there. This is Rosemarie. Call me. I've got somewhere you'll be safe. I'll be at the office for another hour."

"Stupid broad," Hank mumbled. "And the sorry bastard doesn't even call her himself."

He tucked a bottle from the liquor cabinet under his arm and headed out the door. Rachel Mayfield was standing on the deck of her trailer. She'd already been alerted that a major drama was unfolding that involved Doc Attwuld and her next-door neighbor. She was cautious around Hank, though. She'd heard the fights and even called the police on two occasions, only to be told in no uncertain terms by Hank to mind her own business. He scared her. Nonetheless, she had seen Katy leave with Savannah and Dusty, and she made a mental note of what time Hank arrived. She saw him take a slug from a fifth. He looked across the porch and waved his gun at her as he stormed toward his truck. She ducked back inside and dialed the sheriff's office.

Pretty much everybody was calling somebody. Even though she was still at the hospital, Todd Winslow's mom felt obligated to alert her sister. She couldn't let Laura go into town without warning and accidentally find out what her husband had done. Laura had been through this before with Doc, but never at the same level of public humiliation. In the past, Doc had been discreet and then acutely remorseful. As far as she knew, Doc had stayed faithful for the past ten years. Laura had threatened to leave him if it happened again. She might actually do it this time.

"Laura, you need to know," she said over the phone while she waited outside the X-ray room. "I'm at the hospital with Todd. He's been injured in a fall."

"Nita!" Laura voiced sincere concern. "Is it serious?"

"A broken bone or two." She paused. "But that's not why I called."

"What?"

"Call Doc right now and insist he comes home. News is popping like hot bacon grease, and you need to hear the story from him first."

Laura took a deep breath and closed her eyes. "Christmas, Anita. What's going on?"

"A woman again. But at the office, and they got caught."

"Damn him."

"No argument from me. Brace yourself, honey. This one will really stir up the town."

"Oh Lord," she whispered.

"And," said Nita, "get a lawyer . . . a really good one."

Chapter Two

Laura poured two ounces of Jack Daniel's and added ice. It wasn't five o'clock yet, but she expected she would need the drink. She walked back through the kitchen and into the den. The spacious room suddenly felt empty. Weariness crept through her bones as if weights were strapped to her arms and legs. He'd done it again.

She'd known all along that he wouldn't be able to keep his promises. He had always been a magnet for women and vice versa. His boyish, aw-shucks demeanor had seasoned through the years, and he basked in the God-like image people bestowed on him. His regal position as a doctor in a small town proved to be a disaster when it came to his weakness for beautiful women who seemed desperate and helpless. While he leaned heavily on Laura to run the home and raise their two children, the temptation was too great whenever he encountered a damsel in distress. Laura didn't need rescuing. She never had. Their marriage had been founded on something much stronger. She actually loved the ole coot, and despite his flaws, she knew he loved her, too.

The first indiscretion that Laura learned about had surfaced five years after they were married. The banker's third wife became widowed after he suffered a massive heart attack, leaving her young, vulnerable, and very rich. A nasty fight developed over the will as the two former wives and their children leaped into the fray. Doc provided a strong shoulder for the widow to cry on. He worked his magic to keep the bereaved woman's spirits up. Laura had discovered a lot more was up in the process and threatened a divorce. The widow left town. Lawrence begged forgiveness and worked hard to rekindle the trust in their relationship. A diamond ring surrounded by rubies followed. Laura hoped he'd learned his lesson.

Doc met his next fling a few years later: a teacher on an artist exchange program at the community college. Laura never understood why in God's name anyone from Florence, Italy, would ever come to Bixby. But when Doc began to brag about all of the hot Italian blood that ran through his family, as if there was an ounce of Italian anywhere, Laura immediately became suspicious.

The artist broke her arm when she fell from a scaffold, and Doc had treated her injuries. She had painted the side of the town hall with an optical illusion of a tunnel going through the building. Two accidents followed when tourists drove into the brick wall thinking it was a street. Laura was one of the members of the town beautification committee that helped to whitewash over the painting, and she heard the rumors. Not long afterward Doc gave her a new Porsche. The car became a sore reminder of her husband's inability to practice monogamy, and Laura sold the Porsche within the year. She replaced it with an SUV and kept the change.

Their relationship was never quite the same after that, although Doc could still turn on the charm and make her laugh in a way she found completely irresistible. He entertained and cajoled her into believing he was a flawed man who would be nothing without her. The children adored him, and he was a good father. She made a deliberate decision to stay by his side.

She knew that his brief dalliances had nothing to do with love. Some women had husbands who were paramours to the golf course—less humiliating, perhaps, but much more long term and equally costly.

She heard the front door open. "Laura," he called out.

She didn't answer at first, but upon his second attempt she responded. "Back here."

Doc walked into the den, took one look at her face and the drink in hand, and said, "Good idea. Think I'll get one, too." He returned to the kitchen, poured straight vodka into a glass, and added a dash of vermouth. Fishing two olives out of a jar in the refrigerator, he came back to sit across from her. "I take it Anita called?" As soon as Doc had learned that Todd was one of the boys, he knew Anita would be on the phone to Laura within the hour. They shared everything with one another.

"She did."

"What did she tell you?"

"To call a lawyer."

"Have you?"

"Not yet."

"Well, I have," he said. "Harold's on his way over."

"Who is she?" Laura asked with resignation.

"It doesn't matter."

"It matters. Is it someone I know?"

"It's been years, Laura. Honest—years. It was a mistake."

Laura made an effort to swallow the lump in her throat and wiped the back of her hand across her nose.

"Who?" she insisted, fearing a close friend.

"Ohhhhh, Laura." He looked at his wife of twenty-five years, and his voice cracked. "A secretary. The high school secretary. No one, really. I felt sorry for her."

"You felt *sorry* for her?" She looked at him, totally bewildered, her mouth gaping. She rose and walked to the window.

Laura hadn't put on a pound since the day they had met. She had a boyish figure and a short, highlighted bob that was cut so well that no matter what time of day, every hair automatically fell into place. "So tell me what happened before I hear the details from my hairdresser. I need to know whether to hide in my house or simply pack up and leave."

Doc looked at the ceiling and then closed his eyes. "You're going to hate me."

"Probably," she said.

"I got caught with her in the office."

"Anita told me."

He grimaced, knowing this would become the scandal people would revisit for years.

Laura dropped into the leather recliner and covered her eyes. She felt her heart do that funny little irregular blip before it started to race. She took a deep breath in an attempt to control it, even though she knew she couldn't.

"Who caught you?" she asked, as if it mattered.

"Some boys."

"What?"

"They fell in on us."

She stared at him.

"Through the skylight."

She thought of her nephew, Todd. What was he—twelve? They must have been climbing that magnolia tree in back of the building. The office was always full on Fridays. Everyone in town would know by now. "Oh my God. Has it occurred to you what this means for your practice? For your family? The kids?"

His lips twitched. Haley and Brett were both away at college—Haley in her last year of law school, Brett at Wake Forest University. Maybe they'd be spared the news. "We'll manage," he said weakly, only now beginning to think about what he would tell them.

"You're going to get sued. You're going to lose the whole practice . . . and for what? For someone round and soft who walked into your exam room? Lawrence, you . . . are . . . AN IDIOT."

Her stomach knotted, and the bile churned in her throat. The Jack Daniel's that had recently gone down now threatened to resurface. The bathroom off the den was directly behind her. She turned, rushed in, and slammed the door. With the trash can in front of her, Laura dropped her head into her hands, tried to fill her lungs with air and hold it. Then she let the air out slowly. She'd been here before. In a few minutes the wave would crest and then subside. She just had to ride it out. Getting to the top was the hardest. This wasn't a heart attack. Arrhythmia. Tachycardia. Damn it. Why couldn't she control it?

Doc started after her. He knew she had panic attacks. She might be dizzy. He didn't want her to fall. "Laura, are you okay? Can I come in?"

"Hell no. Leave me alone."

He stood outside the bathroom door growing anxious for her. He never intended to hurt her. She was his rock, his anchor in the world. He closed his eyes and wished he could forget this day ever happened.

The door chimes rang.

"Who in God's name is that?" Laura muttered, finding it hard to breathe.

"It's Harold Miller," Doc said, hearing her. He'd called his attorney from the clinic, figuring he'd hear from the police before long and then parents and the newspapers . . . eventually the North Carolina Board of Medical Examiners. He needed Harold's advice. He'd get Harold settled in the living room and come back and check on Laura.

Doc put down his drink, trudged through the kitchen and the formal dining room, and crossed the foyer with the curved stairs leading to the second floor. There were glass panes bordering either side of the entrance, but he didn't bother to look through them. He turned the knob and opened the heavy oak door he had passed through only thirty minutes earlier.

Instead of Harold, a lanky man in jeans and an olive drab army field jacket stood before him. Modest good looks were partially concealed by a black-and-red baseball cap with a prominent "3" on the front. The man raised his arm to chest level.

The first gunshot sounded like a firecracker, and a few seconds elapsed before Laura realized what she had heard. It came from within the house, not outside. She bolted upright and burst through the bathroom door.

The second bullet hit Doc at the exact moment he realized this must be Hank Devine. He fell backward, blood soaking through his shirt. He raised his hand to his chest just long enough to feel the warm, sticky ooze of his life escaping, and then his arm went limp.

Doc lay sprawled on the floor, his right leg caught under his left, his right arm, covered in blood, flung to his side, almost as if he'd been spun around. Laura rushed in and stared straight into the eyes of the murderer before he turned and bolted toward a Ford pickup. The truck ground into second gear and squealed away from the curb.

She scanned the foyer for something to try to stop the bleeding. Doc had thrown his coat and blue cashmere scarf on the coatrack next to the door. She stretched out to grab the scarf and dropped to her knees, immediately pressing it over the hole in his chest.

"Stay with me, damn it," she pleaded. The blood wouldn't stop. She realized that he might actually die. Her mind tried to calculate the shortest distance to a phone to dial 911, and then she saw his eyes meet hers.

"Don't die," she whispered as tears began to pool. She brushed them away. A smear of blood blotted her cheek. What would she do without him? She'd never stopped loving him. "I'm here, right beside you." She didn't know whether he could hear her or not, but she knew deep down she could never leave him. "Hang on, darling."

His lips moved ever so slightly, but she heard nothing. They moved again. What was he trying to say? She leaned closer. His eyes mirrored the crystals from the chandelier above, and for a moment they sparked like little stars as they reflected the light. "Sorry," he whispered, and then his eyes clouded over and the glow disappeared.

CHAPTER THREE

The story hit the front pages and stayed there for days. The scandal consumed the town, with everyone devouring each new tidbit that emerged. It ran on television and radio. The media eulogized Dr. Lawrence Attwuld as a community leader and expressed great empathy for Laura and her children during this tragic period. Tributes to Doc were written in letters to the newspaper. By all accounts, he was a good, albeit flawed man. But then, who was perfect?

Katy Devine, in turn, was described as a desperate victim of domestic abuse. Pregnant and married at sixteen, she'd completed her GED and had worked as the high school secretary for fifteen years. According to her coworkers, she was quiet, dependable, and extremely efficient. She had two teenagers. Her husband was a long-distance truck driver. Those who knew her expressed shock at what they read. She'd never spoken to them of any problems.

When Katy heard that Hank was in jail, she and the kids returned home. A couple of the teachers called with encouragement. "Don't read the papers, Katy," they advised. "At school we know you're the glue that keeps the front office running. Let it blow over."

The memories haunted Katy: the scene in the doctor's office, her flight with her teenage children, Hank's arrest, and the obscene phone calls that wouldn't stop. She requested an unlisted number. Multiple times, she tried to call her brother in Cedar Branch but only got an answering machine.

A week later the doorbell rang. A woman in her midfifties with hair that reflected highlighted streaks between the brown strands greeted her. "Mrs. Devine. I'm Marsha Peabody from the Department of Social Services. May I come in?"

Katy hesitated and then stepped aside for her to enter. Mrs. Peabody chose the sofa over a chair and lowered her ample bottom onto the cushions. She immediately slid one foot out of her tan pump and reached down to rub her right ankle.

"You don't mind, do you? My feet are killing me."

Katy eased herself into a chair opposite her.

"Your children home?"

"In their rooms," Katy said.

"I'll need to talk to them before I leave." Marsha Peabody raised both eyebrows, almost as an apology, and then began to twist one of several chains of beads that cascaded across her full breast. Rings decorated every finger.

"A complaint has been filed," Marsha said softly. "We're required by law to investigate."

"A complaint? Against me?" Katy straightened her back as a nervous quiver surfaced in her voice. "Who filed a complaint against me?"

"I'm not at liberty to say, but I need to ask you a few questions about the abuse and what happened between you, your husband, and the children."

"It's my brother-in-law, Ray, isn't it?" Katy crossed her arms over her chest. "He's threatened to take the kids from me. He came by. I wouldn't let him in the house. He's crazy. Honest to God."

"Are you safe?" Marsha's tone expressed concern.

Katy remembered how quickly things got explosive when Hank and Ray got going. She hesitated but said, "I think I am."

"We could ask for a restraining order if you need it," Marsha said.

"I don't think that's necessary. I told Ray I'd call the police if he came to my house again, and he knows I'm serious."

"Mrs. Devine." Marsha settled back into the couch. "I hate to have to ask you these questions, but I need to know if your husband ever abused your children—emotionally, physically, or sexually."

Katy looked at her, horrified. "No, absolutely not. He wasn't that kind of man."

"Just what kind of man was he, exactly?"

"He . . . well, he worked hard. At one time in my life I loved him. I loved him very much. He tried to make a good living for us. It's just that he came home off the road tired. He drank more and more on the weekends."

"He beat you?"

"He was a mean drunk, Mrs. Peabody. Mean drunks hit people."

"But not the kids?"

"That was different."

"How so?"

"I tried very hard to keep the kids out of our arguments. Most of the time I could."

"Really?"

"I mean, I knew what made him mad. It was the alcohol . . . and Ray. When Ray was here, Ray egged him on." Katy shifted in her chair. She wasn't sure where this was all leading. "Ray had this way of making him think I was always the one at fault—sometimes I was."

Marsha rummaged around in a large canvas bag and pulled out a pad and pen. She began to write down some notes.

Katy looked at her. "Hank never hit the kids. Honest. He did get rough sometimes, but he never hit the kids."

"Rough in what way?"

"He'd holler. Parents holler at their kids. That's not unusual." In a softer tone she added, "He and Dusty went at it a couple of times."

"Over what?"

"You know, father and son things. Who was the boss in the family."

Marsha raised an eyebrow. "Did either of you ever have to go to the emergency room?"

"Once . . . twice," Katy said.

"Broken bones? Internal bleeding?"

"A fractured rib. Some stomach pains. Not Dusty, though."

"That sounds more than just rough to me, but you stayed anyway."

"Mrs. Peabody. Where was I to go? I don't make enough with my salary to support my kids." She paused. "I knew he'd come after me if we left. I was afraid of what he'd do."

"You're sure he never abused your children?"

"Absolutely. I mean, he hit Dusty a couple of times, only a couple, but Dusty had talked back to him. He sort of deserved it."

"Why did you go to Doc Attwuld?"

Katy blanched. She didn't really want to go into the history again. She'd already been through it once with the police. "Hank threw a bowl of hot soup at me. I had some burns on my arm that weren't healing. Doc Attwuld helped me."

Marsha Peabody smiled sympathetically and nodded.

"Really, he did. He cared about me."

Marsha tapped her pen on the pad and snapped it shut. She brightened. "Tell you what. It's lunchtime. How about if you and I go get some hamburgers for the kids. What do they like?"

Katy cocked her head to one side. "Beg your pardon."

"How about hamburgers and fries?"

Katy was confused. She hadn't been out of the house since Doc's murder ten days ago. She didn't know if she could handle the finger-pointing that might occur.

Apparently Marsha had decided they were going out for lunch. She slipped her shoe back on with a grimace and heaved herself up. "My treat. Then, if you don't mind, I'll speak to Savannah and Dusty individually."

"I don't know." Katy hesitated. "People will stare. They'll recognize my picture from the paper."

"Stare?" Marsha said. "Well, God bless them. Let them stare. You can't stay closed up in here the rest of your life. Today's as good as any."

It was past noon, and the high school seniors were taking advantage of their second-semester privilege to go off campus for lunch. Cars looped the drive-through at McDonald's like bees circling a hive. Marsha suggested that Katy grab a table. Katy picked one in the corner with her back to the counter. Marsha planted her hips in line and scowled at a gangly young man who tried to cut in front of her.

In a few minutes, Marsha set a Big Mac, fries, and a chocolate milk shake in front of Katy and took a moment to reposition her jostled necklaces before she slid with some effort into the booth. She flipped the lid on the Styrofoam box, picked up the burger, and took her first bite. She stopped. "Sorry, did you want to say a blessing?"

"No, that's okay." Katy shook her head.

"So tell me a little about your children before I get to meet them," Marsha said, chewing as she spoke.

Katy shrugged her shoulders. "Teenagers—you know. Savannah's a junior, a good girl. She's always tried to keep the peace."

"How so?" Marsha stopped eating only long enough to ask.

"Oh, she could always sense when her father's nerves were frayed, and she tried to intervene when she could. Dusty resents that, but Savannah's the one who cleans up the dishes in the sink, makes the beds, and keeps cold beer in the fridge. If I get held up at work, she'll get dinner started. She's Hank's favorite."

Marsha took a sip of her shake and another bite of her hamburger before she said, "Sounds like the ideal daughter."

The first smile slipped across Katy's face. "She's been a blessing to me. She's got religion now. Started attending the Second Church of Deliverance with some friends from school who wanted her to join their choir. She's quite the believer. Keeps wanting me to go, but . . ."

"But?"

"I don't see where Jesus has done much for us—but I won't stop Savannah. She's got a good group of friends. Several have come by the house this week."

"And your son?"

"Dusty? He's fifteen . . . more quiet and withdrawn. Small for his age. You know it's hard being little when you're a boy." Katy played with the straw and stirred her milk shake, but she didn't take a sip. "Hank's always on his case. Said he had to toughen him up. We argued about Dusty a lot."

"So Dusty got the brunt of his anger?"

Katy eyed Marsha and said firmly, "I got the brunt of Hank's anger."

Marsha nodded. "Uh-huh. So what do you plan to do?" Marsha eyed the uneaten fries on Katy's side of the table. "You gonna eat those, hon?"

"No." Katy shook her head. "Help yourself." She slid the bag of fries over to Marsha. "The school board has asked for my resignation."

"Why? You didn't break any laws," Marsha said.

"They think I'm a poor role model for the students."

"Don't," Marsha said, pulling Katy's fries over to her side of the table.

"Don't what?"

"Resign. You need the job, right?"

"Yes." Katy lowered her voice. "But I had an affair with Doc Attwuld. He's dead, and it's my fault."

"You didn't pull the trigger." Marsha stopped eating and reached across the table to place her hand over Katy's.

"I don't blame his wife for hating me."

"There's not a lot you can do for Mrs. Attwuld at the moment. But you can do something for you and your children. Keep your job, honey. Go back to work."

"You don't think I should resign?"

Marsha waved off her suggestion. "How many teachers and principals have had affairs? They don't have to resign."

The crush of teenagers anxious to get their orders before their lunch break ended became louder. A tall girl broke away from a small brood of friends and inched closer until she stood next to the table.

"Hello, Shaneen." Katy looked up. Shaneen's above-the-knee skirt showed off a stunning pair of bronze legs to midthigh. Katy knew that Shaneen was not a senior and that her clothes didn't meet school standards, but Katy wasn't passing judgment today.

"Miss Devine, you comin' back to work?"

A simple question. A complicated answer. Katy nodded and breathed out a yes without much conviction.

"When?"

"I'm not sure."

"Well . . ." Shaneen stalled a moment and then looked back over her shoulder at her friends. "I gotta go."

"Yeah, see you," Katy said and picked up her uneaten burger.

"Who was that?" Marsha asked.

"One of the students at the high school where I work." Katy smiled. "She's a bit of a troublemaker, but I sort of like her."

"She seems to like you."

Katy shrugged.

"So *when* are you going back?" Marsha asked.

"I don't know."

"When are they expecting you?"

"I don't think they're expecting me at all," Katy said.

"Well, surprise them. You'll be at work on Monday." Marsha pushed herself down to the end of the booth and stood up with some effort.

"Tell you what. I'll get some burgers for the kids, and we'll head back to your house for a bit, and then you and I will get together weekly for a while. How about it?"

Weekly? Katy wasn't real sure, but she didn't argue. This woman had the power to determine whether or not her kids stayed with her. "Sure, okay. That'll work."

❧

On Monday Katy returned to her secretarial desk in the unremarkable front room adjacent to the principal's office. The teaching assistant who had been filling in during her absence jumped for joy, gave Katy a hug, and relinquished the job immediately. Katy answered the phone, handed change to one student in line for a notebook, checked off the school buses as the drivers dropped off the keys, and said good morning to every teacher who walked by. A few were a bit chilly, but most smiled and greeted her warmly. She felt reassured. She was liked. They had missed her.

For fifteen years Katy had kept the wheels greased at Bixby High School. Computers had just begun to find their way into the schools, and she was the first online, picking up the new technology with ease. She knew how to navigate the myriad forms from the central office and how to calm an angry parent better than she could her own husband. No one had ever berated her ability to quietly empathize with the worst offenders. She received far more respect in her job than in her home.

One school bus arrived late, another broke down. Katy stopped the last driver as she walked past her desk to drop off the keys. "Bus number eighty-four between Oakland and Catawba Streets jammed up again," Katy said. "Would you run pick up the kids?"

"Good Lord." The stump of a woman rolled her eyes and swiveled her hips, knocking a stack of attendance sheets off the desk. She grabbed the keys back off the peg and walked out the door.

A parent breezed in to leave a refill of Ritalin for her fourteen-year-old. She appeared surprised to see Katy behind her desk, but chatted for several minutes about exactly how and when to give her son the medication as congestion around Katy's desk peaked.

Shaneen Towers dragged in behind the math teacher, who wore her perpetual frown. Sharp-tongued and disagreeable, the teacher placed her wrinkled hands on her narrow pelvic bones and glared at Shaneen with an icy stare that would have frozen the pavement on a July high noon in any part of eastern North Carolina.

"Well, what do you think of this outfit, Mrs. Devine?" the teacher said, loud enough to stop several students in the hallway running to beat the last bell. She turned and flung out her right arm to highlight the fifteen-year-old girl's ample breasts, unfettered in a braless white halter top. Shaneen shifted her weight, jacked one of her hips higher than the other, and folded her arms across her chest. The flesh under the tight cutoff shorts struggled to escape.

"Shaneen." Katy shook her head and grimaced. She turned to the teacher. "I'll call her mother."

Shaneen dropped into a chair beside the door, poked her chin in the air, and mumbled, "My mama's not home."

"Where is she, hon?" Katy asked.

"Dunno, but she don't care no how."

"Well, your teacher does," Katy said and let her pink fingernails slide through the card file looking for the phone number. "Is she working today at the Red Apple?"

Shaneen puckered her lips and rolled her eyes.

The door to the principal's office opened into Katy's reception area. JD Green skulked out in front of his mother with feigned remorse written across his face. He glanced over at Shaneen, adjusted his posture, and smirked. Shaneen's chin inched higher, and she turned away.

"I don't expect to hear about any more trouble with JD, Mr. Morton," Mrs. Green said as she looked up at the principal. Mrs. Green was big, but Tom Morton was bigger. She grabbed JD's arm with her meaty hand and refocused him away from Shaneen. "You understand, JD?"

The boy squirmed. "Yeah," he sighed.

"What's that you said?"

"Yes, ma'am."

"That's more like it," she said as her son shuffled his big feet in an expensive pair of Nikes. "And you tie them shoes. I didn't pay no hundred dollars for you to be slopping around like that."

"Yes, ma'am." JD leaned down with a swagger and loosely tied his shoes. He turned his head away from his mama and winked at Shaneen. She sneered back. He laid his index finger next to his nose for just a second. Katy caught the exchange.

A bell clamored in the background.

"Go on to your class," Principal Morton said to the boy. "Mrs. Devine will give you a late pass." Then he looked at Katy and added quietly, "When things settle, could I see you in my office?"

"Yes, sir," Katy said, then filled out the pass and called Shaneen's mother.

The late bus arrived. A fresh burst of teenagers scuffled through the hallway in front of the office.

"Glad you're back, Miss Devine," Shaneen said under her breath.

Katy glanced at her. "You're not a senior yet, Shaneen. Stay away from McDonald's at lunch."

Shaneen nodded. "You ain't tellin', are you?"

"Not this time." Katy looked at her and raised an eyebrow, then returned to her paperwork.

The unwelcome change of clothes arrived twenty minutes later with an equally unwelcome mama. "Girl, you can't get yourself dressed proper for school without me? Who you think is going to feed you if I lose my job?" Shaneen's mother slammed a wrinkled grocery bag down in Shaneen's lap.

Shaneen thumbed through the bag of clothes. "Oh, Mama." She grimaced when she saw what was inside.

"You put those clothes on, and I better not have this happen again or I'll bring my housecoat the next time."

"Go on, Shaneen," Katy said. "Go to the girls' room and change. I'll have a late pass for you when you get back." Katy turned to Shaneen's mother. "I'll see she gets to class, Mrs. Towers. You go on back to work."

Katy checked off the teacher's sign-in sheet and recorded the buses that had arrived. In contrast to Shaneen, she had made a point of dressing with modesty today. Her navy-blue knit jumper hung loosely, drawing little attention to her hourglass figure. Her long-sleeved white blouse had a high neckline. She had applied only the smallest touches of makeup: a little lipstick, no eye shadow. Her thick, dark hair was pulled back and held by a large clamp at the base of her neck. Fugitive curls fell loose across her forehead. She appeared inconsequential behind the desk stacked with files and reports that had accumulated in her absence. They would all be properly in place before she left that afternoon.

"You in trouble, Miss Devine?" Shaneen stood in the doorway dressed in the brown bag's change of clothes.

Katy unconsciously pulled a strand of hair away from her face and slipped it behind her ear. "I hope not."

"Papers say your husband killed Doc Attwuld."

Katy didn't answer.

"You should hire that lawyer, Joe Wiseman. They say if you've got the dollars, he'll get the deal."

"Well, I don't have the dollars."

"You don't?" Shaneen seemed surprised.

Katy straightened up her posture and tried to regain the adult role in this conversation. "Shaneen, my husband killed a man. There are consequences."

"Papers say he beat you. I mean to say if any man ever hit me, ever so much as touched me wrong," Shaneen's voice started to escalate, "I'd bash him upside the head with a cast iron skillet. That's what my mama did. My daddy came in all liquored up one night . . ."

Katy held up both hands in an effort to stop Shaneen's rant. She had spent enough time with Shaneen in her office that she'd grown to like her, despite the smart mouth that always got her in trouble, but Shaneen could get loud and loose with her words.

"Your husband going to the state pen?" Shaneen asked in a calmer voice.

Katy pulled out her slip of late passes and handed one to Shaneen. "Probably."

"I could give him my brother's name. He would be a good contact for him when he gets there," Shaneen offered with a rare tone of sincerity. "That's if he ends up at the Raleigh prison."

Katy looked at the girl, unsure whether to laugh or cry. Instead she simply said, "Thank you, Shaneen. I'll remember that."

❧

Tom's office was small. A swivel chair sat behind his untidy desk, and three wooden captain's chairs sat against the wall opposite. He closed the door between his office and his secretary's and motioned for Katy to sit down.

"It's been, what, fifteen years now we've worked together?" he said with a sigh.

"Almost." Katy tried to relax. She could feel the tension in her neck that would probably turn into a headache before the conversation was over. She looked at the former NC State football player opposite her, remembering her first interview with him. Her next-door neighbor had babbled about all the reasons why Katy should never work for a black man in the predominantly black high school.

Tom Morton was a giant who cradled his power like an egg. He'd earned respect from the students and staff as much for his famed history on the gridiron as for his genuine concern for their welfare. In 1974, when the community practically self-destructed over court-ordered integration, he had proven to the few white families who stayed within the public schools that he would be fair. Now, twenty years later, he still practiced the same moral philosophy. He'd been one of the few people who had called Katy after Hank's arrest.

"Things go a lot smoother when you're here," he said.

"Thank you." Katy looked into his face for a glimmer of reassurance that she might keep her job.

Tom settled into his chair, tight lipped. A slight tsk escaped when he finally spoke. "Mrs. Devine." Both of them addressed each other by *Mr.* or *Mrs.* at work, as did the rest of the staff. It showed respect and modeled what they wanted the students to do. "I'm glad you weren't hurt."

"Thank you," Katy said. She swallowed to control the quiver in her voice and looked at her boss.

"I'm afraid we've got a problem," he said.

She bowed her head, embarrassed, her fingers playing with the narrow wedding band still on her left hand.

Tom fidgeted a bit. "I'm sorry that you got caught, but it complicates things."

She didn't respond. Tom knew about Hank. On more than one occasion he had asked her privately if she needed any help. A lot of the staff had personal problems. Tom tried not to be intrusive, but he would often comment that each day it was important to put their own lives in check for several hours and focus on the students and their obligations to serve them.

Katy broke the silence. "I never thought he would shoot Doc."

Tom cleared his throat. "I guess not."

Neither of them said anything for a long minute.

Finally: "This is hard on everybody. I can only imagine what it's doing to Mrs. Attwuld's kids. Do you know them?" Katy asked.

Tom shook his head. "I don't. I hear they're both away at college."

"Would you keep an eye on Dusty for me? I think Savannah's doing okay, but I'm worried about him," Katy said.

"Sure," Tom said.

There was another period of silence before Katy spoke up, her voice faltering. "Am I going to lose my job?"

He looked at her, and she saw the anguish in his eyes. She knew he didn't want to tell her what she already knew. "The superintendent expects your resignation. We really weren't expecting you to come back to work."

"There are other employees who've had affairs. They didn't lose their jobs."

Tom nodded. "They didn't make the front page. No one got killed."

"I didn't kill anyone."

Tom sighed again and focused on his pen, which he kept twisting between his fingers. "Lord, Katy—Doc Attwuld. You got involved with the doctor." He finally raised his eyes to look at her.

Katy's stomach knotted, and she felt a burning sensation shoot into her throat. She stiffened. She rarely challenged anyone, but she needed this job. "What? It would be overlooked if I had an affair with a plumber? I'm not good enough for a doctor?"

"No, no," Tom stammered, his head moving from side to side. "I didn't mean it that way. This just has more consequences," he sputtered, trying to regain the high ground. "The headlines—every article in the paper mentions that you work for the schools, with students. They question you as a role model."

"They made a big deal out of my name, *Devine*. That was unfair," Katy said.

"I'll give you a good reference," he said.

"You don't understand." The control that Katy tried so hard to maintain started to splinter. "I've got kids to support. I can't go even a month without a paycheck."

"I understand. I promise I'll do what I can—I'll give you a good recommendation, make sure you get your vacation and sick leave pay."

Katy sprang up from her chair, her defiance surprising them both. With her hands trembling and a crack in her voice, she said with as much force as she could muster, "I won't resign. I've paid my dues to the North Carolina Education Association. I talked to them. They told me not to resign."

Chapter Four

Katy turned at the mailbox with the familiar "188" on the side, except that half of the first "8" was now gone, and it looked like "1o8" instead. She drove a quarter mile up the rutted dirt road to the old two-story farmhouse. The chipped white paint had grayed considerably since her last visit. She could see two missing boards on one side of the front porch, and the steps would have caused even the most agile child to approach cautiously. The path to the front door was overgrown with grass. She couldn't remember that entrance being used anyway.

Although she and her brother talked on the phone every few months, she'd been back only twice in the past eight years. A flood of memories resurfaced: the color of the soybeans right before harvest; the smell of the dirt when the peanuts were drying in the open air; the corn bursting forth on the stalk and growing from four inches to eight overnight.

Katy heard the rapid pop-pop-pop-pop-pop and recognized the sound even before she looked across the adjacent field to see the old man on the John Deere. It took her a minute to recall his name . . . Slade, Leland Slade. He still wore that brown Quaker hat. As a child she had believed he never took it off, even in bed. Her brothers joked that it was glued to his head.

The sound echoed through her mind and jarred memories from the past. At one time only background noise, she now heard a melody. Pop-pop-pop-pop-pop. The sound reminded her of a television show called *The Reporters* that had aired a few years earlier. At the beginning, the viewer would hear the printing presses running, the same noise that old tractor made.

Just shy of the field sat a landing strip with a crop duster and Cessna 180 parked in a shed. To the left of the runway, between the planes and the house, was a large summer garden. Buckets and a wheelbarrow straddled one row. A bottle of pesticide spray and a pile of weeds told her Sam had been outside.

Two hound dogs announced her arrival, but their antics failed to alert anyone over the noise of the tractor. The screen door to the back porch was unlocked. Katy heard the shower running. The odor from the dirty clothes and sweat hit her as soon as she walked in: outdoor sweat, hard labor sweat, clothes caked with dirt and fertilizer, and boots that had layers of soil packed into the soles and crevices. She had grown up in this house with four boys, and the smell of them lingered in the boards like perfume. She inhaled.

Her brothers had scattered like quail at the sound of a shotgun blast as soon as they turned eighteen. Reese got killed in a motorcycle accident a week after returning from the Grenada invasion as a US Navy SEAL. Gene had a family in Baltimore, David lived in Jacksonville. Sam, the oldest, stayed to help their dad farm. He rightfully inherited the house with fifty acres, but took to the skies and rented out the land to Leland.

When Katy dropped out of school at sixteen and married Hank, Sam had been visibly upset. She'd sent him a note when she completed her GED, and he'd sent her a ten-dollar bill in the return mail. She tried to call every few months. Sometimes he picked up the phone. Sometimes he didn't.

He was singing to himself in the shower—"Big River," that old Johnny Cash song. She stepped over the pile of clothes and skirted around the washer and dryer. She avoided the temptation to replay one of their childhood games where she would pull the curtain and run. Instead she slipped quietly past the shower and sat down in the kitchen to wait.

Dirty dishes sat soaking in the sink. The pine floors needed a good scrub. His wife used to try to keep the place clean despite the years of dirt that had been ground in, but she had left him. Katy wasn't even sure how long ago.

Limp white curtains covering the discolored panes of glass over the sink hid the best part of the day. A schedule stuck in a nail had names and dates scratched beside them—for crop dusting, she guessed. She saw phone numbers tacked up to a stick board by the phone and a picture propped on the window ledge with a nice-looking woman who had her arms around him. Katy didn't recognize her, but she might not recognize Sam either. It'd been a while.

Katy heard him turn off the shower. He walked in with a towel around his waist, dripping water in puddles that pooled on the uneven hardwood. Their family had been blessed with heads of thick hair, and his was still wavy, but heavily salt and pepper now. They all had the Irish blue eyes. He had a moustache with a nicely cropped short beard. She liked it. He still stood tall and straight and hadn't let beer or barbecue ruin his solid figure. Sam walked to the sink, ran a glass under the tap for water, and turned to see her sitting in the chair at the table.

"Christ!" He jumped. He twisted the towel a bit tighter around his waist, and his face lit up like a firecracker. "Sis, you scared me to death. You're early."

"Yep."

"Wait." He took giant steps back to the dryer. "Let me go put on some jeans." He kept talking to her from the adjacent room. "How long you been sitting out there?"

"About ten minutes, that's all."

"You couldn't have done some dishes while you was there?"

"Not hardly." She smiled and tried to remember why she had waited so long to come back. It was mostly because Sam and Hank didn't get along. Hank refused to make the trip after he got back from his long hauls, and he wouldn't let her and the kids go without him. The few phone calls she made allowed her to stay in touch.

"So Hank finally got hisself in jail. You ain't sorry, are you?"

"Sorry about what he did to get there. I'll get a divorce."

"Well, that's been too long in coming. Should have left his sorry ass years ago."

"I guess that's what all the exes say about one another." She felt the tension draining out of her back. What had happened to her that she left this family she loved and let herself be isolated in a town not more than two hours away?

Sam came out of the laundry room, this time in clean jeans and a T-shirt for that new Panthers team they were hyping out of Charlotte. He swooped her up in his arms. "Give me a hug, darlin'. After all those years with that SOB, and look at you. You're still about the prettiest little sis a guy could have."

She returned his embrace and then looked up into his face. Either he was taller or she had shrunk. When had he gotten a full head above her? "It's been tough," she said.

"Why didn't you call me sooner?"

"I tried for days. No answer."

"Sorry about that. Away on a job. I tried to call you. Your phone was disconnected."

"I had a mess of crank phone calls, plus Hank's brother Ray . . . he won't leave me alone," Katy said.

"What's he want?"

"Threatening to take the kids from me."

"He's full of shit. He can't do that." Sam opened the refrigerator door and pulled out a can of Bud.

"I've been meeting with a social worker since April. She seems to think things have been cleared."

He offered a second can to her, but Katy shook her head.

"I should have pulled Savannah and Dusty out of school and just moved right away," she said.

"Savannah." One side of his mouth curled up in thoughtful reflection. "Let's see if I can remember."

She saved him the embarrassment. "She's a coming-up senior now, seventeen, pretty and smart, too."

"I'll bet. Just like her mama," he said.

"No, not like me at all. She's smarter about men. She's got religion. Prays for me, prays for her daddy."

"Hope she's praying for me, too." Sam took a swallow, sat down, and leaned back on the rear legs of the chair.

"I imagine she will be soon. She's real involved with a church—sings in their choir. They've been awfully good to her through all of this. That's one of the reasons I didn't leave. She's on a mission trip with the youth group this week."

"Where'd she go?"

"New Hampshire."

Sam raised an eyebrow and chuckled. "New Hampshire? They having problems up there?"

"Witches. According to Savannah, they've got a witch problem." She didn't question Savannah's religious conversion. "Dusty, now, he's got bigger problems."

"Yeah?"

"He's fifteen. You remember being fifteen? Well, triple it, and you got Dusty."

Sam's smile broadened. "Fifteen wasn't one of my stellar years."

"He's just shut down on me. Mad at me. Mad at his dad. The principal pulled a few of the kids who were riling him into his office and laid down the law, but Dusty's holed up in his room all the time playing that punk rock. It's an effort to get him out the door every morning."

"Life's hard," Sam said.

They settled across from each other in tarnished metal kitchen chairs with torn red vinyl seats. She paused, tried to flatten her hair behind her ears. The weather was humid. Short curls fell across the right side of her forehead. "I need to move, Sam."

"What about your job?"

"I quit. The NCEA told me to sue, but I settled. Wanted to avoid any further embarrassment for me and the kids."

"NCEA?"

"North Carolina Education Association. You pay your dues, and they provide lawyers if you need them."

"So what did the school board offer?"

"They gave me a six-month severance package if I resigned immediately and dropped any further legal action." Her mouth twisted and she shrugged. "I took the deal, but now I can't get unemployment, and no one will hire me. I probably made a mistake."

Sam settled his chair on all fours and leaned toward her.

"Nobody in town wants to offend Doc Attwuld's widow. I understand that, really I do. What's happened to her is awful."

"It's awful for everyone," Sam said. "You, too." He paused. "Did you love him?"

Katy put both elbows on the table and dropped her head into her hands. A lump formed in her throat. Of course she had loved him, but she realized how naïve she'd been to think he'd leave his wife. "I did," she confessed. She looked back up at her brother. "I told him about the troubles Hank and I were having, and Doc Attwuld insisted that I needed to leave my husband. I thought that meant more than it turned out to be. Guess I was a fool, huh?"

Sam looked down at the floor and started to speak, but instead he reached across the table between them and opened his hand. She placed her hand in his, and he squeezed.

"Love makes fools of us all," he said.

Her shoulders relaxed, and a hint of a smile appeared.

"Why don't you come back to Cedar Branch?"

"Is there a lot of talk about me here?" she asked.

"Nah, nobody knows," Sam said.

Katy shrugged. "I remember lots of nice folks. Are the Quaker neighbors still next door?"

"They're around."

"I see the old man's out there." Katy nodded her head in the direction of the noisy tractor.

"Leland? Yeah, he'll never die. As predictable as spring."

"Ever talk?"

"Not hardly, but he's a good neighbor."

Katy got up from the table, went over to the window, and glanced out. "I'm going to rent my trailer."

"You can move in here, you know. This is still your home."

"This house isn't big enough for us all."

"Was big enough for five kids plus Mom and Dad."

"Remember the fights?" Katy snickered.

"Sure do. Some of my best memories." His eyes lit up. "Bring the kids and move. You can have the three bedrooms upstairs."

Sam had said everything she had hoped he would. She still had a home to come to. "I'll think about it. But just you offering—that means a lot."

He sat there staring at her for a minute and then jumped up. "Let's celebrate. What do you want to eat?"

"You cooking?" Katy looked at him, feeling more amused than hungry.

"Nope, but I'm buying. Come on, I'll take you down to The Quaker Café, and we can get lunch."

They drove past Leland's farm. He was still out on his tractor rambling back and forth, pulling a thirty-year-old plow behind him. A rope attached to the rear of the plow allowed him to pull on it at the end of each row to lift the blades when he turned. Katy remembered how he worked from sunup to sundown and then how, at night, not a light shone from his house.

He lived alone, no wife, no kids. As if his size were not already intimidating, at one time a bushy red beard swept across his face like a grass fire. She imagined it would be gray now. Always in dark pants and a plain, collarless shirt with black suspenders, he wore a wide-brim hat everywhere he went. Katy remembered once, when she was little, she'd turned to find him standing quietly behind her. Frightened, she'd run inside and didn't see until later the bucket of strawberries that he'd left on their doorstep.

Nathan and Euphrasia Hoole, an older Quaker couple, had a house on the other side of Leland's. Katy vaguely recalled their children, Chase and Sophie. They had been Sam's age and already in college by the time she started kindergarten.

As they drove toward town, she caught a glimpse of an old cast iron farm bell hanging between two oak posts next to the Hooles' barn. It was similar to the one Leland had in his backyard and another that hung behind the Quaker meeting house. Once used to call for help if the cows got loose or in case of fire, they had become mostly collectors' items.

"We're approaching a population of over eight hundred here in Cedar Branch," Sam said. "Some folks think we need a stoplight."

Sam's house stood in stark contrast to the Quaker homes, which had fresh coats of white paint and black or gray shutters. Chicken pens and gardens could be seen in back. Katy knew that her own childhood home had once belonged to a Quaker family, but when the woman had married a Baptist, she left the Religious Society of Friends, or Quakers, as they were commonly called. Evidently in those times, if you married out of the Quaker meeting, you were no longer considered a member.

"I see you've got that plane you always dreamed of," Katy said.

"She's a honey," Sam said with a nod. "I love being up in the air away from the crowds."

"Right," Katy joked. "A lot of congestion down here in Cedar Branch."

"I'm telling you, Sis, I'm flying with the angels up there."

"How much do the angels pay you?" Katy asked.

"I do okay." Sam smiled. "I do some crop dusting and have a gig in Colombia where I go every couple of weeks."

"South Carolina?"

"South America," Sam said.

"You're kidding?"

"Nope. I'm spraying those coca bushes to try to halt the flow of cocaine into our country."

Katy dropped her jaw in surprise. "I don't believe it."

"You don't? Who do you think's trying to protect the youth of America from themselves? Just good ole boys like me. Work for a private contractor out of Fort Worth."

"You aren't afraid of getting shot?" Katy asked.

"Only person who ever took a shot at me was a woman," Sam said and winked. "Fortunately, she couldn't aim straight. Unfortunately, she don't live so far away, and I hear she's started target practice."

They passed the town sign with a small board underneath announcing "Bird Sanctuary."

"Don't remember that," Katy said.

"Can't shoot at birds in the town limits. People . . . yes. Birds . . . no."

Sam hadn't lost his sense of humor. Each memory brought her closer to wanting to return home. "Why not?"

"You might hit someone's huntin' dog or pet by accident."

"You're kidding."

"Nope. Some years ago Maggie Kendall—remember her? The Judge's daughter?—fired at a bunch of pesky birds and accidentally killed a neighbor's dog. That's the cause of the whole thing."

Katy laughed. She felt almost giddy. The last few months had been brutal . . . rejection after rejection for secretarial, receptionist, cashier jobs in Bixby. She didn't even make it to the first round of interviews despite the solid reference that Tom Morton had given her. Dusty moped through the school day and came home to isolate himself in his room. Savannah was the only one encouraging her and trying to keep their spirits up.

They passed the Quaker meeting house on the left. The one-story cedar-framed building included a wide porch that wrapped around three sides. Katy had only been inside once. Her father had insisted the entire family attend the funeral of a Quaker elder. She remembered the service as if it were yesterday. No music, no preacher. Pews arranged in a square so that they all faced the center where the coffin rested. There were no flowers anywhere. Everything looked so plain and drab that she wished she had brought a handful of spring daffodils that grew plentiful along the border of most fields. Everyone in the service sat still, their eyes closed.

"What they doing?" she had whispered to her mama.

"Listening for God," her mother had whispered back and shushed her.

To the delight of her brothers, after ten more minutes Katy whispered again. "Mama, I'm listening, but God ain't talkin'." This sent her brothers into a fit of giggles, which stopped abruptly when their father gave the one closest to him a good pinch.

After some time, one of the older Quakers stood up. It was easy to tell which ones were Quakers because they dressed plainly like Leland— no suits or ties.

The man who rose spoke briefly about the deceased's faithfulness to God, and after he sat down, another Quaker man stood and said a few words. Two women followed. Finally someone in a suit and tie got up to speak, and afterward, to Katy's surprise, her own father rose to his feet.

With his bald head bowed and his calloused hands shaking, he seemed unsure whether to speak or sit back down. Then in a voice that trembled, *quaked* even, he said, "He loaned me money once and didn't ask for it back. I never forgot.

"Years later," her father stammered on with great difficulty, "when I finally saved enough to repay him, he wouldn't take the money. He simply told me the Lord had given him some extra, and he didn't need no more." Her father took out a handkerchief and wiped his nose and then added, "That money was a big help to my family."

Katy had never forgotten that day; the courage it must have taken for her daddy to stand up in the middle of all those people, telling the whole town how they'd been broke. Her older brothers slouched and then fled to hide in the car as soon as the service ended. Katy thought only about how some folks had enough money to give away and not worry whether they'd ever get it back. That's what she wanted some-day . . . to have that much money.

They passed the post office and the bank. Old red-and-blue Esso signs still hung in front of the gas station and repair shop. The Quaker Café came next with a flood of memories—her first job. She'd waited tables that summer, and Hank had stopped in for a hamburger and fries. She'd fallen for his James Dean image and the idea of leaving behind the little enclave of farmers and Quakers who seemed trapped in a time warp. He was eighteen; Katy only sixteen and pregnant by the end of the summer. Her mother cried. Her father signed the parental consent form for the baby's sake, then took to the fields and didn't speak.

The pharmacy and the hardware store were directly across the street from the café. Red North Carolina brick embraced every building as a statement to a small Southern town that refused to fall but couldn't stop the crumble.

Sam turned right into one of the five parking spaces in front of the café, and they walked in. Miss Ellie Cartwright, the owner, stood at the register. She was in her late seventies, and her face wore the lines of time while her hair held a dark hue from numerous dye bottles. Nonetheless, Katy recognized her immediately. Although a thick layer of makeup wrestled to keep age from overshadowing Miss Ellie's once-beautiful face, a flattering floral dress showed off her still-admirable figure.

Miss Ellie stood tall and erect in blue high heels that defied the demands of her job. Picking up a pair of reading glasses from the counter, she slipped them over the end of her nose and switched her gaze back and forth between each customer and the register keys as they told her what they'd had to eat. There were no cash receipts.

Sam picked up a rag from the sideboard and wiped off an empty table. He pointed to the chair opposite him before pulling out his own. "This is my darling little sister, Katy, in case anyone here don't remember," he announced to no one in particular. "She may be cute and a little shy, but she's smart as a fox, so don't say I didn't warn you."

A few people turned and nodded politely. A couple tipped their hands in the air in a half wave. Katy slid into the wooden captain's chair and pulled it closer to the table. She cut her eyes toward six men finishing up their hamburgers and fries on the other side of the room at one elongated table. She thought she recognized Doc Withers, much older but unmistakably one and the same. The man at the other end with the badge and gun was obviously the Sheriff. Two other men had on suits, and the last was dressed in khakis and a collared knit shirt.

Katy immediately recognized him as Frank Busby. The soda shop in the pharmacy he'd run had been a popular place for teenagers. "Frank Busby still own the pharmacy?" Katy asked.

"Nope. Sold it to a Quaker couple around the time you left. The guy with him, the balding one, that's Chase Hoole. Grew up two houses down from us. He's the pharmacist now, although Frank still steps in to help out from time to time."

"Nathan and Euphrasia's son. I remember," she said.

"Chase's son, Adam, and his wife, Heather, have moved back to town. They got a little girl." Sam rose from his chair. "Sweet tea?" he asked as he went to retrieve two glasses from the sideboard and put them down on the table. "Adam's assistant principal out at the high school. Euphrasia and Nathan still going strong. In their eighties now."

"I heard Judge Kendall died," Katy said.

"Yep. So did his daughter, Maggie. She died the same year. Cancer."

Katy had been a good twenty years younger than Maggie. She barely remembered her, other than the fact that the Kendalls practically owned the town. "What happened to all that Kendall money and Cottonwoods Plantation?"

"Got spread around. Josh Cartwright, over there," Sam said as he gave a furtive glance toward the broad-shouldered man in the short-sleeve polo shirt at the back table, "Miss Ellie's son, he got Cottonwoods. There's a story . . ." Sam said and then stopped. Miss Ellie approached them.

"Miss Ellie, remember Katy?"

Miss Ellie brushed the strand of hair from her eyes and pulled out one of the chairs and sat down. "Well, certainly I do. You worked here one summer for a couple of months." She held an order pad and pencil, but seemed more interested in sitting than taking an order at the moment. Bright red nail polish decorated a working pair of hands lined with bulging blue veins and age spots. "Where do you live now, Katy?"

"A couple of hours away. I'm thinking of moving back."

"New job?"

"Nope, a divorce," Katy said without saying more.

"Uh-huh." Miss Ellie didn't prod. "You got children?"

"A fifteen-year-old and a seventeen-year-old," Katy said.

"Well, bring them on down, and I'll give them each a free hamburger and fries when they get here."

"Thank you, ma'am," Katy said. "I'll do that."

"So what can I get you two for lunch? I've still got a couple of pieces of fried chicken left."

Sam looked over at Katy. "Fried chicken would be great," she said.

"And I'll take a hamburger and fries."

As Miss Ellie walked away, Katy looked around. "She runnin' the place all by herself?"

"Pretty much. Has Teensy in the kitchen. A string of waitresses come and go."

"She seems kinda old to do all this."

"Never underestimate Miss Ellie. She's running on all cylinders."

Katy glanced around at the eight square wooden tables near her and the two smaller ones pushed up against the wall. The suits sitting at the longer table in the back were hotly debating a court case. Three elderly women at a table in the corner eyed Katy and whispered.

Over Sam's shoulder, Katy saw one of the women rise and approach. Dressed primly in a cotton skirt and white blouse, she wore pumps and stockings. Her gray hair appeared to have been removed from tight overnight rollers and never combed out.

"Hi," she said as she reached the table. "I'm Helen Truitt. Are you Katy Devine?" Katy noticed that Sam didn't stand but leaned back in his chair, keeping his hand on his glass of iced tea. "You look so familiar."

Katy flushed.

Sam jumped in. "I think you have her mixed up with someone else, Helen. This is my sister, Katy O'Brien. Same last name as mine."

"Oh." Helen looked confused for a moment and then seemed to brush it off. "I thought you resembled someone. Well, it's nice to meet you, Miss . . . O'Brien? I should remember you, but I worked full time when you were younger and didn't go to that end of town so much."

No one spoke. Helen's eyes darted between Sam and Katy, and then she awkwardly returned to her seat.

Katy looked at Sam. "She's going to put it all together."

"It don't matter," Sam reassured her. "Nobody pays her no mind."

CHAPTER FIVE

After an offer in July from one of the new assistant teachers to rent her trailer, Katy packed everything up and moved with the children into the three upstairs bedrooms at Sam's. Savannah parted with her friends amid tears and vows to call and write daily, but she made the most of the new situation by helping Katy unpack boxes and rearrange furniture. Dusty, on the other hand, moved from his bedroom to the upstairs without much more than a transfer of his boom box. He remained cautious around Sam. Sam gave him space.

"For two weeks every month, the house is all yours," Sam said before he headed to Colombia to destroy more coca plants. "Leland's always next door if you need help, or you can go to the Hooles. I'll bet before the week is up Billie McFarland shows up. She can't stand not knowing the skinny about anybody new in town."

Billie arrived the next day in a burgundy Land Rover and climbed down wearing ruby slacks and a cherry-pink blouse. Her Scottie, Webster, immediately jumped from the Rover and began to taunt the two farm dogs with a back and forth jig while he nipped at their feet. The barking brought Katy to the door, where Billie handed her a basket of warm blueberry muffins and then swooped up Webster and pushed her way past Katy to escape the canine antics.

Billie McFarland seemed a contradiction to everything in Cedar Branch. Color coordinated from her toenails to her new rage short haircut, she could have just walked out of Saks Fifth Avenue.

"I'm Billie McFarland," she said by way of introduction. "Been in Cedar Branch for twelve years now, which makes me a newcomer. From New York City, which makes me a Yankee. I use that as my excuse for everything I do." Billie talked as she carried Webster through the porch and kitchen and into the living room.

"I've heard about you," Katy said as she followed her and put the muffins on the coffee table next to a half-empty bag of potato chips. Boxes littered the sides of the walls, and extra furniture cluttered the room. A new television stood out as the main focal point, with a battered brown sofa and two equally worn recliners sitting opposite it. "Sam showed me your picture at the café."

"You noticed?" Billie said with obvious pride. "My husband painted that. The woman in the middle is Maggie Kendall. Did you know her?"

"Not really. She was quite a bit older than me. Lived on the other side of town."

"It's a big town," Billie said and motioned to the stack of boxes. "Still settling in, are you, hon?"

"This is just temporary until we get a place of our own. It's going to take a miracle to merge my furniture and Sam's into the same house." Katy started to motion to a chair, but Billie was ahead of her and sat down on the couch instead. "We're filled to overflowing. My children and I are going to put the place into some order while Sam's away."

Webster scooted next to Billie's hip, cocking his head, alert for any surprise attack from the outside dogs. "Kids still sleeping?" Billie asked.

"Teenagers. They'd sleep all day if I let them."

"When school starts, that will take care of that," Billie said. She crossed her legs and started to pet Webster as he fidgeted up and down on his short hind legs. "Got a job yet?"

"No," Katy admitted. "We've barely arrived." Katy took this woman in with keen interest. She was maybe in her early sixties, but she had a great cut and a good dye job—so maybe late sixties. Billie looked like a woman who could afford a good dye job. Nonetheless, Katy was pleased. Someone had dropped by to welcome her to the community. She had a visitor. The only visitor they had in Bixby during her time with Hank had been Ray. When he came, she disappeared into the bedroom.

"Miss Ellie could use some help at The Quaker Café." Beside her, Webster groaned, got up, and did two turns on the sofa, then settled back again, apparently convinced the outside dogs had lost interest in his whereabouts.

Katy raised her eyebrows, somewhat surprised. "Is there a job?"

"There's always a job. It's just a stopover for everyone looking for something better. You should ask," Billie said.

"What does she pay?"

"Minimum wage, but you're attractive and would probably do okay on tips. Tax free. Lots of men in there. They like a pretty girl, especially ones with . . ." She waved her fingers in front of her breasts. "You know, good credentials."

Katy blushed and then let out a laugh. "You're not kidding."

"Of course not. I'm as serious as a heart attack. Speaking of which, several of those men have had one, so don't go overboard on short skirts and cleavage. We've been through that once already. Died right there at the table."

"Who did?"

"The Judge. You haven't heard that story?"

"At the café?" Katy's eyes got wide.

"Right there. It was a terrible night." Billie rolled into her story of how Judge Kendall had died during dinner two years ago and no one even noticed.

As Billie talked, Katy remembered the newspaper articles. Of course she remembered. After all, he had been a prominent figure in town when she was a child, but she hadn't heard the details.

"I can't imagine," Katy said. "The Judge dying over his meal. They didn't tell you that part in the state papers."

"Suppose they didn't want to mention the chicken and dumplings."

"Probably wouldn't have done much for business," Katy said, and suddenly she and Billie were sharing the same joke.

"You're right," Billie said and added, "and then Maggie, the same year." Billie's tone turned somber, and Katy thought she heard her voice crack. "That was really sad." Billie waved her hand in front of her face as if she could brush the memory away like a pesky fly. "Enough about that. So what about you?"

"Not so much to tell," Katy said. "Going through a divorce. I grew up in this house."

"Heard your ex shot your lover," Billie said without skipping a beat. Katy was speechless.

"He was the town doctor, right? Boys falling through the skylight." Billie broke into laughter. "My God, what a sight to behold. Him with his pants down. You couldn't make up something that funny. Everybody read about Katy Devine."

Katy stared wide-eyed at Billie in disbelief. "Mrs. McFarland, my children are upstairs."

"I'm sorry," Billie said, catching herself and adjusting her tone. "I didn't mean to be insensitive. It's just that some people said—" She stopped herself before she completed the sentence.

"Mrs. McFarland, I had feelings for him, and he is dead. My family has been through a terrible period, not to mention Mrs. Attwuld and her children. That's the reason I've brought my children back to Cedar Branch. I had to get out of town. My presence was painful for everyone. I'm changing my name back to O'Brien."

"Billie, do call me Billie. And I apologize. It will all be a nonissue in this town. Nobody cares." Billie did a mock zip up of her lips. "Enough. Let me get us some coffee, Katy O'Brien. Cups in the kitchen?"

Katy stood and followed Billie, watching helplessly as Billie took control of things, putting the kettle of water on the stove and rummaging through the cupboards until she found the jar of instant. "Is this all Sam has?" she asked without expecting an answer. She stepped back into the living room, patted Webster on his head, and returned with the blueberry muffins. Billie sat down at the table. "There now, there's nothing that a good cup of coffee and a warm blueberry muffin won't make better." Billie picked up a muffin and tore it into four pieces.

They sat in silence for a few awkward moments as they sipped coffee. Billie seemed to be leading up to something. Finally: "I have to ask you this. I hope you won't be offended, but I want to be sure you've considered your options. Are you planning to sue the practice?"

"Sue?" The thought had never crossed her mind. "For what?"

"Malpractice, sexual harassment. I'm sure there are a dozen things you could sue him for," Billie said.

"He's dead. I can't sue him."

"You can sue his estate, and you can sue his office. You know he had to have malpractice insurance."

"He didn't force himself upon me."

"You were a patient in his office. He held a position of trust. And there you are, a victim of domestic abuse, coming to him for help."

Katy blushed. "Does everyone in town know all this?"

"Goodness, I get the newspapers. You think we don't read over here in Cedar Branch?"

"Sam said nobody's heard."

"Lord, everybody's heard. Nobody in North Carolina thinks there's anything between I-95 and the Outer Banks," she mused. "Heck, we are the entertainment capital of the state. Much more creative with our scandals. Comes from breathing Roundup and drinking swamp water. The *News and Observer* should pay us."

Billie rose again to retrieve a butter dish. "Doc knew that your husband abused you, didn't he?"

"Are you always this blunt?" Katy asked.

"Yes. I'm from New York. We don't beat around the bush."

"He could get mean when he drank," Katy said, unsure how much more to say. "Doc wanted me to leave him."

"Why didn't you?"

"I hadn't figured out how to support my children on my own. Plus, I was afraid of what he'd do."

"And here you are, on your own, without a job." She put a slab of butter on her muffin. "Everything you were trying to avoid, you now have to face."

"What seems right one minute doesn't always feel right later on," Katy said. She felt defensive and looked out the window past Billie. Why must she always apologize to everyone?

"Honey, put your head on straight. Your husband attempts to isolate the family so that you'd see him as your only source for support. He drinks and makes you think that every time he loses his temper it's your fault. And then to teach you a lesson, he insults you, hits you. He's got you so conned into believing that it's your responsibility to make things right that even when the police come you make excuses for him. Am I right?"

Katy lowered her head but didn't say anything. She felt at fault—kind of pathetic, like a soiled dishrag. This was exactly how Hank made her feel. She hated that feeling. "You're right," she said.

"My husband is a retired psychiatrist," Billie said. "I hear him talk about this all the time. You were emotionally vulnerable. The doctor took advantage of his professional position to seduce you. Another man . . . another *man*, for crying out loud . . . pretends to be your savior and takes advantage of your insecurities. You gotta break this cycle. For your kids. For yourself. You don't want to raise a daughter who lets some creep beat her up or a son who thinks he has a right to knock women around, do you?"

"*No!*" Katy said, her eyes wide at the thought that her children would copy such behavior.

"Then sue the bastards. Reclaim your life. 'I am Woman,' remember? 'Hear me roar' and all that hogwash." Billie started swaying her arms in the air from side to side as she sang the first stanza of the Helen

Reddy song. "Roar, for crying out loud. Roar. Help your children under-stand that you have rights, too, and those rights were violated."

Katy sat back, a bit stunned. "I couldn't do that to Mrs. Attwuld. She didn't do anything wrong."

"You wouldn't be doing anything to her. The medical practice has insurance. It would be the insurance company paying out, not her."

"You think I should do this?"

"Are you kidding? Yours is one of the best cases I know of. You ask those lawyers down at The Quaker Café. I'll bet one of them will take it in a heartbeat."

"Really?" Katy didn't begin to know how to approach a lawyer. "Why would they talk with me?"

"Talk with you? Why, honey, if there's a nickel to be made, they'll fight over you. You're money in their pockets. But settlements don't come easy. Lawsuits are a game of endurance and wits. They take time."

"How do you know all of this?" Katy asked.

"I told you. I'm from New York City. We suck up lawsuits like car fumes."

Katy gave a faint smile. "I'll think about it," she said.

"See there, just the thought has you looking better. Lift up your head. Think like a winner. Action creates energy. Energy gives you power." Billie added, "While you're thinking, why don't you wait tables and help out Miss Ellie? If she closes the café, the town will dry up. Swear to God."

"Well, some money coming in is better than nothing at all . . . until I get a better offer," Katy said.

"You'd be front and center to the best shows playing in town. There are days I'm tempted to go volunteer just for the entertainment."

❧

Katy rounded the house on her afternoon break from the café and saw what she'd feared. She had agreed to work the lunch and dinner shift with a three-hour break between two and five. In the back of her mind, she knew this gun thing would come up. She had hoped not quite so soon.

"Sam, who gave you permission to teach my kids to shoot?"

Three heads turned in her direction. A board propped across two logs was decorated with empty soup cans.

"I didn't know I needed permission. Just thought a little target practice would be healthier than sitting on their butts watching TV all day," Sam said. He turned back to Dusty. "Steady. When you're ready, take the shot."

The gun fired, striking dirt somewhere in the woods.

"I hoped that weeding the garden and keeping the place picked up would keep the kids busy. Even fantasized that the three of you might decide to scrape and paint the farmhouse."

A collective moan rippled through the air.

"They need to know how to handle a gun, Katy. Most of the boys around here have a gun in their hands before they're ten. Neither of them can even hold the dern thing right. Gotta feel the weight, absorb the kick, strengthen the wrist muscle."

Dusty turned away from his mother and fired the last shot in the Remington six-shooter. The cans remained unscathed. He was still a boy in frame and temperament. He'd hit a growth spurt before long and probably grow as tall as Sam, but for the time being Katy knew he resented the fact that so many of the boys were waking up inches taller each day while he seemed destined to be stuck in a holding pattern.

"Put that gun down, Dusty," Katy ordered.

Dusty paused, surprised by his mother's assertive tone, and looked instead at his uncle for a rebuttal.

"Listen to your mother, Dusty," Sam said.

Dusty glared at her, his blond bangs brushing across his eyebrows in Tom Sawyer fashion. He turned suddenly. "You can't tell me what to do," he said to his mother.

"Hey, boy." The sharp crack in Sam's voice came instantly. "Don't you speak to your mother like that. I want to hear a 'yes, ma'am,' or this is the last time you touch any of my guns."

A lull and then a hesitant, "Yes, ma'am" followed before Dusty dropped the gun and stormed to the house.

"Young man." Sam's voice was stern. "You come back here and pick up that gun. What did I tell you? Don't ever put a gun on the ground, and breech it and check to make sure it's empty before you holster it."

"That's exactly what I'm talking about," Katy complained. "He's not ready for the responsibility of a gun." She looked at Savannah. "Go on inside. Let your uncle and me talk about this."

"Maa-maa," Savannah whined. She bit her lip and turned around slowly. She'd been playing with makeup and had penciled in a line around her lips, giving her a puckish look. It was kind of appealing. Her honey-nut eyes looked away in despair, and Katy almost regretted the fact that she'd interrupted this moment they were having with Sam.

"I'm sorry, sweetheart."

"It's just so boring out here. This is the only thing that's any fun."

"School starts soon. You'll meet new friends," Katy said.

"Couldn't we at least go to church?"

Katy looked over at Sam, who avoided any eye contact. "I'll look around and see. Maybe we can find something," she said without much conviction. Church had never been her strong suit. She assumed that Savannah's conversion to religion had been more a factor of friends than faith.

Katy dropped down cross-legged into the grass and waited while Sam supervised Dusty as he picked up the gun and breeched it. Then Dusty followed as Savannah trudged away, her thick ponytail swinging from side to side.

"I know what you're trying to do, and I appreciate your desire to teach my kids responsibility," Katy said, "but I don't like guns."

"They're not children, Katy," Sam said.

Katy knew that all too well. In Bixby, the first day of hunting season had practically turned into a school holiday because the absentee rate was so high, especially with the white kids.

"It's in the same category as drinking and sex," Sam continued. "You better teach 'em, because they're going to be trying both whether you want them to or not."

"Guns scare me. Hank had two in the house. Used to threaten to kill me and wave them around like a wild man when he got drunk."

Sam reared back and stared at her. "He threatened to kill you?"

Katy regretted her words instantly. "We walked a fine line when he was drinking. I never really believed he was capable of killing anyone until now."

"God Almighty, Katy." His voice escalated. "Your kids see their dad threaten their mom with a gun, and you think it don't matter? Did you call the police?"

"Wasn't much the police could do. Our neighbor called them a few times. When they showed up, it made Hank all the madder. Things got worse."

She wanted to shift the conversation away from trying to defend her decisions. In retrospect she seemed so foolish. "Why don't you teach them to fly that plane instead?"

"That asshole." Sam started to pace. "Why didn't you leave him? I'd have come and got you." He picked up the six-shooter and the Winchester.

"It was my problem. No need to get the whole town involved," she said. "I didn't want to embarrass the kids." She stopped and then blurted out, "Sam, I was afraid."

"He better damn well stay in jail, because the next time I see the son of a bitch . . ."

"Stop it." She didn't want to talk about the past anymore. "We're startin' over here."

Sam holstered the pistol. His face was fraught and his voice tense. "They're my guns, Katy. I keep them in my house."

Katy noticed a hint of hostility in his voice and realized that this could be the first of other lifestyle issues to come. "Lock them up, will you?" she asked.

"I could do that," he said, "but how do you plan to protect yourself if Hank ever shows up and I'm not here?"

"He's going to jail for a very long time. I'm not going to spend any more of my life being afraid of Hank Devine," Katy said with as much confidence as she could muster. If she said it often enough, she might even believe it.

CHAPTER SIX

Katy put a basket of hot biscuits in front of Billie's husband, Gill. Paint splatters covered his khakis, and a frayed gray T-shirt with "PRINCE-TON" printed boldly across the front hung on him, two sizes too big.

Despite his reputation for a sharp, sarcastic wit that was unfamiliar to the typical Southerner, Katy discovered she quite enjoyed waiting on him at the café. Gill and Billie came in a few times each week, and Billie always stopped by to visit when Sam flew to Colombia. Katy had become fond of them both.

Gill looked up at Katy with puppy dog eyes. "So what's the special tonight?" He asked the same question every Thursday even though the menu never changed.

"Your choice of fried chicken, chicken and dumplings, or Salisbury steak," Katy announced as if only moments earlier she herself had learned the chef's specials for the evening.

"Hmmm, let me think about it."

Billie brushed him off with her hand and looked up at Katy as if to say *don't pay any attention to him* and focused instead on the man across the table from her. "Katy, this is Joe Wiseman. I don't think you've met. He's a lawyer." Billie nodded, prompting Katy to speak. Katy said nothing.

"Joe works out of Westtown. Only up here every month or so when he has a court case in this area."

Katy remembered Shaneen had mentioned him, and she'd heard his name brought up at the VIP table in the back of the café. Joe pushed back his chair, partially stood, and stretched out his arm to Katy.

"Glad to meet you," he said. A thick gray horseshoe moustache curved around his upper lip and down either side of his mouth almost to his chin. His rumpled hair appeared unkempt. Since he moved in and out of the prison system to meet his clients, he chose not to insult them further with a fashion statement. He clearly nurtured his image.

"What can I get for you?" Katy asked.

"Fried chicken. That's all I ever order here," Joe said.

"Salisbury steak," Billie said.

"Chicken and dumplings for me, and I'll pay you extra if you put chicken in it." Gill flashed Katy a wicked smile that she returned. Then she departed to the kitchen to get more biscuits. She always did her best to keep the big tippers happy.

Helen Truitt entered with the Barker sisters and Mary Law, the Methodist Church organist. All widowed and approaching eighty, they convened several times a week to assess the moral and social conduct of the town's inhabitants. More often than not Helen's acid comments could be heard throughout the café. She could hatch a nasty rumor in the course of a forty-five-minute meal and spread it like poison ivy. Miss Ellie made an admirable effort to limit Helen's verbal barrages.

Katy placed four glasses of sweet tea on a tray and headed over to their table.

Without looking directly at Katy, Helen pulled out her chair, and with her nose lifted and her eyes inspecting the dust on the light fixtures, she said, "We'd like Miss Ellie to serve us." She kept her hands on her chair, but did not sit down.

Katy was confused. This hadn't happened before. Then she flushed when she realized Helen had made the connection. The snub was personal.

Miss Ellie always kept one eye on Helen whenever she came in. Immediately she rose to her feet and walked over to greet them.

All four wore their Sunday best. "Such a shame," Helen said as she eyed the other patrons in the room.

"What's a shame, Helen?" Miss Ellie asked.

"Dress standards. You would think when one went out in public, one might be the least bit concerned about their appearance, but not any longer. Some people look as if they're walking out of the tobacco fields instead of into a restaurant." She spoke as if she were reading lines from a script long ago cut from a screenplay.

"By the end of the day some people are just tired and grateful someone else is doing the cooking," Miss Ellie said.

"Possibly," Helen continued. "Such a poor example for the next generation. No wonder children today have so few social graces."

"Would you ladies like to have a seat?" Miss Ellie asked.

"Ellie," Helen said, her voice lowered to emphasize the importance of what she intended to share. She motioned with her finger for her hostess to bend down closer. "That girl you hired." Helen turned her head and nodded to Katy. "She was involved in that murder over in Chowan County. She's calling herself O'Brien now, but her last name is Devine. She's the one who had the affair with the doctor." Helen's lips pursed with satisfaction that she had just revealed a startling truth.

"I know," Ellie said and straightened up.

Helen ran her hands across her skirt to smooth out the wrinkles. She seemed disappointed in Ellie's lackluster response. "I just thought you should know *whom* you've got working in your café, that's all."

"I knew that when I hired her." Miss Ellie offered them an ingratiating smile. "Now, if you ladies would still like to have dinner, I'll ask Katy to take your orders."

Mary Law, hungry and not willing to be turned away, blushed a deep rose and interjected, "We wish to order, Ellie."

Helen hesitated and then seated herself.

Miss Ellie's son, Josh, walked into the café, greeted the four women with a routine, "Good evening, ladies," and headed back to the VIP table. His starched shirt collar and the crease in his pants suggested a man who expected perfection. Rumor had it that his career had been with the CIA, but he scoffed at any attempts to reveal his government activities, preferring to say only that he once worked with the State Department.

Katy showed up with country-style platters of rice, gravy, pole beans, slaw, and tomatoes, which she slid between Billie and Gill before serving their entrées. As she put down the plate of Salisbury steak, Billie touched her arm and whispered discreetly, "I told Joe about your situation. He thinks you've got an open-and-shut case."

Katy blushed. She had no desire to get into a public discussion of her personal history in the middle of the café. She turned to get refills of water and tea. When she came back, Joe looked up. As he bit into a chicken leg, fried crumbs showered down and nestled along the sides of his moustache. A moan of appreciation escaped, and he nodded in approval at the taste. "We'll talk," he said. "Give me your number, and I'll meet you down here one afternoon after work."

Katy felt her pulse quicken, and she scrawled her phone number on a napkin and pushed it toward him as inconspicuously as she knew how. Gill pretended not to notice. "Give me a couple of weeks," Joe said between bites. "I'll call."

A lawyer might actually sue Doc Attwuld's estate on my behalf, Katie thought. Good Lord. Her mind began to imagine the controversy she would create in Bixby. Laura Attwuld would be humiliated all over again. If people thought she was an opportunist before, they'd think she was a gold digger now. She started to second-guess making such a decision. She didn't want to revisit the scandal. Hurrying into the kitchen, she leaned against the refrigerator, closed her eyes, and raised the back of her hand to her forehead.

"What's the matter, baby?" A woman's voice as deep and smooth as the first swallow of a good bourbon jolted her from her trance. "That spit of a Yankee didn't get 'nuff chicken in his dumplin's?"

Katy looked across the metal counter at the broad back of Teensy Anderson. She was shaking the grease out of a basket of chicken in one hand and doing the same to fries in the other before dumping them under a heat lamp and pulling a sheet of biscuits out of the double oven, all in one continuous motion. Teensy had been there forever. She'd started working at fourteen alongside her grandma at a time when she wasn't even allowed to sit and eat her own cooking in the front room. When the Quaker owner sold the restaurant and her grandmother passed on, Miss Ellie appointed Teensy as head cook. Head cook basically meant the only cook, but it gave her supervising status over the dishwasher and more control over the white waitresses than they cared to admit. Cross Teensy and your orders came out burnt, and the tips dried up. No one wanted to endanger the reputation of the food at The Quaker Café. Good service relied on a good cook. And Teensy was *good*—one just had to take a taste of Miss Ellie's famous biscuits, which Teensy made daily.

"Nothin'," Katy said. "Joe Wiseman's out there."

"Something wrong with his chicken?" Her eyes flashed under a pair of eyebrows that could have provided shade for hummingbirds. She clearly didn't like Joe Wiseman bad-mouthing her chicken.

"Chicken's fine." Katy hesitated. "He wants to talk to me about filing a lawsuit."

"And . . . ?" Teensy slipped two more patties of ground beef onto the grill and threw a pile of sliced onions on top of the ones already there.

"I just don't know how all this legal stuff works, and I don't need any more trouble in my life."

"Listen here, honey." With her hand gripped around the spatula, Teensy leaned on the counter, the whites of her eyes so white that her pupils looked like black holes. "There's always someone slow walkin' behind. You gotta stay in front of 'em."

Katy feigned a weak smile. She wasn't sure if that meant she should or shouldn't do what Joe told her. She liked Teensy. She'd honestly forgotten all about Teensy from when she first worked at The Quaker Café years ago, but Teensy remembered her. White folks remembered white folks, but Teensy remembered everybody—who to trust and who was trouble. "You weren't no trouble," Teensy had told her when she'd walked into the kitchen and been reintroduced. "You were just young and stupid."

"What do you know about Joe Wiseman?"

"I hear people talk." Teensy slapped two buns on the griddle and then flipped the burgers onto them with onions on top of one and fries on both.

"What do they say?"

"They say he be the go-to man when you got trouble."

"What if you're not in trouble?"

"Pshaw, everybody got trouble. I got trouble. You got trouble. It's just some knows how to make money off trouble. Joe Wiseman's a rich man . . . a rich man knee-deep in trouble." She shook her head. "I swear, what some folks won't do to make a livin'." She slung the two burgers across the counter. "Order up."

❧

Several weeks later and two hours away, Laura Attwuld got a visit from her lawyer.

"Joe Wiseman? She's retained Joe Wiseman?" Laura's voice reverberated across the room, and Harold Miller flinched. Laura remembered the murder case from five years ago. Wiseman had defended a client accused of a heinous crime in Chowan County and raised enough doubt in the jury's minds to have him set free. The verdict was not well received among the locals in Bixby.

Harold watched Laura. She always appeared so controlled in public. Perhaps that's what was expected of any prominent person's wife, but he knew she had a breaking point, and this might be it.

As executor of Doc's will, he was doing his best to tie up loose ends, but Doc's office affair and subsequent murder had made things very complicated. Wiseman presented a further problem, one Harold had hoped to avoid.

"Joe Wiseman is a criminal attorney." Laura looked at Harold, confused and frightened. "What has he got to do with me?"

Harold shifted his position in the living room chair and removed his steel rim glasses. He set them down on the adjacent coffee table. "He may file a malpractice suit against the office."

"You mean she's suing *the office*? Can she do that?"

"Doc violated medical ethics. The practice could be held liable," Harold said without flinching. Laura dropped into a chair. He let her absorb the first shock before he hit her with the second. "Joe might also bring a suit against Doc's estate."

There was another long pause before Laura could find words. "I don't believe what I'm hearing," she said. "I'm the one who was wronged. I've done everything I was supposed to do: stood by his side, raised the kids, kept his house, did the community thing . . ." Her voice trailed off. Neither spoke for a minute before she asked, "Why's he doing this to me?"

Harold didn't respond for a minute. She already knew the answer, and he did, too. "Wiseman's just a lawyer like any other. He takes the cases that come through the door—especially the ones that might make some money," Harold said in a monotone.

"He's not just a lawyer, Harold. He crushes people." Laura became rigid, tight lipped, jaw clenched. "What does he want?"

"He's fishing. Trying to find out what the practice has in insurance and what the estate has in assets. I ran into him over at the courthouse yesterday asking for a copy of Doc's will."

"He can get that information?"

"A will's a public document. Anyone can request a copy," Harold said.

Laura looked at him in disbelief. "Anyone?"

"That's the law."

"This isn't fair." She got up, walked over to the cabinet, and reached for a bottle of Jack Daniel's, but thought better of it. Instead, she turned and said, "Harold, you know what my financial situation is. Can't you give me any good news?"

Harold tried to find something to reassure her, but at the moment everything was in limbo. These things took time, more time than most people could afford to wait. The life insurance company had denied payment based on a clause that voided the policy if the policyholder died in the act of a criminal offense. In North Carolina, adultery was still on the books as a criminal offense, although it was used more often in cases that involved alienation of affection. Sexual misconduct on the part of the doctor would likely be deemed malpractice, and had he lived, Doc would have certainly lost his medical license. But there were cases in which criminal charges of adultery had been upheld.

The life insurance company had obviously decided to hold on to its playing cards and see how the game would unfold. They might be able to avoid a large payout. Harold thought he could win, but he'd have to fight it out with them.

To make matters worse for Laura, no doctor wanted to take over a medical practice that might be in the middle of a major malpractice suit. Without a doctor, there was no practice. Without a practice, no money came in to offset the bills.

"I'm working on it," he said. "We'll reach a settlement eventually." He meant that, but he couldn't predict how long it might take. Hank's murder trial could delay all negotiations.

"Our savings will only go so far." Laura walked into the other room and came back with a Kleenex. This surprised him. He'd never seen her cry, even at Doc's funeral. "I was counting on that life insurance policy. Wake Forest is expensive. Next year's tuition is due before long. I don't know what to tell my son."

Harold stood. "Can I get you anything?" he asked.

"No, no," she said without conviction. "I just need to figure out my options."

"Listen, I'll talk to Wiseman and see if he'll go after the medical practice insurance and leave Doc's estate out of the mix. I don't think he has a lot to gain by attacking you. He's bluffing, trying to force a deal."

Laura wiped her nose and nodded.

Overwhelmed by her thoughts, Laura watched Harold walk down the sidewalk and get into his BMW. Surely it would be easier to just make a quiet out-of-court settlement between the insurance company and that girl. That's why you had insurance. But if Wiseman went after Doc's estate, she'd have to fight. More lawyers, more money down the drain. This was a nightmare.

If another doctor interested in the practice didn't surface before long, she'd have to hire accountants and medical attorneys to work through the records and close the office. That cost alone was staggering. Either way, Doc had left her with far more problems than a simple affair. But what affair is ever simple?

CHAPTER SEVEN

Sam sat on the couch, beer in hand. He and Dusty munched on a bag of Lay's potato chips and watched a Buffalo Bills–Pittsburgh Steelers game. Katy helped Savannah piece together the fringe along the edge of her uniform. She had been selected as a flag girl after the assistant principal, Adam Hoole, encouraged Savannah to try out for a vacancy that occurred over the summer.

Adam had stopped by several times to speak to Dusty and Savannah after visiting his grandparents, Euphrasia and Nathan Hoole, two doors down. A man with seemingly endless energy, he bubbled with enthusiasm about the school and community. On a more personal level, he and his wife asked Savannah to do some babysitting for their two-year-old, Mary Beth.

Savannah seemed to be adjusting. She jumped at the opportunity to be a flag girl with the band, and she'd made a friend who picked her up for church every Sunday. She joined the church choir and encouraged her mother to go, but Katy couldn't. She worked Sunday lunches at the café.

Dusty, on the other hand, had no interested in church, and he still struggled to just get up and out the door every morning.

Katy's attempts to discuss all that had happened between her and Hank remained awkward. She apologized to Savannah and Dusty for many things, but she let them know that the most precious gift she had was the two of them.

The Steelers took an early lead with a touchdown and field goal. Outside, the two dogs began to bark. The distraction annoyed Sam, and he glanced between the front windows and the television. "What's that ruckus out there?" He motioned irritably at the door as the yapping became more intense. "Dusty, go see what's bothering those dogs, will ya?"

Dusty groaned. He liked Sam better when he didn't order him around. He went to the window, looked, paused, and then walked over to the door and took a second look. He turned abruptly. "There're turkeys all over our yard," he hollered. "Turkeys, goats, *and* pigs."

Just then, they heard the clanging of a bell from Leland Slade's backyard.

Katy went to the kitchen window. "We've got a barnyard circus out there."

"Lord, Leland's Thanksgiving turkeys." Sam shook his head and heaved himself off the sofa reluctantly. Animal chaos occurred a couple of times a year, but it seemed to be getting more frequent. Leland would forget to close a gate and get distracted by another chore. The animals would make a break for the road, and it would take a couple of hours to round them all up again. Sam didn't mind the chase so much, but he did mind missing his football game.

"Dusty, get those mouthy dogs and lock them on the back porch. Katy, grab anything with a stick at the end, brooms or dust mops."

Two decades had gone by since Katy last tried to catch a pig. They were smart critters. As for goats and turkeys, she'd never corralled one in her life.

Savannah and Katy gathered brooms and mops. Fifty yards stretched between the fenced-in area around the barn in Leland's yard and the ditch that ran along the road in front of his house. The garden and runway were between Sam's house and Leland's barn, along with the field of corn that Leland had harvested.

Sam grabbed two mops. "I'll try to get ahead of them and turn 'em back. Don't let the critters cross the ditch down there." He pointed to a tom and three hens pecking at the ground near the house. "Try to head them back toward Leland's."

Not quite sure exactly what to do, Katy started lightly thrusting her broom at the turkeys. "Shoo, go on home now," she said, but the brownish-black tom puffed up the beard across his chest and started to spread his tail. An array of chocolate-brown feathers three-quarters of the way up fanned out into a white-and-black wigwam pattern to the tip and sprayed across his backside. His triple-toed feet pranced in place, and he yodeled and advanced on her. Katy jumped back. The red snoods on the hens' heads became erect, and they scampered in three different directions.

The bell clanged again, after which Leland trudged through the field of sawed-off stalks carrying a pail of corn. He took long strides across the landing strip. Bent and wearing his wide-brim hat and a weathered coat, he seemed resigned to an afternoon of catch and carry.

Sam moved in front of the flight of turkeys. He slowly turned to face them and gradually extended the mops he held in each hand outward. Ever so cautiously, he raised and lowered them in slow motion. Looking like a Frankenstein with arm extensions, Sam continued with drawn-out strides across the yard, getting the attention of any strays.

Most of the dozen or so turkeys reversed their flight and headed back in the direction of Leland's, sometimes at a run. But their escape remained erratic. A few sidetracked to the left or right. The pigs, in contrast, took off around Sam like football linemen headed for the end zone.

"Keep 'em outta the road!" Sam yelled at Dusty as two forty-pound porkers headed for the highway. Dusty braced for the charge. With legs firmly planted on the ground, he moved into a tackle position.

"Don't!" Sam screamed across the yard, sending the turkeys into a flurry. Dusty lunged for the pig headed straight at him. He caught only air and tasted dirt as the pig scampered between his legs and Dusty hit the ground on his stomach. The pigs disappeared into the roadside ditch. Righting himself, Dusty followed suit over the slippery embankment that was still damp from a midweek rain. Two pigs wearing shiny coats of muck reappeared up the bank, invigorated by the chase. Dusty emerged wet and dirty.

A pickup rolled to a slow stop on the highway behind him. Phil and Nanette Harper climbed out of the Chevy truck with their fifteen-year-old son, Ben. Local farmers, they were Quakers who had moved to the area ten years earlier in search of a small community and a few acres of farmland. They made themselves available to lend a hand wherever needed. Helping Leland corral his animals had turned into a routine event.

Adam Hoole pulled in behind the truck in his Honda Accord. His grandparents lived next door to Leland, and he had long ago learned how to recapture Leland's fleeing livestock. He laughed with the Harpers as they unloaded long sticks and buckets of oats and corn from the bed of the pickup.

"Hey, Leland," Adam called, "did you break the news to the turkeys about the upcoming Thanksgiving party?"

Leland looked up, hinted at a rare smile, and shook his head. Taking the pail of corn, he pulled out a few handfuls and threw the kernels in a small circle. This got the attention of the turkeys in his vicinity, who gobbled their way over to the new food source and clustered together to peck at the ground. Adam did likewise where he stood, and Phil and Nanette stepped outside the ring of turkeys, took their long sticks, and moved into a circling maneuver similar to Sam's.

Ben, a few inches taller than Dusty, walked over and handed him a bucket of corn. "That pig will follow you if you offer him food. Throw a bit out."

"Thanks," Dusty said, embarrassed that the other boy had seen his dive into the ditch.

"Stand still. Stand still," Ben coached. "Just throw a little out and let him come to you. That's it," he said as Dusty followed instructions. Carefully they dipped the pail close to the ground for the pig to get a taste and then walked a few feet ahead of him. The pig hesitated, but then started a slow stroll behind them back toward Leland's farm. Before long, another pig had become interested and moved alongside. He grunted at the first pig to get his head in the pail, and Dusty poured some of the kernels on the ground.

"My name's Ben Harper."

"I'm Dusty."

"I know. I've seen you at school. We've got North Carolina history together."

"You Quaker?" Dusty asked.

"Yep."

"You don't look Quaker."

"Yeah? How's a Quaker supposed to look?"

"I don't know," Dusty conceded. "Sort of old fashion, I guess—wearing black and white. Not jeans and a Tar Heel sweatshirt like you."

"Bet you don't even know which ones are the Quakers at school," Ben said.

"No," Dusty said. "I don't."

"You're thinking Amish. We're not Amish. Besides, the Amish don't even go to our school. They have their own."

"What about Leland?" Dusty nodded at Leland across the yard in his black trousers and suspenders, the broad-brimmed hat on his head.

"That's just Leland. He's hung on to the old ways."

"Oh," Dusty said, embarrassed that he didn't know much of anything about either the Quakers or the Amish.

"How you like school?" Ben asked.

"Not much."

"I've seen those guys making fun of you."

Dusty grimaced.

"Jim Gorman, Greg Russo, and Carl Newcomb. They're always picking on new kids," Ben said.

Dusty shuffled his feet uncomfortably.

"They give Quaker kids a hard time. They know we won't fight, so they tease us to see if we'll take a swing."

"And you don't do anything?" Dusty asked.

"Mostly I ignore them."

Dusty started thinking about the jokes the boys made about his mama. Every time they snickered, he wanted to bust their chops, even though he knew they would beat him to a pulp. "I wanna knock out their teeth," he said.

"Naw, that never works. There are other ways to get even."

A burgundy Land Rover pulled into the drive, and Webster could be heard barking from the backseat. Billie McFarland climbed down dressed in puce jeans and a salmon-pink sweatshirt. "I heard the bell and figured the turkeys were loose. Threw on my sweats and came right over."

Sam groaned. "Keep your mutt in the car," he yelled.

Billie shot Sam a defiant look, but Nanette Harper came to her side immediately. While no one ever questioned Billie's good intentions, Nanette knew she needed guidance, and Billie deferred readily to any-one who raised the animals that she depended on to marinate, grill, or roast.

Giving Billie a hug and then handing her a pail of corn, Nanette said, "See that pig over there with her piglets? See if you can tempt her back to Leland's by offering her some corn. Just hold the pail low to the ground, give her a taste, and walk forward a few steps at a time. If she comes, the little ones will follow."

Delighted to have a task, Billie headed in the direction of the sow, carefully sidestepping any droppings from the turkeys' flight. She pulled a handkerchief out of her pocket and spread it on the ground in front of her before she went on bended knee and started talking to the mama as if they were planning to have tea together.

Mama pig grunted, eyed the corn, and snorted. Billie threw some kernels on the ground, and the piglets danced in place. "Well, hello there, darlings. You all going for a stroll today? Perhaps we could amble on home now before nightfall and the big bad wolf comes knocking at your door?"

"Billie, watch that ole sow. She gets mean if you get close to her young'uns," Phil shouted. "Don't touch them."

Billie stood, backed away a bit, and rearranged her handkerchief. This time she poured a pile of corn on the ground, which got the mama up and moving.

Savannah helped Sam usher the first of the turkeys back toward their pen. "Put them in the barn," Leland said. Savannah did a double take. She'd never heard Leland speak before. The man did talk.

"Better start looking toward the woods," Adam said, motioning. "Once we lose daylight, they'll roost or hide under shrub. Make a good meal for a fox or coyote."

One of the pigs followed Katy closely as she dipped the bowl of grain down repeatedly to encourage him to catch up and get a nibble. A second pig eyed the departure of his buddy and finally turned homeward. But three of the goats still stood defiant on opposite sides of the yard, with no apparent desire to relinquish their newfound freedom. The men and boys branched out in an effort to tighten the circle around one goat at a time.

After thirty minutes of touch tag, Adam caught the rear end of one of them and wrapped his arms around her middle. The second goat took off into the brush. All eyes turned to the black goat still in the middle of the yard.

"Okay, Dusty, let's you and me get this one." Sam stared her down while the remaining posse circled around. "I'll keep her focused on me while you come up from behind. No fast moves. Take it slow until you know you're in grabbing range."

Dusty glanced over at Ben, who nodded his approval. The goat didn't move. The rectangular pupils stared out of their yellow irises. "Come on, ole girl. No one's going to hurt you," Sam coaxed. They inched in closer. "Steady and ready," he signaled to Dusty.

Having eyed the commotion from inside the Land Rover, the little black Scottie could stand his isolation no longer. Collecting his courage, Webster leaped without warning through the open window to the ground. The farm dogs confined to the porch barked in loud protest. Their nemesis was free. They were not. Dusty lunged from behind the goat just as she put her head down and charged forward. She landed a blow directly into Sam's crotch.

Sam yelled in pain, collapsed, and withered on the ground like a man struck by lightning.

"Ooh!" Phil and Adam called out in unison. "That hurt."

Katy burst into laughter.

Phil squatted down next to Sam. "Want any help?" Sam raised his hand and shook his head without speaking. "Okay, we'll check back." Phil moved on. "Man down. Let's see what the rest of us can do."

Adam saw that Billie had momentarily stopped romancing the pigs. "Get Webster out of here," he called to her.

"Sorry, sorry." Billie put her pail on the ground and left mama pig to devour the contents while she retrieved Webster and lectured him on his inappropriate behavior. On her way past Sam, she leaned down apologetically and whispered softly, "I'm so sorry. It won't happen again." Her apparent regret appeared to do little to soothe him. Sam hunched up on all fours and began a slow crawl to the porch.

By the time the sky darkened and the animals were contained, Dusty and Ben had cemented a friendship. Dusty gave Ben a high five and went inside to change out of his filthy clothes. Buffalo had lost, and Sam lay on the sofa with a bag of ice between his legs. Katy looked at them. "Pretty pathetic, you two. Not the best day, huh?"

Dusty turned toward his mom with a smile she hadn't seen in years. "The best day ever."

CHAPTER EIGHT

Katy entered the dining area with more servings of fried chicken and butter beans. The first wave of churchgoers stood in line to pay Miss Ellie. The Baptist minister always shortened his sermon to allow everyone to get a head start on the Sunday buffet. First the Baptists, then the Methodists, who got more preaching but were assured they'd be first in line to the gates of heaven. The out-of-towners arrived from the county's various other churches forty-five minutes later. Diners understood they were to eat and leave, knowing they occupied coveted seats. Turnover was fast. Tips were good.

Katy reset two tables and placed four chairs around each. Someone behind her rattled a glass of ice. "Miss," came a voice that brought back bad memories, "I could use a refill."

She added the napkins and silverware to the cleared table, steadied her nerves, and picked up the pitcher of tea on the sideboard. Katy turned. Hank's brother, Ray, sneered at her. Wearing a NASCAR sweatshirt, he bent over his plate with his elbows on the table and one hand holding up a glass. Long, thin legs in jeans stretched under the table to the chair opposite him. Three years older than Hank and about twenty pounds heavier, he had lost the earthy appeal that once made him so irresistible. His chiseled nose was now flattened, enhancing his bad boy image that attracted some women. When she'd been younger, those same qualities in Hank had attracted her. But Hank had always been softer than Ray—the same daredevil ways but not nearly as nasty.

Fight, she thought. Someone had gotten in a good lick since she'd last seen him.

"Long time no see," he said as she approached and refilled his glass.

"Shaved your head?" She eyed the buzz cut that revealed a scar above the right ear. "Looks terrible."

He laughed. "You always had a way with words."

She had no reason whatsoever to be civil to this man. He had harassed her unmercifully.

He rubbed his hand over the top of his head. "Job thing," he said. "Medic."

She sniffed. He was the last person she'd want to see in an emergency.

"You moved. Didn't give us a change of address." He raised an eyebrow. Katy said nothing. "Saw your kids at school on Friday."

Katy took a step back. Her surprise pleased him. He liked the idea that they hadn't told her. "Their daddy sends his love. He wanted to know how they're doing. They ain't been to see him since he lost his senses after what you done."

Heads turned.

"Stop it," Katy whispered under her breath. "I'm not having this conversation with you."

Ray shrugged. "Nice-looking kids. I think Dusty looks more and more like his dad, don't you?"

Katy could feel her mouth go dry. She looked desperately around the room, not knowing who could hear them. "I can't talk now."

"I'll wait," he said. "I got time."

"We need the table."

"Don't see no reserved sign sitting on it."

Katy's hand trembled. He noticed—let his eyes wander down her frame and raised an eyebrow. "You look good, Katy. You gettin' any while Hank's locked up?"

She couldn't stand the pleasure he got from tormenting her. She turned, put the pitcher back down on the sideboard, and disappeared into the kitchen. She walked into the employees' bathroom and locked the door. She needed a minute to calm herself.

Normally Miss Ellie would have noticed something was wrong, but on Sundays everyone moved at top speed to get as much food out as fast as possible. Katy couldn't hide for long. Things would get backed up.

Katy returned to the kitchen and yanked three baskets of hot biscuits from under the warmer. She swung around so quickly that one basket tipped, and several biscuits hit the floor like pieces of gold falling down an elevator shaft. Teensy stopped. She looked out from under her bridge of eyebrows. "Something got you spooked, gal?"

Katy scrambled to pick up the biscuits and discard them. "My brother-in-law's out there. He's got me rattled."

"'Bout what?" Teensy didn't take lightly to mishaps during her Sunday lunch.

"He's been making hateful phone calls. Now he's out there telling me he's been to the school to see my kids."

"So read him the riot act. Get rid of him."

"You make it sound easy."

"Sam in town?" Teensy asked.

"Yeah."

"Call him. Tell him that thug's here."

Katy nodded. She pushed through the swinging door to the dining room. She'd call Sam as soon as she had a spare minute, but right now Ellie needed all the help she could get. Maybe Ray would just get up and leave.

For the next thirty minutes she tried to ignore him, but whenever she turned to see if he'd left, ice ran through her veins as memories surfaced—the menacing looks and crude jokes he always made at her expense. The house was dirty, the food lousy. She was too slow, too messy, too fat, too stupid. Hank mirrored whatever mood Ray was in.

Why is he here? she kept asking herself. *What does he want? And what did he say to Dusty and Savannah?*

Ray nursed his glass of tea and a dish of banana pudding until the Sunday crowd thinned. Katy carried out the remainder of the dishes and swept the floor before she took off her apron and went to his table.

She'd been rehearsing what she'd say to him, mustering up her courage. She hadn't called Sam because she wanted to handle this herself—wanted him to know she had changed. She pulled out a chair, sat down, and tried to look him in the eye. His stare bored holes through her.

"I don't want you seeing Savannah and Dusty again," she said. "I'm not taking them to see Hank, and if they subpoena me to go to court, don't expect any good memories to come to mind."

"Katy, darling." Ray's voice lowered in mock sweetness. "I'm surprised at you. I can't believe you ain't more concerned about Hank, given what all you done. He loved you so much, and you screwed around behind his back. There weren't nothin' that happened you didn't cause."

Katy shot out of her chair so fast that it tipped over backward. The few remaining customers in the restaurant turned in her direction. Billie's words ran through her head. *Don't raise a daughter who lets some creep beat her up.* "Get out, right now." She turned, walked to the door, and opened it for him.

Ray rose slowly. Pulled out a five and three ones. Threw them on the table. He righted the downed chair and made a long question mark with his face as he looked innocently at the gawkers in the room. As he walked out the door, he grabbed her wrist and pulled her behind him. Once outside his voice turned spiteful.

"You think you can just move, change your name, and let Hank rot in jail? You think I'm gonna let you keep the kids?"

"That's over, Ray. Social services promised me there's no way you're getting them." She strained to get away, but his grip tightened.

"You think? Let me tell you what I think. I think you killed the doc and set Hank up. Doc used you and then dumped you. You're the one should be in jail, and ain't no way I'll let Hank take this rap for you. He'll walk away from this, and he'll take the kids with him."

Katy had seen his anger escalate like this before. Instinctively she tucked her chin down and raised her free arm in front of her face to protect herself from a possible blow.

"Hey, you!" A bulky black figure emerged from around the outside corner of the café. Still wearing her white apron, with her shoulders hunched and her fist clenched, Teensy measured equal degrees of width and height to Ray. "You let go that gal right now."

Ray stopped. He looked at Teensy and laughed. "What you gonna do if I don't, nigger woman?"

From behind Teensy's back came a black cast iron skillet that moved with the same agility as a swordsman's blade. She honed in on his truck. A loud crack burst through the air. The side window of Ray's Silverado shattered into a thousand pieces.

"You fat bitch!" Ray shouted as he let go of Katy and lunged toward his truck.

"You better believe it. I am a fat bitch." Teensy had already raised the skillet with both of her hands over her head and took out the back window before Ray crossed the empty parking spaces.

He eyed his rifle, now dangling like a broken limb between the glass and the rear seat. "Goddamn it!" he screamed. "I'm going to blister your black ass."

Teensy clutched the skillet like a baseball bat, moved back a yard, and planted her feet solidly on the pavement. "Mmmm-mmmh, you sure got a mouth on you. Come on." She rocked her hips and shifted her weight to her back leg. Raising the frying pan over her right shoulder, she said, "Give it your best shot."

Ray hesitated just long enough for Teensy to know she'd won. Ray yanked open the truck door and revved up the engine before kicking it into reverse. "This ain't over."

Not until he'd cleared Main Street and headed out of town did Teensy turn and look at Katy. The smell of fried chicken clung to Teensy like honey on a biscuit. "Too bad about that truck. I ain't seen exactly what happened, did you?"

Katy stood wide-eyed, her mouth agape.

"Must've hit the lamppost while backing out. We should clean it up."

"Thank you," Katy whispered. She bent down slowly to pick up a couple of larger pieces of glass. "I didn't know what to do."

"Then you better learn, child," Teensy said. "Ain't nobody can boss you around unless you let 'em."

"You don't know Ray. He'll be back, and he'll be mean." Katy almost shuddered with fear knowing he'd be out for revenge the next time she saw him.

"Then you get meaner. You get louder. You get bigger." Teensy eyed her grease-stained apron from hip to hip and dropped her hands on either side to emphasize the expanse. "How you reckon I got so big? It weren't from hiding behind some man's pants leg. I've been at the table for every meal and got my share of what was coming."

"You've been lucky, then," Katy said and realized as soon as it slipped from her mouth what a foolish statement she'd made. She knew little about Teensy's private life, but she knew no one black had grown up in rural North Carolina in the 1940s living an easy life.

Teensy sucked in the air around her and straightened her back. "You think? You come meet my husband sometime. Bedridden for three years now. I kiss him good-bye every morning after his sister comes, not knowin' whether he'll be alive when I come back. Raising three of my grands. They're a joy, but they got to be fed. It ain't luck that keeps me goin.'"

"I'm sorry," Katy apologized. "I know better."

"You just remember this when you start feeling sorry for yourself. The only one who decides who you are and what you do is you. Now." She made an effort to bend over and pick up some glass and then gave in to her girth. "You go get a dustpan and a broom, and let's clean this up."

Chapter Nine

After the great barnyard escape, the Harpers invited everyone over for dinner the following Sunday evening. Only Leland declined the invitation. Around the table, talk turned to the upcoming turkey slaughter at Leland's. It was time to get them dressed for the Thanksgiving sale.

Sam would be gone that week, he confessed with some relief. Phil and Ben encouraged Dusty, Savannah, and Katy to join them. Helping Leland with the chore had become sort of a tradition within the Quaker community, and the school excused students whose parents sent a written letter explaining their absence.

"A lot of helping hands make light work," Nanette said. "Besides, we have some fun."

"He pays you," Ben told Dusty. "You'll make some money at the end of the day."

"Of course, it's all in two-dollar bills," Phil laughed.

"What?" Dusty asked.

"That's just one of Leland's many quirks. He believes that if all the farmers would pay for everything they owed with two-dollar bills, then the state would realize how important farmers are to the economy. He figures it's a simple way to make a powerful statement, and he has visions of two-dollar bills filling up the cash registers across the country."

"Do the farmers do it?" Savannah asked.

"A few did at first," Phil said, "but when you're talking about paying for fertilizer and equipment with two-dollar bills, well, you get into a whole lot of paper money. The vendors don't like it, and the banks finally just stopped ordering more two-dollar bills and told people they were out. It got too cumbersome."

"But not for Leland," Nanette said. "He found a little bank that orders them for him."

"Yep," Phil said. "Leland pays for everything, and I do mean *everything*, in two-dollar bills. The local stores have a cigar box under the counter marked 'Leland' to put his money in when he comes in."

"What about taxes?" Sam asked. "Does he send the government a manila folder filled with two-dollar bills?"

"Taxes?" Phil laughed. "Don't think for a minute Leland pays any taxes. He considers taxes a means to support war, and he stands by the Quaker testimony of peace. He won't support the military in any form."

"But taxes don't all go to the military," Sam said. "There's Social Security, health care, and education."

"He doesn't pay into Social Security and doesn't receive any," Phil said. "He has no insurance and pays his bills in cash when he goes to a doctor, which is rarely. Says he won't question God's good judgment when his time comes."

"He's a very generous man," Nanette added. "He makes regular donations to the local food banks and educational funds. He figures he's supporting his own community in the best ways he can."

"How does he get away with it and not get arrested?" Katy asked.

"It's pretty simple," Phil said. "He never makes enough money to have to pay taxes. Leland knows to the penny what he can make every year without getting taxed. After that he just gives his food away."

"What an interesting man," Katy said. "How many turkeys does he raise for Thanksgiving?"

"Leland started out with a batch of a hundred biddies about eight years ago. He got 'em free with an order of a hundred pounds of chick feed," Phil said. "He put them in the grain bin when they arrived till he could get a pen ready and then flipped the wrong switch the night he went out to water them. The fan went on instead of the light and sucked them all up to the top. If they weren't dead going up, they were dead coming down."

Savannah grimaced. "That's terrible."

Phil chuckled. "We're not raising pets. We're running a business. We make mistakes like everybody else."

Savannah didn't seem terribly reassured.

"After that Leland had all this chicken feed and no chickens. So he went out and bought a batch of turkey poults. He put this batch in his attic in a plastic kids' swimming pool to keep them warm and not to make the same mistake again with the grain bin. When they got too big for the attic, he built a pen outside, but they've been getting loose once or twice a year anyway. Working with Leland, you have to just expect the unexpected. He's a character."

"It's really a lot of fun." Ben tried to soften his father's version. "Really."

Dusty wasn't yet convinced, but if Ben was going to be there, he'd go, too.

&

The ash-colored Silverado with the gun rack in the back window pulled off the road across from the Hooles' home. The windows had been replaced.

Ray Devine watched the commotion at the adjacent farm. Four cars and three trucks, all with more than eight years of wear on them, wedged in angular positions around Leland's driveway. In twos and fours, men and women gathered in back of the house pushing wheelbarrows of firewood, large pots, and utensils. Smoke drifted above the roofline.

Across the harvested cornfield, Ray watched Sam throw a duffel bag over the seat of his Cessna and check his plane before climbing in. He taxied to the end of the lengthy grass runway. From a covey of pines, he turned the plane to face the road and began to pick up speed before lifting up over the highway and heading south.

Good, Ray thought. *He's out of the way.*

Katy walked briskly out the porch door. She pulled the hood of the sweatshirt over her head and crossed the runway before trudging across the harvested field of corn to Leland's. Moments later Dusty came out the door behind her. Ray watched from a distance as the boy zipped up the front of his sweatshirt, stuffed his hands into his jean pockets, and followed her lead.

Ray shifted the Chevy into first gear and rolled into the right-hand lane. Katy and Dusty were a good forty yards from the highway, and neither bothered to look up at the truck. It passed them going in the opposite direction and then slowly turned into the drive. Savannah came out of the house, book sack over her shoulder. Curls peeked out from under a red knit hat. She struggled with a pair of gloves and didn't notice the truck until it pulled into the drive. Ray rolled down the window. "Can I give you a lift to school?"

"Uncle Ray?" She glanced in the direction of her mom and brother, who were about to disappear around the back of Leland's house.

"Saw your dad this week. He asked me to stop by and give you his love. I got some more letters for you. He misses you and Dusty a lot."

Ray had been dropping Hank's letters off to Savannah at school once a month for the past four months. Dusty wouldn't come near the truck, but Savannah had taken the letters and had given Ray some in return to take back to her father. Gradually, she'd become more willing to talk.

"I don't know." She hesitated. "Some friends pick me up. They'll be here any minute."

"I'll wait with you. You can go with them if you like." Ray leaned across the seat and opened the door. "It's cold. Climb on in a minute."

Savannah paused. It was cold. She didn't plan on riding to school with him, but they could talk for a few minutes. Her dad's letters were having an effect. He wrote: *I'm innocent. This is all a terrible mistake. I regret anything I ever done to hurt you, Dusty, and your mom. I love you all and realize now more than ever what having a family has meant to me.*

She threw her book bag in first before grabbing hold of the bar and pulling herself up.

"How's my daddy?" she asked.

"To be honest, honey, he's going out of his mind. He can't believe what's happening. Feels like his whole life has been ripped away from him."

Savannah hung her head and scraped some of the pink polish off her little fingernail. "He wrote me he's going to the church services they have there."

"Oh yeah. I've started going to church, too. We're both praying that things will work out so the family can be back together. He's forgiven your mom, even after all she did to him," Ray said.

Savannah twitched her lips and looked away.

"I mean, he needs her forgiveness, too. He says he's talked to the minister a lot. He knows he didn't always treat your mom the way he should have."

A baby blue '88 Honda pulled into the drive, and the two girls in the car looked up into the Silverado somewhat confused. Savannah rolled the window down. "This is my Uncle Ray," she said. They waited for further explanation. "He's going to take me to school today. I'll meet you there."

"You sure?" said the larger of the two girls. They recognized the Silverado from school. Savannah had told them some of the history, and it wasn't all good.

"Yeah." Savannah nodded.

"How 'bout Dusty?"

"He's gone to Leland's to help kill turkeys. He and Ben Harper got outta going to school."

"You not going?"

"It sounds awful. Cutting turkeys' throats and pulling out their feathers and innards." Savannah scrunched up her nose and shook her head so that her curls bounced around her neck.

Ray smiled. "Really? You going with me? That's great. I've got something your dad wants me to ask you."

The two girls wheeled their vehicle around and headed down the drive. They turned left and sped off, ignoring the thirty-five miles an hour speed limit. Ray followed more slowly and waited until he'd cleared the town limits before he spoke again. "Your daddy really wants to see you."

"I can't." Savannah shifted in the seat. "My mom won't let me."

"You're seventeen. You don't need to go with your mom. I'll take you."

Savannah didn't say anything. She watched the car with her friends in front of them speed out of sight.

"He needs to see you, really bad. He needs to know that his kids still care about what happens to him." Ray waited for an answer. When none came, he backed off a bit. "That's okay. I understand. You might pray on it and figure out what Jesus would do."

"I pray for him every day," Savannah said softly.

"What do you pray for?" Ray asked.

"I pray for Mama and Daddy, and Mrs. Attwuld and her kids. Somebody killed their daddy, and they've got no one now, too. Did Daddy do that, Uncle Ray? Did he really kill Doc Attwuld?"

"No, baby. No, he didn't. He's been set up, and you need to believe that."

"Who did, then?"

Ray paused. He knew Savannah would bolt if he suggested Katy's name. "Your mama wasn't the only one Doc Attwuld was messin' with. Who knows? Another woman? Another angry husband? Your daddy just got the blame, that's all."

Ray stopped to let his words sink in. When he thought he'd given her enough time to consider what he said, he added, "He's a changed man. Really. Are you reading his letters?"

"I am. I write back, you know that. I give you the letters."

"Is Dusty reading them?"

"He's read a couple is all. He thinks Daddy is guilty."

"That's why it's so important for you to see your father—so you can tell Dusty how much he's changed. If you could talk to your dad, you'd know."

They drove the rest of the way in silence. Ray had learned enough about women to know when to push and when to let them feel like they were in control. He wanted to keep building this relationship with Savannah. He didn't want her to get scared and bolt.

Ray had several different ideas on how to get Hank out of jail. Blaming Doc's murder on Katy was one of them. If that didn't work, there were others, but he needed to keep as many options open as he could. No telling which way the dice would roll.

❧

Leland's backyard felt cluttered. Where normally a few oak trees separated the house from the barn and the turkey coops and pigpens, now a dozen men and women in jeans and flannel shirts scurried about. Two fires were going with iron cauldrons of water heating on top. Ben fed one of the fires with split oak, while his mother helped several women unload large pots from the back of a truck. Ben's father and two other men were rigging up some kind of contraption with a hook and a crossbeam. Katy had already joined Nanette Harper and seemed to be getting introduced to the other women.

Adam Hoole, the assistant principal, spotted Dusty from across the yard and gave him a wave with a friendly smile. Evidently skipping school to kill turkeys was as good an excuse for him as it was for Dusty.

"Your uncle not coming?"

Dusty flinched and turned to see Leland towering over him. The few times Leland spoke always surprised him. He never recognized his voice. "No, sir. He's gone for two weeks. Flew out this morning."

Leland nodded. "Stay close to Ben. He'll show you what to do."

Dusty approached the warm fire. This could be as good a job as any, just keeping the wood burning. Ben slid another log under the cauldron and squatted on his haunches. Dusty hunkered down beside him. Ben saw him and beamed from ear to ear. "You came?"

"You thought I wouldn't?"

"Wasn't sure."

"So what do we do, just keep the fire going?" Dusty said hopefully.

"That and a little bit more. Come on, I'll show you."

The pigs had been moved to an enclosed area behind the barn, and two cows and a horse stood in a back field. The goats remained skittish, and the turkeys knew instinctively this was not a day to celebrate. They darted from one corner of their pen to another.

"Our job is to catch them." Ben nodded in the direction of the turkeys. "I got a system that works for me by snagging a foot and then grabbing them by the legs. You gotta be careful, though. The toms have a spur, and the wings are strong enough to break a bone if they hit you good."

Dusty raised his eyebrows. He'd been concerned about blood and guts, and Ben seemed more focused on broken bones. "What'll we do once we got them?" Dusty asked.

"You'll see." Ben fidgeted with a long, thin rope he pulled out of his back pocket. "I'll make a slip knot and lay this in the middle of the coop. You chase the turkeys in the direction of the noose, and when one steps in, I'll pull it."

"Then what?"

"Then we stuff 'em in one of those burlap bags over there," Ben said, motioning to a pile of old feed sacks in the corner, "and Leland and my dad will take it from there."

Dusty remained skeptical, but so far Ben hadn't talked about knives or cutting or blood, so he decided he was good. "When do we start?" he asked.

Ben looked around and saw that the water was almost boiling and that the men had the hook hung from the crossbeam. Though Ben stood taller than Dusty, he probably didn't carry much more weight. If his dad was any indication, Dusty figured Ben would probably grow to six feet long before Dusty did. He might even be good basketball material if he hit a spurt this year.

Phil saw Ben and Dusty checking out their setup and hollered across the yard, "Think we're ready for the first one."

"Now," Ben said, and the two of them opened the door to the pen and scooted in. The turkeys scampered to the opposite side. Ben laid a circular twelve-inch noose in the middle of the pen and then moved to the side, holding the two loose ends of the rope close to the ground. "Go shoo them in this direction," he said.

Shooing wasn't as hard as Dusty thought. The turkeys automatically ran away as soon as he approached them, but none seemed inclined to step in the noose on their first stroll across the pen. "Keep 'em moving," Ben called. "We don't want them stopping to think." Dusty wasn't convinced that turkey thinking presented a problem.

Pretty soon one turkey stepped in the noose and Ben pulled, but not fast enough. The turkey ran to the other side and gobbled his acknowledgment of successfully outsmarting this game of jump rope. Ben went to the middle of the pen to readjust the noose, and the turkeys took a short breather.

"It works," Ben said in an effort to reassure Dusty that he knew what he was doing. "Run 'em again."

This time around, Ben snagged the leg of a turkey, and the bird nose-dived to the ground and began to flap wildly. Ben was on him in an instant, grabbing both legs and holding the turkey upside down. "Here!" he yelled. "Hold his legs while I get a rope around them."

Dusty obeyed, feeling the unexpected weight as the bird flapped his wings trying to free himself. Dusty held tight with both hands, knowing that other eyes were on him. Ben looped a rope around the legs and then grabbed one of the burlap bags. Ben slipped the bag over the turkey's head and around the rest of his body until only the legs were sticking out. "Now watch this," he said. Encased in the dark sack, the turkey suddenly calmed.

Ben's dad was waiting at the gate to take the bag from his son, and with long strides that matched his height, he carried the victim to the crossbeam. Slipping the loop between the turkey's legs over the hook, he tied a small rope around the bag near its thighs. Within seconds, the turkey stuck his neck out of a hole in the bottom, and Leland slit his throat so quickly Dusty didn't realize what had happened until the blood began to drain onto the ground. "Oh!" Dusty gasped.

"Isn't that something? They do it every single time—stick their necks out like that."

"Is that why they say *don't stick your neck out?*"

"Probably," Ben said.

From that point on, the processing of the turkeys went through an assembly line of steps that had been practiced and refined. By the time the first turkey bled out, Ben and Dusty had caught the second. After they delivered him to the gallows, they loaded the first one on a wagon and pulled it over to the wooden tables that stood at waist height next to the cauldron.

Nanette Harper and Anna Reed grabbed the legs of the dead turkey with the strength and certainty of pioneer women. Each holding a leg, they dunked the body headfirst in and out of the hot water while Nanette occasionally pulled at a feather until she was satisfied that they were loosened. Then they swung the turkey onto the table, where it was immediately assaulted by the other women, who cut off the large wings at the joint and plucked the feathers.

After four turkeys had been killed, Phil spoke to the boys. "Hold off a bit until the women catch up with the plucking. We don't want the dead ones sitting around too long."

Ben motioned to Dusty. "This is when we check the wood for the fires, and then if we're lucky, Pam will have biscuits coming out of the oven about now." Sure enough, when they walked into the kitchen, the smells engulfed them.

Pam Sibley pulled out a sheet of hot cheese biscuits and smiled at the boys. "Just in time," she said. A motherly woman not much taller than Ben, she was rounded slightly from her own good cooking. Her eyes shone with kindness. "Coffee and hot chocolate on the stove. Help yourselves."

Leland's kitchen was much like Sam's, part of a house built in the fifties that had never been remodeled. Both the stove and the refrigerator looked dated, although clean and organized. Leland had nailed up some open shelves for his mugs and dishes, nothing as elaborate as a cabinet. Anything one needed was in sight.

Dusty followed Ben and grabbed a mug. "This is Dusty. He lives next door," Ben said as a brief introduction.

All the women stopped their lively chatter and turned to greet Dusty. "Of course," Heather said warmly. "I'm Adam's wife. Euphrasia and Nathan are my in-laws. That's our daughter, Mary Beth," she said, nodding in the direction of a two-year-old. "Your sister helps out and babysits her sometimes." One by one the others stepped forward to offer a handshake.

Once when Dusty's grandparents were still alive and Dusty was visiting them, he awoke under the warmth of flannel sheets to the smell of bacon and biscuits wafting up the stairs. He had heard laughter and was met with smiles when he entered the kitchen. Surely all of these women lived in homes like that. A thousand times since then he had hoped to wake up in such a family again. A thousand times he'd been disappointed. His mother was usually too busy trying to get everyone out the door to school or his dad was home for the weekend and silence prevailed.

Two women on the back porch gutted the turkeys while those inside prepared lunch for the crew. Pam stacked her biscuits in a basket and headed outside to feed those weathering the cold. Dusty heard slight applause. Pam would make similar trips out and back throughout the day with sandwiches, soup, cheese toast, and the most delicious chocolate chip and walnut cookies Dusty had ever eaten.

By four o'clock they had killed and cleaned sixteen turkeys. People stopped by throughout the day to pick up their orders. Most of the turkeys weighed between twenty and twenty-five pounds, but two or three were over thirty-five pounds.

"Lord, Leland," Billie McFarland groaned as she loaded her turkey in her Land Rover. "Whichever turkey you've picked out for me for Christmas, you stop feeding him right now. He can't grow another pound or he'll be too big to fit in my oven."

Leland said nothing. He went to retrieve the other animals from the field and return them to the barn before nightfall. Never before had Dusty felt so exhausted. He realized that Leland and Phil must feel the same at the end of every day. And when Leland handed him twenty two-dollar bills, Dusty felt a burst of pride.

CHAPTER TEN

Billie and Gill pulled up the drive to Sam's house just shy of nine o'clock on New Year's Eve. The farm dogs greeted the approaching Land Rover with loud and furious barking while Webster yapped at them out the window. Gill sat in the passenger's seat, looking like someone doomed to another round of psychoanalysis with a patient who continued to blame his life on everyone else.

Katy opened the back door. "Just a sec," she called. "Getting the kids straight."

Celine Dion could be heard in the background belting out "I Can Dream."

"No alcohol, got it?" Katy raised her eyebrows and looked straight at Savannah and then Dusty. Dusty sat on the sofa next to Ben. The two of them shuffled through the videos sitting on the coffee table. Sam had bought the family a VCR for Christmas, and they'd been watching movies nonstop throughout the Christmas vacation. Savannah was in the kitchen with her carpool friends, Julie and Amanda. They were tackling a homemade pizza and had just loaded on three different kinds of cheese.

"Mom . . ." Savannah skewed her mouth as a reprimand.

"I'm just saying." Katy really didn't expect any trouble. They were all good kids. "It's not allowed."

"We got it." Savannah gave her mother a dismissive look. "Go. We're okay."

Katy disarmed the dogs with a firm down command and walked past them to the back door of the Land Rover. She wouldn't be doing this if Billie hadn't twisted her arm and insisted on picking her up. It had been years since she'd been invited to a party. For Hank, a party meant burgers and beer with a bet riding on whichever ball game he was watching.

According to Billie, an invitation to Cottonwoods on New Year's Eve could not be snubbed. This would be the first year the party would be hosted by Miss Ellie's son, Josh, who had moved into the old plantation home a year earlier. The transition had stirred up speculation as to whether or not he'd maintain the old traditions. Billie insisted it would be an opportunity for Katy to meet some people her age; people from out of town who didn't frequent The Quaker Café.

Katy suspected the invitation was more a courteous gesture on Miss Ellie's behalf and that her presence would hardly be noticed. She was not very high in the pecking order in town, and she felt increasingly uncomfortable that someone might be there who knew about her past.

She climbed in the backseat and immediately felt underdressed. Billie wore a tantalizing pink cashmere wrap with a hood that draped fashionably long across her shoulders. Gill had on a top hat and held on to the silver knob of a cane braced against the seat. Even Webster outshined her. He had on a bow tie and a rhinestone doggie vest.

"Wow, I'm hardly dressed for this party." Katy grimaced as she considered her black pantsuit and shamrock-green blouse, even though the blouse showed enough cleavage to draw some attention. She had changed blouses four times before giving herself permission to go ahead and wear it. The only warm coat she had was a double-breasted peacoat she'd gotten from Goodwill five years ago. The coat had served her well on a daily basis, but it left much to be desired in night fashion.

"Nonsense," Billie said. "Gill bought his top hat at a thrift store and wears it just to show off. Me? I look for any excuse to dress up in this town."

"Billie," Katy laughed. "You dress up every day of your life."

"Not like this I don't," she said as she wheeled the Land Rover, which she lovingly referred to as Tank-Tank, past the dogs and back down the drive. "You look fine. People will show up in everything from jeans to formals. You'll look better than most."

"I'm really quite nervous." Katy shifted slightly in her seat to accommodate Webster. "I won't know a soul."

"You know us, don't you?" Billie said. "Everyone who comes into the café knows you. If you get uncomfortable, just sit down and entertain Gill. He usually props himself up in a corner and stares into space. You'd add considerably to his image."

A grunt came from the passenger side of the front seat. "I'd like that," Gill said, "you and me. We'll let Billie entertain the crowds, and we can get snockered somewhere together."

"Where's Sam tonight?" Billie asked.

"Has a date. Meeting some woman in Westtown at a dance club."

"Oh." Billie perked up. "Who?"

"Don't know. He told me not to expect him home till tomorrow since they'll be up late drinking."

"At least someone is getting laid," Gill said.

"Gill." Billie shot him a look. "Manners, please. We've a guest with us this evening."

⤛⤜

Cars stretched around the block, up the drive, and off into the yard around Cottonwoods. A police car sat out front, and Police Chief Andy Meacham stood in uniform to the right of the first of the twenty steps vaulting one floor up to the main piazza and formal entrance. Josh greeted guests at the top.

"Expecting trouble, Andy?" Billie asked as they walked by him.

"Nope," he said and flashed all three a smile. "Just helping Miss Ellie to discourage the underage drinkers. They see free beer and hope that once things get going nobody will notice them slip in."

"Good luck with that," Billie said and started up the stairs.

Chief Meacham looked younger than his thirty-eight years and thus usually failed to be much of a visible threat. On the other hand, he provided the perfect match for small-town demands. He'd grown up in Cedar Branch. His parents still lived there, and they knew everyone in town. Crime proved to be fairly predictable. Andy spent most of his days checking on Main Street's businesses and assisting with traffic around the school. Occasionally someone wrote a bad check or couldn't pay their charges at the grocery store. Andy would make a quiet visit and help get things straightened out. On rare occasions, there might be some shoplifting or a DUI charge. Andy knew how to be discreet and to resolve things without publicity.

"Good to see you, Miss Katy," he said with a slight tip of his hat.

"She's my date tonight," Gill said, placing his hand in the small of Katy's back and nudging her forward. Gill didn't plan to lose his seating partner before they'd even gotten inside the house.

"This is the place to be if you want to feel older and less attractive at the end of every year," Gill said as he took Billie's wrap and Katy's coat and made his way through the sea of humanity and up the stairs to the private quarters behind the upper floor's formal living and dining rooms. While he enjoyed eyeballing the youthful flesh, he had become increasingly aware that no one eyeballed him.

He threw the outerwear on a pile of coats lying across the bed in what had once been Maggie Kendall's suite. During the time that she and her father had inhabited the house as adults, the Judge had the run of the downstairs, and Maggie had taken over the second floor. Since both of them ate almost every meal at The Quaker Café, the fact that the kitchen was on the bottom floor made little difference to either.

Like the Judge, Josh had set up his living quarters on the ground floor. He had considered turning the top two floors into a learning center as part of the Kendall Foundation, but to date nothing had been done. The future of the old plantation home still seemed to be in limbo.

Katy scanned the room for anyone she might know. Over in the corner she saw Helen Truitt and the Barker sisters sipping cups of punch. The Methodist minister, Richard Shannon, and his wife were caught in the women's snare at the moment. Katy wouldn't mind talking to Richard if he could ever break away. He'd always seemed to be interested in her and her children when he came into the restaurant.

Someone tapped her shoulder, and she turned to see Adam Hoole, the assistant principal, and his wife, Heather. "Good to see you here," he said. "You remember my wife?"

"Oh." Katy turned with relief. She liked Adam a lot, and she remembered Heather from the turkey slaughter day over at Leland's.

"How are Savannah and Dusty doing?"

"Good," Katy said, nodding. "Dusty seems to be happier. Has a couple of friends . . . Ben Harper's one."

"Ben's a great kid. He and his mom and dad do a lot for the school and our Quaker meetings. Won't find better folks."

"Will they be here tonight?" Katy asked, hoping to place herself next to someone she'd be comfortable with for the remainder of the evening.

"Might . . . don't know. Could be they're downstairs on the first floor. This place gets so crowded you can stay the whole night and still not see everyone."

Katy spotted Billie, with Webster tucked under her arm, making her way through the room. Wherever she was, people stopped to scratch Webster's head and admire his vest and bow tie. Off to one side Gill had settled onto a sofa. As the Hooles turned to greet another friend, Katy excused herself and walked over to sit next to him.

"Thought you'd deserted me," he said.

"Hardly," Katy said. "I'm looking for a safe place to land."

They sat together quietly. Gill surveyed the room and made comments on the faces, the clothes, the balancing act that occurred with cups, bottles, and plastic plates piled high. He noted who had already had too much to drink and who was headed in that direction and who he predicted would be worth watching. "They used to serve everything on crystal and china," he said. "As the alcohol consumption and crowd grew, however, there was too much breakage. But nobody serves anything on china and crystal anymore." He sighed. "Damn shame. The aristocracy is doomed."

The music got louder, and voices adjusted accordingly. "They're dancing downstairs," Gill casually mentioned, "in case you want to join them."

"I'm really out of practice." Katy blushed slightly. "Go ahead if you like. You don't have to sit here with me."

"I haven't danced in years, not since Princeton, actually," Gill said.

"So what do you do for fun?" Katy asked.

"I paint," Gill said. "What do you do?"

"Oh." She arched her eyebrows. "My kids are my fun. If they're good, I'm good."

"You could have more, you know. There is life besides kids."

"What do you suggest?" Katy asked.

"Well, I was thinking you may want to meet more people your own age. You're too young and attractive to spend the evening next to an old geezer like me."

Katy looked at him out of the corner of her eye. "Are you trying to dump me?"

"Not in the least," he said. "I'm damn near speechless to have such a beautiful lass at my side, but if you find someone else to take you home, I won't be offended."

Katy hesitated and then rose. "I'll go down for a half hour. If I stand in the corner by myself for longer than that, I'm coming back up here."

"That's fair." Gill motioned to the stairs on the other side of the room. "I won't hold my breath."

The steps descended into a large area with a kitchen to the left and a family room to the right. A marble island acted as a divide and was currently covered with an assortment of liquor bottles and plastic cups. French doors led out onto a patio that seemed almost as congested as the rooms inside, despite the cold. Men crowded around a large outdoor grill.

A sofa and several chairs had been pushed back against the wall as "Achy Breaky Heart" blared from a CD player. About twenty women stayed in step to a line dance in the cleared area. Katy counted four men in the group as she stood with her back against the wall on the bottom step. She felt both conspicuous and out of place.

She might get herself a drink, she thought. She hesitated. A woman across the room opened a cooler and pulled out a Mountain Dew. A soda, Katy thought. At least if she had a drink in her hand she might blend in. She'd made a commitment to stay down here thirty minutes. She looked at her watch. Three minutes had passed.

Katy walked around the dancers and squeezed behind the backs of two intertwined groups who shouted conversations between one another. She pulled a Mountain Dew out of the cooler, flipped the tab, and picked up a few chips from a side table.

"Dickel and Dew?" a man next to her said.

Katy turned to make sure he was speaking to her. "Sorry?"

"You like Dickel and Dew?" He nodded to her soda can and raised his own.

She flushed. "It's just Mountain Dew, that's all."

"I could put a little Dickel in it for you, if you like. It's good stuff."

"I don't know."

He didn't push it, just tilted his head slightly and grinned. Not a lot taller than she was, perhaps only a few inches, he had an angular jaw and square shoulders. A buzz cut of blond hair gave him a marine-type look.

"Name's Mike. Mike Warren." He held out his hand.

"Katy," she said, taking his hand in hers for a brief shake. It was surprisingly warm.

"You're the new gal at The Quaker Café, right?"

She cocked her head. "I don't think I recognize you."

"I usually stop in to pick up sausage biscuits and coffee on my way to work. I'm a contractor . . . mainly electrical, in case you need anything wired." He showed off a set of white teeth. "You're not there for the breakfast shift."

"Nope, I'm not," she said.

"You dance?" he asked.

"Not really," she said.

"Then this is what you should do," he said as he eyed the line dancers. "It's *not really dancing*."

"Achy Breaky Heart" ended, and after applause by those paying attention, the "Electric Slide" started up, and the line reformed.

"Come on." He reached for her hand. "This one is easy. I'll show you."

She hesitated, but he had already grabbed her free hand, and with the Mountain Dew still in the other, she let him pull her out on the edge of the floor.

"It's basically a four step . . . to the right—step, step, step, step. To the left—step, step, step, step."

Katy giggled nervously but followed his instructions.

"Back—two, three, four. Now step forward, rock back and forward again with a kick step, and turn. All over again."

As they turned, Katy found herself at the front of the line rather than the side. Mike talked her through it a second time, and she kept up with him. He was right: the dance was easy.

Mike began to improvise. He got looser, wiggled his hips more, and sometimes double-stepped so that he was doing eight steps for her every four. Once he went down on a knee and did a fancy twirl on the turn, and those around him applauded.

By the end of the dance Katy was laughing. They walked back over to the counter, and Mike poured more Dickel into his Dew. "A little Dickel?" he asked her.

"Okay, just a little," she said.

After a swing dance, "Macarena" exploded over the speaker system, and Mike pulled her back onto the floor. Katy shook her head, but let herself be nudged forward. "Simple. Simple," he assured her, "but leave your Dew on the counter. You'll need both hands."

❧

Joe Wiseman stood next to an antique credenza in the upstairs dining room. He had seen Katy O'Brien edge her way past him and head downstairs a half hour earlier, but had not caught her attention. He liked the idea that he knew she was there but she didn't know he was there, particularly given the entrance of Harold Miller and his wife, Kristen.

The parties at Cottonwoods were legendary, with most of the political and legal power in eastern North Carolina congregating every New Year's Eve to slap each other on the back and drink their way into what they hoped would be another lucrative twelve months. Begun by Judge Corbett Kendall's parents, the gala quickly became known as the high society event of the year, with a rather selective guest list. But the Judge had turned the annual party into an avenue to repay favors and negotiate new deals. His daughter, Maggie Kendall, more of a populist, started inviting all of her friends, regardless of their political leanings. After that the guest list became unpredictable.

Gossip swirled about who would or would not be included on Josh and Miss Ellie's list. Katy's presence had surprised Joe.

"Joe." Harold stretched out his hand.

"Harold." Joe returned the shake and then gave Kristen a kiss on the cheek. "Good to see you, darling."

"Where's Maryanne?" Harold asked.

"One of the kids is a bit under the weather. She decided to stay home tonight."

In contrast to Joe's jeans and hunched posture, Harold was well dressed and stood erect. He ran his hand across his receding hairline and adjusted his metal frame glasses. He was not particularly attractive, with a beak for a nose, thin eyebrows, and extremely large earlobes. But his designer clothes and lean torso resonated with success. Kristen, ten years her husband's junior and a former North Carolina beauty queen, could have been in a trench coat and still dazzled the crowd. This evening she had chosen a midnight-blue empire dress with a revealing neckline. Every man admired her as she glided through the room on the arm of her husband—lucky sod—the geek who hit it big in both his professional and personal life.

"Sometime we should talk," Harold said.

"No better time than the present," Joe said and smiled.

Harold glanced at Kristen, who took his cue and broke away to speak with another couple. "It's about Katy Devine."

"You mean Katy O'Brien?" Joe feigned confusion, but he knew exactly what Harold wanted. He'd been expecting a call ever since they ran into one another at the courthouse.

"Right. Katy O'Brien . . . whatever she's calling herself now. I'd suggest slowing down on any lawsuits. She may be charged before this is all over."

"Charged with what?" Joe didn't like surprises. He prided himself on knowing the facts before insider gossip became fair trade among paralegals.

"The DA's office is having a hard time putting together the evidence against her husband. Hank swears he was on the road at the time of the murder. To date they can't prove otherwise."

"Are you kidding? A neighbor identified him."

"Neighbor seems a bit confused now."

Joe realized he hadn't stayed on top of this case. He, of all people, knew better. Many a time he'd hung a jury with one snippet of information that threw into question someone's testimony.

"So what are you trying to tell me?" Joe asked before a smile snaked across his face. "Oh . . . come . . . on. You don't mean to tell me they might go after Katy?" Joe shook his head. He'd been in this business a long time, and he knew the moves that were used to get other lawyers to back off. He was skeptical. "Hell, Harold, she was with her kids. They'll testify."

"Kids lie to protect their folks. Depending on the judge, he may or may not let them take the stand."

"And Doc's wife?"

"She was in shock. She'd never seen Hank Devine before. Could have been anybody wearing a NASCAR hat. I'm just suggesting that if your client acts like a gold digger and has no alibi . . . well?"

Joe laughed and raised a can of Bud in acknowledgment. "Thanks for the tip, Harold."

⚘

Joe moved around the room for several more minutes and stopped to speak at some length with Miss Ellie and the Hooles. He wanted to find Katy O'Brien before Harold did, but he didn't want to alert Harold that she was there.

Harold wouldn't expect to see Katy, and if he discovered her at an exclusive party, tipping the bottle back in suggestive attire, Harold might paint a picture for the jury that Joe didn't want. Eventually he headed toward the stairs.

The speakers were booming, and at the edge of the line dancers Joe saw Mike Warren grinning from ear to ear as he tried to help Katy master the "Cha Cha Slide." *Oh Lord*, Joe thought to himself, *the Dickel and Dew man.* He stood on the sidelines until the song ended and then caught her attention and motioned them both over.

"Joe." Mike stuck out his hand. "You decided to honor us with your presence this evening."

"Hey, Mike." Joe grabbed his hand, and they did a shake and fist bump. "Thought I'd try to get here before you tore up the place."

Mike let out a guffaw. "Stop that, man. You'll give this little lady the wrong impression."

"Kidding . . . only kidding. Would you let me speak to my client for just a minute?"

Mike raised his eyebrows and stepped back. "Your client?"

"For just a minute," Joe said.

"Well, sure, but I want to hear the rest of the story when you're done." Mike gave a slight bow and headed back to pour a little more Dickel in his Dew.

Katy flushed, and the color ran into her cheeks, even though she wasn't sure why she felt embarrassed. She hadn't expected to see Joe Wiseman show up in the crowd. And she most certainly hadn't expected him to come looking for her.

"I hate to spoil your fun, Katy," Joe said in a sincere tone, "but I really think it's best if you go on home tonight."

"Why?" She was confused. "Is there something wrong with Mike?"

"Mike? Hell no. He's the salt of the earth. His company built half the homes in the county. It's just that there are some other lawyers here, and it may not help your case if they decide they want to describe how much fun you were having at a party nine months after you cheated on your husband."

Katy felt her cheeks warm and her neck get hot. She stammered, "I'm—I'm—I came with the McFarlands."

"I'll get you a ride," Joe said. "You've had some drinks anyway."

"Not much."

"Yeah, that's what they all say." Joe led her toward the patio door on the ground floor.

"What about Mike?" Katy looked over her shoulder and saw him in the center of four other men involved in some jovial exchange.

"I'll deal with Mike, and I'll tell the McFarlands," Joe said. "I'll find your coat and be back in a second."

Once outside, Joe ushered Katy over to Chief Meacham. "Andy," he said, "Miss O'Brien needs to go on home. Could you find someone to give her a lift?"

Andy's eyes brightened. "I'll take her myself," he said. "My pleasure."

CHAPTER ELEVEN

Andy saw the truck before Katy did—the ash-colored Chevy Silverado was parked beside the porch. He'd seen it around town on more than one occasion, although never at Katy's. "Looks like you got company," he said when he pulled up the drive. Andy saw her stiffen. "Everything okay?" he asked.

Katy felt the bile building in her gut as the anger began to surface. "Somebody I don't like much," she said.

"Want me to go in with you?" Andy asked.

All kinds of thoughts surfaced: hiding behind a man's pants leg, not being a wet dishrag, being meaner, bigger, and louder. Marsha had suggested she simply stay clear of Ray. Call the police if he bothered her, but she hadn't seen her social worker in months now. She might as well learn to deal with this situation on her own.

"Thanks, Andy. I'll handle it," she said and bolted out of the car. She stormed through the porch into the living room. Two electric heaters burned furiously in separate corners of the room. Three large pizza boxes lay open with partial pieces still remaining. Plastic liters of Coke and Sprite sat on the counter. Ray was hunched over a napkin on the coffee table, pen in hand, with the five teenagers on either side while the movie *Ace Ventura* played unobserved in the background.

"Hi, Katy," Ray acknowledged her. "I was just drawing a map for the kids, explaining to them about Desert Storm and how I became a medic." He flashed an ingratiating smile. "Thought they'd know where Kuwait is, but they don't."

"What . . . are . . . you . . . doing . . . in . . . my . . . house?" Katy spat out the words.

"Came to wish everyone a Happy New Year. Didn't know you'd leave the kids to go partying." Ray spread his arms, palms up in a helpless gesture.

Savannah sensed an impending confrontation and didn't want her friends to witness scenes that she'd known in the past. "He brought pizza, Mom. We weren't real sure what to do."

Katy's voice shook. "You didn't know what to do? I thought I made that pretty clear."

Dusty looked at Ben, Julie, and Amanda. He didn't know how much they all knew. He had never told Ben his father was in jail, only that his parents were getting a divorce. He hadn't wanted to let his uncle in the house, but Savannah hadn't asked him before she opened the door.

"Out." Katy pointed to the door. "Get out this minute, and don't come back."

Ray stood, a shit-eating grin plastered on his face. "Sorry, kids," he said, shaking his head. "I only came to say hello from your dad."

Ray rubbed his hand over the bristle on his head before putting on his fatigue jacket and picking up the NASCAR cap off the table. "Just thought it'd be good for the kids to have a man around."

"They got a man around," Katy shot back.

"Oh yeah? If I recall correctly, your man's in jail because of you," Ray said as he brushed past her and out the back door. The dogs commenced their barking. Katy waited until after she'd heard the motor on his truck turn over and then walked to the porch door and stood, her heart pounding so hard she could hear it. After she saw the lights of his truck drive out of sight on the main road, she saw Andy's cruiser pull out from the other side of her house and follow in the direction of the Silverado. She hated to admit it, but deep inside she was glad Andy had been there.

She turned her attention to Savannah and Dusty, acutely aware of the other teenagers in the room. "We'll talk about this tomorrow," Katy said.

Embarrassed in front of her friends, Savannah stood. Besides, they knew something her mother didn't. They knew that she'd been seeing her Uncle Ray at school. "Dad's changed, Mom. Uncle Ray's been bringing me Dad's letters. He's changed, really."

"Letters? He's been bringing you letters? Since when?"

Savannah turned to her friends in search of an escape. "Come on. Let's go up to my room." Tears brimming in her eyes, she bounded past her mother and up the stairs. Her tight jeans exposed hips that had rounded into those of a young woman.

A sense of looming despair washed through Katy. She remembered that she herself had given birth at Savannah's age. How well she knew the impulsiveness of youth . . . the conviction of a seventeen-year-old who believed she saw life more clearly than her parents. How many things she would take back if she could do it all again . . . but not Savannah and Dusty. She loved them more than they could know, and she felt them slipping away.

Dusty and Ben quietly settled back in front of the *Ace Ventura* movie. Ben seemed uncomfortable, not accustomed to family fights. Katy wondered if he'd tell his parents. She hated the idea that Phil and Nanette would know that her tawdry past was revisiting her in Cedar Branch. She didn't want this incident to tarnish the relationship between the two boys.

Dusty stared at the television screen blankly, his arms across his chest. The only person yelling in the room had been her. She couldn't prove that Ray had threatened her. While she was out, the kids had invited him in. He'd left promptly when she'd asked him to.

She'd call Marsha Peabody on Monday morning. At the very least she'd talk to Adam Hoole at the school. She didn't want Ray allowed in the parking lot talking to her children ever again. Perhaps she should try to get a restraining order, but on what grounds?

CHAPTER TWELVE

The day after the holiday celebrations, the café was packed. Teensy pivoted like a freight train around the kitchen. She hurled the food from one counter to the other and slid six plates of bacon and eggs across the warmer at Katy. "Hot pot of grits coming off in a sec." She threw a glob of margarine on top and began stirring. "Biscuits on the way."

"The lady out there who just ordered poached eggs . . ." Katy said.

Teensy glowered. Poached eggs were not her strong suit, and she bristled whenever anyone ordered them. "Yeah? She want some creamy stuff on top now?"

"No, she wants to buy my trailer."

"Yeah?" Teensy stopped for a minute and pursed her lips. "So sell it to her, 'less you planning to haul it over here." Teensy's attention was on the biscuits now. Timing was critical, and the biscuits were what made The Quaker Café famous. Burn a batch and everything got backed up. There was a rhythm to cooking for a lot of people that couldn't be broken.

"What do you think I could sell it for?" Katy asked.

"How much you still owe?" Teensy asked with only partial interest.

"Eighteen thousand."

"What do you think it's worth?"

Katy thought. She'd put it on the market nine months ago for $35,000, but hadn't gotten any takers. So when the woman in the dining room had expressed an interest in buying it, Katy had agreed.

"I think it's worth thirty-two thousand," Katy said, suddenly aware of the possibility of a cash influx that she badly needed, "but I'd take less."

"How much less?"

"Twenty-eight . . . maybe twenty-five."

"So ask for thirty-two thousand."

Katy nodded and started to retreat to the dining room. She turned and added, "See, the problem is I don't own it outright. Hank's name is on the mortgage, too."

Teensy snorted as she filled two bowls with hot grits. "Well now, baby child, that puts spit in the jelly, don't it?"

"I'd have to go see him. Get him to agree."

"He likes money, don't he?"

"Yeah, but he doesn't like me much."

"I never seen that being in love was required to make a deal."

"But what would I say to him?"

"Say, 'I got a deal for you. Take it or leave it.' That's all you gotta say."

Katy paused. She hadn't seen Hank since the murder. Lord only knew what nasty things he wanted to say to her. The hair on her neck stood up just thinking about it. "What if he starts yelling? Starts calling me names?"

"Hell, you ain't figured that out yet? Stand up. Give him the finger and walk out." Teensy slid two eggs sunny-side up onto a plate and threw four pieces of bacon on top. "See, the best part is—you can. He can't."

Visiting hours at the Chowan Detention Center were between two and three thirty on Wednesday and Sunday afternoons. Katy called in advance to schedule an appointment and didn't tell Sam or her children.

They had fifteen minutes. She preferred to be in and out in five. She sat down on the opposite side of the partition and tried to steady her nerves. She wanted to control her voice; keep her words succinct, direct, and firm.

Katy watched the guards escort Hank to the visiting room. He approached with the caution of a caged lion, scanning the room until he saw her. His eyes locked on her, and she made her first mistake. She looked down. She regretted that immediately and looked back at him.

His hair, slicked back, reflected grease. Streaks of gray that hadn't been visible before were tucked around his ears. As if he could read her thoughts, he raked his finger across the side of his head and sat down.

"Well, well, well, look at the little whore who dropped by to see me. You bring the kids?"

"Kids can't come," she said, ignoring the insult.

"Savannah can. She's over sixteen."

"I've got an offer on the trailer."

He leaned on the back two legs of his chair and smiled. "And you need my signature."

She nodded. She had practiced squaring her shoulders in the mirror, sitting up straight. *Don't bow to him*, she reminded herself.

"Then what? You take Savannah and Dusty and skip town again?"

She stuck to her script. "There's about eight thousand dollars after the loan is paid off. We'll split it half and half. You still have your eighteen-wheeler."

"It's gone. Repossessed."

"I don't care," Katy said. "My money helped buy that trailer. I want my half."

Hank scratched the side of his nose and let the silence weigh between them. "I need a lawyer who can do something," he said. "Not the wuss the court appointed. That Joe Wiseman. You get me that Joe Wiseman fellow, and I'll sign the papers."

Katy swallowed hard. She knew he'd want something, but Joe Wiseman hadn't come to mind. "Joe Wiseman can't help you, you're guilty," she said.

"Not guilty," he countered. "They can't prove a thing."

Katy tried to keep to the subject at hand. "Who do you think's going to pay Joe Wiseman?" she asked.

"Sell the trailer, take the eight thousand, and get me Wiseman. I see Joe Wiseman in front of me, then Savannah can bring me the papers and I'll sign them."

Katy bristled. "Why would I do that?"

"To show your family you're sorry for all the trouble you've caused. You owe me that," he said.

She stood, turned her back on him, and walked out.

❧

Katy had planned to arrive at Bixby High School after all the buses had left, but traffic was light, and her visit with Hank had taken less than ten minutes. When she walked inside, the smell of chlorine told her the custodians had already scrubbed the bathrooms. An unexpected wave of nostalgia hit her. For a moment she wanted to feel the hum of activity around her desk again. The school had been her safety zone.

A twentysomething woman sat amid a pile of papers and file folders. A nameplate partially revealed the words "Lucy Si. . ." something. The math teacher stood next to Miss Si-something jabbering on about lost lesson plans she'd left for a substitute.

"Wasted time. I return to a class out of control and two weeks behind," she fumed.

Miss Si-something shrugged her shoulders and simultaneously peeked at herself in a small mirror balanced against the accounts book. She pulled a jar of lip gloss out of her upper desk drawer, dipped the end of her pinky into the rose color, and ran her finger over her lips.

The teacher looked up and noticed Katy. "Well, Ms. Devine." She exhaled in exasperation. "I hope you're here to reclaim your job."

Katy saw a file folder slip away from the nameplate and caught the last part of her name. Miss Simpson scowled. Katy returned an appreciative smile. To her memory the math teacher had never delivered anything close to a gracious remark to her throughout her fifteen-year tenure at the school.

"No," said Katy. "I'm here to speak to one of the teachers. I hope you've been well."

"Only as well as is acceptable, given what's acceptable these days," the teacher said and gestured to the clutter in front of them before she turned and stormed out the door.

"Thank God, she's gone," Miss Simpson whispered under her breath. The three o'clock bell rang. Katy turned to watch the students burst through the hallway and saw Shaneen sitting in the corner chair to the side of the doorway.

"Shaneen," Katy said. "You're exactly where I saw you the day I left."

Shaneen twirled a strand of her long hairpiece between two fingers and cut her eyes at Katy. Her skirt conformed to the two inches required below the knee when she stood, but she didn't hesitate to cross her legs when seated and reveal an ample display of her shapely calves and delicate ankles. She was indeed a beauty. In a city where she might have access to a modeling career, she would have at least gotten an interview. But small-time Bixby offered her little hope for anything more than an early pregnancy.

The door to Tom Morton's office opened, and JD Green came shuffling out, though this time without his meaty-handed mama. Shaneen uncrossed her legs and shifted in the chair.

"You've about hit my last nerve, JD." Principal Morton scowled with obvious exasperation. "I'm about this far away"—he drew his thumb and forefinger together an inch apart—"from kicking you out for the rest of the semester. I don't have time to spend on you every day. You understand?"

"Yeah," JD mumbled.

"What's that you say?" the principal bellowed. Even Katy jumped. She'd never heard Tom raise his voice to such a level.

JD straightened immediately. "Yes, sir." From the corner Shaneen let slip a guffaw, but caught herself when the principal shot a warning glare in her direction.

Tom looked away from JD and saw Katy standing next to her old desk. His tight brow relaxed, and he regained his composure. "Get out of here," he said to JD and then turned to Shaneen. "You stay right there, young lady, until after I speak to Mrs. Devine."

Shaneen nodded.

Tom stepped back and extended an arm toward his office door. As Katy walked through, he turned to Miss Simpson. "See if you can manage to let me have a five-minute conversation without being interrupted." Then he closed his door.

More papers lay in piles on the desk, and several boxes sat stacked in the corner. Katy yearned to dive in and straighten things out for him.

"God, we miss you around here," Tom said. "Sit down, sit down." He gestured. "How are you?"

"Some good days, some not so good." Katy removed folders from a chair in order to have a place to sit and placed them on the floor.

"Sounds pretty normal." A grin warmed his haggard face. "Got a job?"

"I'm waiting tables."

"You should be managing an office instead."

"Well, if you hear of anything."

He smiled. "What brings you here?"

"I had hoped to sell my trailer, but it's not going to work out. I need to talk to the staff member who's renting it and tell her."

Tom glanced at his watch. "Last bus loads in ten minutes. You can see anyone then."

"Well, I won't keep you." Katy started to rise.

"No, you're a nice interruption." Tom waved her back down in her seat. "Tell me what's happening. When's the trial?"

"April, so I'm told."

"Will you have to testify?"

"I hope not."

"That's for the best. You and the kids stay away from the courtroom if you can."

Katy bit her bottom lip and pushed a loose curl back behind her ear, an unconscious response she had when not sure what to say. She didn't want to discuss that part of her life again. She knew the trial would reclaim the headlines. She hoped to be far removed from the ordeal.

A small tap broke the silence. Miss Simpson peeked in. "Shaneen's going to miss her bus if you don't let her go."

The principal let out a groan.

"I'll take her home," Katy said.

Tom looked at Katy, took a moment to consider the offer, and then accepted. "Tell Shaneen to sit tight. She'll just have to miss her bus." The door closed, and Tom stood, indicating that the visit was over. "Sorry, I gotta . . ." He cocked his head toward the outside office.

"No, no, I understand," Katy said.

He stepped to the door. He'd been an imposing figure once. Now he seemed less formidable. "I don't know if I'll make it to retirement. It's gotten worse since you left."

Katy stood, looked up at him, and wished that she could offer the support he'd given her during her chaotic life with Hank. "Thank you for what you said. I heard you put up a fight for me in front of the school board." She placed her hand on his forearm, and he responded by taking her hand in his and squeezing with unexpected force. For an awkward moment he seemed not to want to let go.

"I wish I could have done more," he said.

Katy blushed, not sure why the moment felt so intimate—she and this man exchanging an unspoken bond of admiration behind a closed door. "I'll be outside when Shaneen's ready," she said.

⇜⇝

Shaneen slid into the '88 Dodge Shadow.

"Seat belt," Katy prompted. Shaneen reached behind her to pull the belt across her chest. Katy noticed her fingernails were bitten to the quick.

"Stay in school, Shaneen," Katy said as they drove. "You've just got one more semester."

"I will." Shaneen stared out the window.

"You know, you've got potential, you could go places."

"Places?" Shaneen said and shrugged. "Like where? Cedar Branch?"

Shaneen's put-down hurt a bit, but Katy knew her well enough to overlook it. "Oh, I was thinking bigger—maybe New York, Chicago, Los Angeles. You're that pretty. Pretty enough to maybe do some modeling for a clothing store or ad agency."

Shaneen perked up. "You really think so?"

"Yeah," Katy said. "I really think so."

Shaneen puckered her lips and rocked her head to the left. "How would I go about that?"

"I'm not so sure. Maybe look into some modeling schools in those places. I could ask a friend of ours, Mr. Hoole, at our high school, or I bet Mr. Morton would help you . . . if you were serious."

Shaneen thoughtfully nodded her head up and down.

"So what's happened since I last saw you?" Katy asked, expecting a flood of tittle-tattle.

"Nothin'."

"Nothin'? I don't believe that. You used to be my main source of information." They turned into the low-income housing units. Tricycles, bicycles, and Big Wheels—some whole and some in parts—lay about. A few windows had been boarded up, and several screens showed signs of damage. Boys just home from school ignored the January cold and started a game of pickup basketball under the naked hoops.

Katy pulled to a slow stop in the parking lot. Shaneen opened the door. "Thank you, Miss Devine. You really think . . . ?"

"Yes," Katy said strongly. "I think there's a lot more to that woman inside you."

Shaneen paused, looked at the floorboard, and said in rapid fire, "They say you got the roots on you."

Katy looked at her in surprise. "What?"

"Roots. Folks say that man put the roots on you."

"What do you mean? Who said what? What man?" Katy grabbed Shaneen's wrist as she started to slip out.

"JD told me. He saw that Silverado at the root doctor's."

"Roots?" Katy looked at Shaneen incredulously. "I don't even know what that means."

"It means you got trouble," Shaneen said, obviously not wanting to go into any more detail. "You got bad trouble, Miss Devine."

CHAPTER THIRTEEN

More than five months had passed since Katy first sat with Joe Wiseman the previous August and signed papers to initiate a lawsuit against the medical practice. Billie had been right. These things took time.

Meeting with Joe in the small room off the dining area of the café used mostly for private groups, Katy hoped he would finally have something encouraging for her. She still wore her apron even though the lunch crowd had left. She sat in one of the metal folding chairs set up around the extended table.

A box of Valentine's Day candy from Hoole's Pharmacy across the street sat next to Joe on the table. He caught her looking at it, picked it up, and placed it in the chair next to him. "For the wife," he said. She nodded.

"Thanks for taking a minute here. I just need to be honest with you. Harold Miller tells me that the case against Hank may not be as tight as we once thought," Joe said.

Katy blinked once and again, not sure what he was telling her.

"It appears that some of the witnesses are folding."

She raised her hand to stop him, as if bracing herself for the blow that would come. "Are you kidding? Do you know what he'll do if he gets out?" Her eyes darted around the room as though to escape the consequences of a not-guilty verdict. "Hank will kill me."

Joe grimaced. "I didn't mean to scare you. I just have to be honest so you know what to expect. The defense may try to suggest that there were others with a motive and opportunity. You, maybe."

Her eyes opened wide and then searched his in an effort to see if he might be joking. Ray had talked like that, but that was Ray. She hadn't expected to hear it from Joe. "I didn't kill Doc. I loved him."

"That's a shaky defense," Joe said. "Every juror knows some version of how an affair ended in murder. I've never asked you before, but I need to know where you were at the time of the murder."

"I went to the school. I had a key, and the kids and I spent the night on the mats in the gym."

"Did anyone see you?"

"Savannah and Dusty. They were with me the whole time."

"Anyone else?"

"No." Katy couldn't believe what was happening. "I didn't want anyone to see us. I knew what Hank would do if he found me."

"I believe you." Joe touched her arm in an effort to calm her. "I know you had good reason to be afraid, but I'm telling you because I think it's important that you know that what you do between now and Hank's trial may be open to criticism."

"Why?"

"The insurance company may be looking for ways to make it look like you trapped Doc in a compromising position and planned to sue him afterward or . . ." Joe paused. "Hank's lawyer may suggest you had a motive to kill Doc yourself and let Hank take the rap."

Katy pulled away. "I can't believe a jury would believe any of that."

"I'm a lawyer, Katy," Joe said calmly. "I've stopped predicting what a jury will believe. All it takes is for one juror and one wrong impression to sway a verdict."

Katy stood up, turned away from him, and looked out the window. The curtains were stained and dingy. She felt as limp as they looked.

"It's going to be important," Joe said, "between now and the trial not to do or say anything that could give the wrong impression in front of a jury."

"Like what?" Katy turned, not understanding what he meant.

"Like leaving your children and their friends unchaperoned on New Year's Eve. Being seen at parties drinking and coming on to the local Dickel and Dew guy."

Katy's face turned crimson. Dusty and Savannah were teenagers, for heaven's sake. A party, a couple of dances, a blouse she hadn't worn in years—was nothing she did above reproach? She stood speechless.

"Look." Joe got up and walked over to her. "I don't want to upset you. I'm just giving you some idea of what might go on in a courtroom. It's all about perceptions . . . getting people to see things your way instead of the other fellow's. It's not pretty. It's not fair, but it happens. You need to be prepared."

Katy steadied herself and sat back down. "What do you suggest?" she asked.

Joe tightened his jaw. "For the next five months you are the model of respectability. You're a hardworking single parent who devotes every hour she can to her children. Be at your job on time every day. Attend PTA meetings. Go to church. Don't smoke, drink, dance, or swear. Keep your opinions to yourself and any male admirers at bay."

Katy sighed.

"And . . ." Joe paused a moment and put his fist up in a defiant gesture, "I'm going to sue the insurance company for a million dollars in damages."

Katy looked at him in disbelief. She could see the headlines already. *Jilted Adulteress Sues for a Million.* "They hate me already," she stammered. "It would make me look guilty for sure—like I planned the whole thing just to get money."

"Katy." Joe leaned in close. "You could put your kids through college . . . buy a house with the money."

"I can't do that. I can't sue Laura Attwuld."

"It won't cost Laura Attwuld a nickel. I promise you."

Katy started to chew on one of her nails. The memory of the slander and insults that had surrounded her in Bixby resurfaced. "They'll come after me like a pack of wild dogs."

"No, they won't. They'll want to hush it up and settle out of court."

"What makes you say that?" she asked.

"Rumors have popped up about other affairs. The last thing the medical practice wants is another lawsuit from some other woman. They'll want out of this quietly and quickly."

"Other women besides me?" Katy asked. Why had she not heard this before? Had she been so gullible that she'd been the only one in town not to know? Could she feel any more stupid?

Joe skipped over her question. "If the affair happened outside of the confines of Doc's office, we'd only have the option to go after his estate. But with the medical office involved, well, the office is insured for just this kind of thing. What you have in your favor is that people witnessed the encounter: the boys in the tree and the staff who rushed into the room. You got him dead center." He paused and then added, "No pun intended."

Katy blushed and found herself unable to look him in the eye. "It does sound like I set him up, doesn't it? No one's going to pay me a million dollars."

"Nope, probably not that much," Joe conceded. "It's all a game, really. But I have no intentions of letting Harold Miller dictate my agenda. He's trying to scare me off. I just want to send him a message. I could make things much worse for his client."

"I don't want to make things worse for Laura Attwuld. Besides, a lawsuit might encourage them to accuse me of murder."

"*Might* is like an unloaded gun, Katy," Joe said. "Without a bullet or someone who pulls the trigger, it's all for show. Harold's flashing his guns. He's bluffing."

"What if he's not?"

"Well, we'll stir that pot if it boils."

Katy felt defensive. No one had rallied around her after the murder. The press had painted a one-sided picture of the events, and the popularity contest came down in Doc's favor. She had been a desperate woman caught in a cycle of abuse. "People in Bixby loved Doc," she said. "They love his wife. She got hurt, too. I don't want to be the reason she gets hurt more."

"Look." Joe locked onto her eyes. "This trial is not about you. It's about Hank. I only mentioned the possibility because I want you to be prepared for anything that might happen, but you are *not* the one on trial."

"But you said . . ." Katy interrupted.

"I said what I said to warn you that Hank's lawyer may try to raise enough questions in the jury's minds to convince them someone else could have killed Doc. And he may do that by casting disparaging remarks at you."

"And if he's successful?"

"Then we'll go to trial together, and I'll give the newspapers enough history on Doc Attwuld's past indiscretions to create a publicity frenzy for months."

Katy said nothing for a few moments. She wished that she felt completely confident in Joe's assurances, but she didn't. Hank just had to be convicted or he'd come after her and the kids. "Who's handling Hank's case?" Katy asked.

"Howland and Matthews, a couple of law partners in Edenton."

"Are they any good?"

"They're young."

"You're saying they're not that good?"

"Nope, I'm just saying I'm better," Joe said.

"Do you think Hank will be convicted?"

"Probably."

"Can you guarantee that?"

Joe couldn't guarantee anything, but the more he thought about it, the more pissed off he was at Harold Miller. "I guarantee," he said.

⁓

Savannah sat on her bed, Hank's letters in a shoebox in front of her. Dusty looked at her skeptically—his arms folded, his chin tucked into his chest.

"I think he's changed. I really do," Savannah said.

Dusty frowned.

"Listen to this," she said, unfolding one. *"Another day has gone by. I haven't seen either you or Dusty in nine months. I've had so much time to think and pray about all that's happened. I was not the best father to you and I can see that now. But I want to have another chance. I realize now how much I love both of you. Please pray on it. My life is worth nothing without my children."*

Dusty shrugged his shoulders. "So?"

"Doesn't he sound different to you?"

"No," Dusty said.

"Oh, come on, Dusty. He does sound different. He said he loved us."

"You, maybe," Dusty said. "He never loved me. He thought I was a wimp."

"Not so." She paused and then said, "I want to go see him."

She had Dusty's attention now. "Mom won't let you."

"Uncle Ray said he'd take me."

"Don't go." Dusty stood. "He beat up Mom. He hit on me. You're the only one who got off scot-free."

Savannah bit her lower lip and looked away. "I think Jesus wants me to go," she said. "Jesus teaches us to forgive those who have wronged us."

Dusty opened his mouth wide in a silent scream.

"If I go, will you keep it a secret from Mom?" Savannah asked.

He didn't say anything.

"Please."

"Maybe," Dusty said and walked out of the room.

~⚮~

Savannah's friends pulled their car off the road at a prearranged site on their way to school.

"You're sure about this?" Amanda asked when the Silverado pulled in behind them.

"Yeah," Savannah said. She opened the door, climbed out, and gave a partial wave to Ray. "I gotta do this, but you can't tell a soul where I am. Promise?"

Amanda shrugged.

"Dusty?" Savannah raised her eyebrows in a soundless plea.

Dusty had learned long ago not to repeat what he saw. He wouldn't tell.

An hour later Savannah walked into the Chowan County Detention Center with Ray and waited nervously in the sterile lobby until her name was called. She left her pocketbook with her uncle and passed through a gray door on the right-hand side where a female guard asked for her identification and any items in her pockets. Without small talk or so much as a hello, the matron waved a metal detector up and down Savannah's body before allowing her to step through the second door. She sat down on a round steel chair anchored to the floor in one of the three booths and faced a bulletproof partition.

He was thinner. His high cheekbones made his face look longer. Hank's charcoal eyes misted when he saw her. "Hi, baby," he whispered as he sat down and leaned into the mic. "I've missed you."

"Oh, Daddy." She hadn't really thought through what she'd say to him. Uncle Ray had forewarned her that they'd only have fifteen minutes, but that her dad just wanted to see her.

"How've you been?" he whispered.

"We're all good."

"How's your brother?"

"He's okay. He wanted to come, but Uncle Ray says you have to be sixteen." She was conscious of the fact that she'd lied, but she wanted to make him believe they all cared what happened to him.

"Listen, kiddo." Hank stopped and looked straight at her. "Oh God, you're beautiful. I just want to hug you so bad." Savannah's lower lip began to tremble. He noticed. "Listen, I want to tell you I'm sorry. Sorry for anything I ever did to hurt you or your brother."

She brushed away a tear with the back of her hand. "That's okay, Daddy." She let the words slip out without giving them much thought. What good did it do to let anger fester inside? She'd learned that in church.

"I've stopped drinking." He tilted his head and tried to make a joke. "They don't keep it in the fridge, and you're not around to get it for me."

She smiled.

"Do you think you could give me another chance?"

"I'll try," she said. How could she not at least try? She used her sleeve to wipe away the tears that had started to run down one cheek.

"Does your mother know you're here?"

Savannah shook her head.

"I understand," he said. "Now stop the crying." He wanted to reach through the glass and brush her hair back from her face. Such a small thing to be denied. What hell.

"What's happening at school?" he asked, hoping to get her to talk more.

"Nothing much," she said and struggled to regain her composure.

"Come on, tell me anything. Everything," he encouraged her. He needed to control the lump forming in his own throat.

"I'm a flag girl. I sing in the school chorus. I'm going to church. I sing there, too."

"That's good. That's really good. Praying for me, ain't ya?" Hank said.

"All the time, Daddy," she said. "I pray for you and Mama and Dusty."

"That's my girl."

"You didn't kill him, did you, Daddy?" She had to ask. The question nagged at her continuously. Taking someone's life cut to the core of everything she'd come to believe as evil. "Uncle Ray says you've been framed."

Hank grimaced and looked down at the metal ridge between them. Why was it so hard to lie to her? "Yeah, baby. I was framed," he said.

She seemed relieved. "I'm praying that this will all be over one day—that we'll all forgive one another."

Hank's right foot practically tap-danced with the jitters, but he kept a straight face. Why in the hell should he ever forgive Katy? He lowered his eyes. "Maybe so, baby," he said.

"They got chapel here?" she asked.

"There's a chaplain that comes in on Sundays."

"Do you go?" She hoped he'd say yes.

"Every chance I get," he said. "I'm a changed man." He flipped the subject. "How's Dusty doing?"

"He's got a good friend. They spend lots of time together."

"Yeah? Doing what?"

"Just foolin' around. His friend, Ben, and him help Leland Slade some weekends. He pays 'em in two-dollar bills." She smiled.

"Yeah?" Hank smiled back. "Can you spend those things?"

She nodded. "Ben's dad's got horses. They ride sometimes, and Uncle Sam is teaching him some about flying."

"Well I'll be. That would be something if he learned how to fly," Hank said.

"I got my driver's license. Hoping to get a summer job. I get to use Uncle Sam's truck when he's out of the country."

Hank shifted uncomfortably. That should've been him teaching his kids to drive.

"What do you do every day?" she asked.

What did he do every day? My God, he plowed through every day like a pack mule walking the side of a ridge. "Hey," he said, "what about those 49ers? That makes five Super Bowls they've won. That's something, huh?"

A buzzer sounded, and Savannah jumped, startled by the noise. The visitation time was over. Hank cocked his head at the guard in hopes that he'd give them a few more minutes, but the rules were the rules. "Tell Dusty I miss him, will ya? Maybe he'll take me for a ride in his plane one day?"

"I'll tell him, Daddy," she said as her father rose to go.

"And baby, thanks for coming. You're the best thing that's happened to me since I got here."

CHAPTER FOURTEEN

Ata took the ten silver dollars one by one, closed his eyes, and slowly ran his tongue over each. He rubbed them between his fingers, spit, and tossed four to the side. "No good," he said.

"I'm willing to risk it," Ray said. "Let's get this deal over with."

Ata stared down at the remaining coins as if he might not continue, but then held out his hand. "Heart dirt?" The nails of his two pinky fingers were long enough to make each digit the same length as the second finger on each hand.

Ray pulled a pouch of dirt from the pocket of his army fatigue jacket. The task had sounded easy. Collect some dirt that covered Doc Attwuld's casket over his rotting heart, exactly one year to the hour of Doc's death.

Ray had gone to the cemetery late on March 18 and parked his truck well out of sight. Shadows slipped into nightfall. A dog howled. He sat on the ground behind a crypt waiting for the exact time. The wind picked up. A squirrel scampered up a tree and caused him to jerk. At exactly six o'clock he moved to the right side of the grave, pushed his pocketknife into the ground, and started to take stabs at the earth to loosen the soil.

Then there was someone else. The lights from a car ricocheted through Spanish moss. Ray ducked back behind the crypt.

Laura Attwuld emerged from the car and walked tentatively into the graveyard. She was a handsome woman. That word came to his mind, as did *angular, firm*. He had considered ways to approach her to express his regrets. He'd passed her once in the grocery store, and on another occasion he'd seen her go into the post office. But he feared that his likeness to Hank might further cement the memory of his brother in her mind. He'd also considered the possibility that the similarity between the two of them could rattle her enough to admit she wasn't really sure who she'd seen the night of the murder. So he'd chosen not to speak to her. Now he sort of wished he had.

He watched her. She held a dozen red roses. Something caused her to stop. She seemed slightly fearful. She looked in Ray's direction. He stiffened.

He could feel her staring at the crypt for what seemed to be an extraordinary length of time. What was she doing here at night? Commemorating the anniversary in the same way he was? What the f—? Was she looking for heart dirt, too?

She approached Doc's grave, started to drop the roses, and then hesitated. She leaned down and fingered the fresh soil. Stood and scanned the cemetery. Finally, she spread the loose dirt even with her foot and placed the flowers on top. She walked back to her car.

Ray lay flat as her car lights circled and disappeared down the road.

He returned to the grave, set aside the flowers, and did a mental calculation of where the coffin lay six feet under him. He tried to imagine a body stretched out across the top of the grave in order to get the proportions right. Ata hadn't specified how deep to go or how much to get. He went down three inches and then began to collect dirt and deposit it into the sixteen-ounce plastic jar he'd brought along. Seeing the hole he'd left, he looked around for a place to retrieve some filler and then thought screw it and laid the roses over the displaced earth.

❦

Ata nodded and looked over at the burlap bag. The chicken inside let out a feeble squawk and then resumed her struggle to escape.

Ata calmly tucked the bag under his left arm and motioned Ray deeper into the woods. "You know blood?" he said, and Ray said nothing. He'd seen blood. Nothing new. The hen clucked several times and grew silent, aware perhaps that her fate had been sealed.

Moonbeams peeked through the overhead branches and danced along the ground as the wind gusted at the tangles of Spanish moss. Ata stepped swiftly, avoiding the knotted underbrush with skill. Under a live oak where the vines hung heavy enough to reach the ground, he stopped. He began to gather sticks and small branches.

Ray kicked away the scrub to clear a small circle of clean earth. He knew there would be a fire. There was always fire involved in this sort of thing. Still, he had hoped he wouldn't have to be involved at this stage. He'd thought he'd simply tell the root doctor what he wanted, pay him, and leave.

Once the fire burned hot, Ata folded onto his haunches. Not many years older than Ray, dressed similarly in jeans and a sweatshirt, he could have been anyone on the street in Bixby, except for the fingernail thing. A house painter between eight and five, he gave himself away with his accent when he opened his mouth. He was West African, and he'd brought his ancestors' superstitions with him—the ability to influence the spirits and foresee the future.

Ata sat by the fire. Nothing. They waited for what seemed a long time.

"What are we waiting for?" Ray asked.

"Spirits," Ata said.

Jesus, Ray thought, *what've I got myself into?* If he wasn't so sure there was something to all of this he'd call the whole thing off, but he had reason to believe. When he'd been in Kuwait, a buddy gave him something he called *roots* as a good luck charm to keep him alive. On a particularly dangerous patrol, they took mortar fire, and the guys on either side of them were hit. Ray and the buddy who'd given him the roots weren't.

When he returned to Bixby, he was surprised to discover that finding a root doctor wasn't all that complicated. The Southeast had a thriving business of root doctors practicing juju and the power to predict or alter the future depending on how much you were willing to pay. Ask the right people, show them the money, and you could buy a myriad of remedies for whatever you needed.

Ata held out his hand. "Picture," he said.

Ray dug in his pocket and pulled out the picture of Katy. "Have the spirits arrived?" he asked.

Ata grunted and motioned for the picture to go in the fire.

Ray didn't hesitate. He'd fix her. She'd screwed up his brother's life from the very beginning. She had it coming. She was just like their mother—pathetic, closing herself off in the bedroom, pretending like nothing was going wrong. He tossed the picture. The edges curled, and a flame incinerated Katy's image in a sudden burst.

"Now, dirt," Ata said.

"In the fire?" Ray asked.

"On the ground."

"Anywhere?"

Ata nodded.

Ray poured out the heart dirt in front of the fire and then jerked back. A miniature dust devil danced in the air and blew some of the black earth back in his face. He swore under his breath and brushed it from his eyes. Ata watched . . . lowered his gaze . . . said nothing.

Then Ata moaned, and the lament started somewhere in his gut, filled his lungs, and escaped like the groan of an alligator. The night echoed the sound. The trees seemed to shudder. The moon disappeared behind a cloud, and Ray felt a cold chill blow across the nape of his neck.

"The silver," Ata said without opening his eyes.

"Where? In the dirt?"

He nodded, eyes still closed.

Ray pulled the remaining six silver dollars from his opposite pocket and dropped them all at once. Two rolled out of the center and onto the bare ground. Two lay catawampus on top of one another, and two disappeared into the brush.

An owl screeched. Ray felt the muscle in his calf tighten and thought for a moment it would cramp. He gritted his teeth—stood up—flexed his foot—it started to subside, and then another sharp pain caught him in his thigh. The spasm crippled him temporarily. He groaned involuntarily. Ata held out his hand in a way that felt more like a warning than an offer to help. Ray's face contorted and slowly relaxed as the cramp began to ease off.

Ata gently removed the docile hen from the bag and in one uninterrupted motion slit her throat.

Ray recoiled. This simple act surprised him, even though the chicken's demise had been foreshadowed.

The chicken flapped headless around the ground. Blood streamed from the open neck wound, the head dangling precariously by a piece of skin.

The wind stilled. The night sounds ceased, and the death dance ended. Ata sat motionless. Blood lay splattered across the heart dirt and coins.

Ata stood and did a slow bow. "Your brother is free." Ray started to speak but was quieted with a gesture. Ata picked up a stick and bent closer to the ground.

"Here," Ata said, pointing his stick at two silver dollars that had rolled free from the heart dirt. Ray nodded. "These two walk away."

"Me and my brother?" Ray asked.

Ata ignored him and continued. "Two escape harm." His eyes scanned the ground as he ran his stick lightly through the leaves in an effort to see where the coins might be.

"What about those?" Ray said, pointing to the two coins toppled together.

Ata shifted the coins apart. Both were covered in the blood of the chicken, although the one on the bottom had been more protected.

"You wish to know?" asked Ata.

"I paid to know," Ray said.

"Somebody dies."

"Who? Katy?" Ray asked. It must be Katy. It had to be Katy.

Ata tightened his lips, separated the branches one by one within the fire, and began to throw the dirt on them to extinguish the flames. When it became obvious he would say nothing more, Ray left the dead chicken and the six coins where they lay and walked away.

Chapter Fifteen

Saturday's lunch crowd at The Quaker Café was more boisterous than usual. The weather pushed people indoors, and those living alone came to join in the excitement of basketball in a room filled with UNC fans. Frank Busby, the retired pharmacist, spent most of every day between the café and the pharmacy across the street, talking with whoever came in. His good friend, Henry Bennett, could be counted on to join him for almost every meal. Between the two of them they had a medical remedy or financial cure for whatever ailed the town.

Timmy Bates sat next to the television. "I'm excited," he said, clapping his hands like a child, though actually he was in his forties. Henry Bennett stood behind Timmy and placed his scarred and weathered hands on Timmy's shoulders in a fatherlike gesture. The citizens of Cedar Branch kept a watchful eye on him as they would any other eight-year-old, and they did so with love and compassion as a tribute to his dead brother. Timmy had lived in back of his brother's peanut processing plant until Marshall died of a heart attack at fifty-seven. When Marshall's widow, Eloise, sold the plant and moved to her family home in Greensboro, she made arrangements for Timmy to live in an old trailer she owned on a piece of land near town. She'd had the trailer furnished for him but had discouraged him from cooking for fear of a fire. She sent Miss Ellie a monthly check to cover Timmy's meals at the café.

"Who you rooting for?" Frank teased him. "Duke?"

Timmy looked horrified. "NO, not Duke." He shook his head, and everyone laughed. Nobody would dare root for Duke and sit down in The Quaker Café on this particular day.

March Madness was Timmy's favorite time of year. North Carolinians became fixated on the annual rivalry among the big players in the state: UNC-Chapel Hill, NC State, Duke, and Wake Forest. The café overflowed with joviality and bracket debates, which began the preceding month and ran all the way to the finals. In the 1980s, the regulars had talked Miss Ellie into putting a portable television in the corner of the café so that everyone could follow the NCAA tournament while the Tar Heels rolled to victory. Other than basketball, bad weather, and an occasional news event, she insisted the TV remain turned off. "If I am kind enough to fix your meal, at the very least you can pay attention to me instead of that silly squawk box," she'd say. For the most part patrons honored and fulfilled her expectations.

"What will this be? The seventh or eighth time if they win?" Miss Ellie asked.

A Carolina team had played in the NCAA Final Four eleven different times and won the ACC tournament all but four. More than a few people thought their winning streak was directly related to where they sat and what they ate at that exact time every year. Superstitions were hard to break, and patrons had already settled at their historical tables and were ordering the exact same things they'd ordered a year ago.

Fifteen years earlier, Charlie Voyles had missed a game because his wife unceremoniously scheduled a vacation in a location so remote that the television wouldn't pick up the station. He was furious. He called friends and asked them to videotape it for him and then made them promise not to tell him who won until after he viewed the tape. The Tar Heels won. The next year he went to The Quaker Café, and the Tar Heels lost to Duke by one point. The following year he and his wife returned to the vacation spot, where he sat glued to a fishing pole while friends taped the game, and the Tar Heels won again.

From that point on Charlie taped the game every year and watched it three days later, and woe to anyone who told him the score before he had seen the video in its entirety. Creating the right environment for Carolina was serious business in restaurants, bars, and homes. The Quaker Café didn't want to be held responsible for a loss.

On this particular day in 1995, twenty people squeezed around the television cheering at a raucous game between Duke and Chapel Hill. Bracket sheets blanketed the county, and betting on Duke ranked next to treason. With Mike Krzyzewski on leave for the year, Tar Heel fans bragged that UNC would burn Duke like piss on snow.

Gill McFarland sat at a table next to the window taking in the scene. Frank made his rounds during the pregame show and took the opportunity to console Gill about Syracuse. "Why you sitting way over here, Gill? That was one heck of a game against Arkansas. New York can stand proud."

Gill didn't particularly need consoling. He'd come for lunch since Billie wasn't cooking, and had he remembered that half the town would be in frenzy mode this time of day, he might have alleviated his hunger with a brie sandwich. But here he sat, and the psychoanalyst in him studied the crowd.

Katy moved between the tables refilling glasses and keeping the hamburgers and fries coming. She still viewed basketball with caution. In former years, Ray had always been at their house for the games. She guessed he and Hank bet heavily on the scores, and the games could end with a raucous celebration or an uproar of profanity. Either way, the drinking was always a prelude to trouble.

This was the first time since her childhood she didn't feel threatened by the final score. She'd left Dusty and Savannah at home with Sam and a mountain of snacks in front of the television set. No doubt Sam would show them how to bet on the point spread.

"Katy." A grin stretched across Mike Warren's face. He'd been making more of an effort to show up at The Quaker Café on weekends since New Year's Eve. A couple of times he suggested he and Katy might drive up to Westtown for dinner on her day off, but she'd declined, remembering Joe Wiseman's words of caution. "Wanna get something to eat after the game?"

She smiled. "Looks like you're getting something to eat here."

"There's a place in Westtown we can dance. You'd have fun."

"I don't know, Mike." She was weakening. "We'll see."

Gill waved her to his side of the room, which gave her the excuse she needed to turn her attention somewhere else. "Any chance Teensy might make me an omelet?"

"You might have to wait a bit until she gets the hamburgers off the grill."

"I'll wait," he said. "Billie's meeting me here. No telling how much longer she'll be."

By halftime, the café brimmed with jubilation. The Tar Heels appeared to be on their way to an easy victory. Miss Ellie got herself a chicken salad sandwich and sat down at the VIP table to join in the lively banter. But a winning streak can turn on a dime, and at the beginning of the second half, Duke rallied in an unexpected sprint of activity and took the lead, at first up by two points and then six and suddenly by twelve. Miss Ellie finished her sandwich and stood up, as did several others. Victory seemed to be slipping away.

Gill watched with interest as people's body language changed from festive to acute stress. A few disappeared into the bathroom. Food orders stopped. Miss Ellie started to clear tables and retreated to the kitchen.

Richard Shannon, the Methodist minister and a Duke graduate, got up quietly and headed to the door.

"Leaving, Reverend?" Gill asked. "They need your prayers more than ever now."

"I can't stand this. I'm talking to God about basketball," Richard said, shaking his head. "I'm conflicted. Got to leave and clear my thoughts."

Gill watched the minister out of the picture window. He got into his car and pulled away, leaving the only free parking space for two blocks.

Billie McFarland burst through the café door. "Is Duke in the lead?" she gushed. Onlookers nodded without taking their eyes off the game. As always her pink ensemble set her apart from the Cedar Branch locals, but if she'd shown up in a different color, the town would be awash with rumor.

Billie had promised to deliver food for Meals On Wheels and couldn't believe her misfortune to be given the day of the championship game. She didn't track the basketball games as closely as the North Carolina diehards and just hadn't expected UNC and Duke to both make the finals. So she got stuck and felt obligated to fulfill her commitment.

"You should see everyone up at the nursing home," she blurted out. "People in wheelchairs are walking. Those on life supports have opened their eyes. A man who hasn't spoken in ten months screamed an expletive across the room that made three women wet their pants.

"Isn't this amazing?" She sat down across from Gill and waved at Katy. "A BLT, hon. And a glass of sweet tea." She turned to Gill. "Can you believe the frenzy?"

"It's a Civil War reenactment." Gill sniffed. "The Yanks versus the Rebs, rich versus poor, in state versus outsiders." The rivalry rattled the locals something fierce.

The score bounced back and forth as Carolina reclaimed lost points and each team traded the lead. The noise in the restaurant intensified. Miss Ellie moved back in front of the television and rocked up and down on her heels while others sprang out of their chairs screaming. As the final buzzer sounded, the score was tied, and the game went into overtime.

Miss Ellie rushed over and urged Gill and Billie out of their chairs. "Come over here for good luck. We've got to have everyone cheering."

Gill seemed amused and showed little inclination to move, but Billie rousted him up. "This really is serious stuff. You don't want to be accused of jinxing the game. They'll do that, you know." Gill got up without conviction. He moved to the back of the pack and watched the commotion.

In overtime Carolina was leading by three points and had a chance to clinch the game in the final seconds at the free throw line. A roar went up as the ball left the player's hand followed by a collective groan as deafening as the sound of ice caps falling in Antarctica. The ball missed.

With seconds remaining, Duke hit a thirty-seven-foot three pointer to send the game into a second overtime and the crowd into pandemonium. Even Gill started to watch as the second five-minute clock ticked into double overtime.

Suddenly, as if the elevated tension in the café itself had released a pressure valve and the walls of the building could no longer withstand the strain, the squeal of brakes pierced the air and the front window exploded into a thousand pieces. Chairs and tables cracked. Broken glass sailed through the air.

Miss Ellie fell as her knees buckled. Katy dropped a tray of sweet tea and fries and slid to the floor. A piece of glass pierced Billie's right arm. Blood appeared. Instinctively everyone else covered their faces and ducked. Gill McFarland stood numb, staring in disbelief at Helen Truitt's '86 Cadillac, which sat parked in the front half of the café. The table where he and Billie had been sitting only moments earlier lay somewhere under the front tires.

Mike Warren was one of the first in town to purchase a cordless battery-operated phone. Unaware that he would prove its value at this accident and that the new device would be purchased by dozens of people afterward, he picked it up immediately. Mike had participated in similar drills as a member of the rescue squad, but this was the real thing. First call 911, he knew, and then check for casualties. The town siren went off barely seconds after he made the call.

Mike's small stature was deceptive. He'd been hauling lumber from the time he was ten. After completing an engineering degree at NC State, he'd returned home to help manage his dad's construction company. He jogged daily, lifted weights, and served with the volunteer fire department and emergency management squad. He'd pulled his best friend's son from a truck wreck, delivered two babies on the way to the hospital, and been on the scene in the aftermath of fires, domestic violence, gun shootings, and farm accidents. They may have been members of a small redneck town, but he'd stake his life on every guy on the team.

Standing up, he yelled out over the commotion, "Who's hurt? Anyone hurt?"

Broken glass crunched under people's feet, but the majority seemed more dazed than injured. Henry Bennett, the person closest to Mike, looked up. "I'm cut, but I'm okay," he said. "Check the others."

The sleeve of Billie's pink sweater gradually bled into rose and then red, but she appeared either unaware or unconcerned. She yelled to Mike, "Over here. It's Ellie."

Miss Ellie lay on the floor with blood streaming from her forehead onto the pastel tiles. Mike knelt down beside her, pulling the napkin dispenser off the table and pressing a handful of them against her head. "Hold this," he said, conscripting a startled Gill into action. "Apply pressure while I check her pulse. Someone get me a clean towel."

Katy disappeared into the kitchen.

"Someone call Josh." Billie barked out her own orders. "Tell him his mother's been hurt."

"You're bleeding, too." Gill looked up at his wife and for the first time saw the blood on her sweater.

Billie wasn't paying attention. She had spotted Timmy Bates. He had curled up into a fetal position on the floor and was shaking violently. She went to him. "It's all right, honey," she said as she folded her arms around him and stroked his hair. "Sometimes people get hurt, but we'll get this mess straightened out. Everything's gonna be all right."

Dr. Withers came within minutes to triage the cuts and bruises. The rescue squad arrived and took Miss Ellie and Helen to the hospital. Josh phoned later that Miss Ellie had a mild concussion. Evidently Helen had blown a fuse at home, knocking out her television, and in her excitement to see the final minutes of the game, she had jumped in her Cadillac and headed to the café. Seeing the empty parking space in front, she'd inadvertently hit the gas pedal instead of the brake as she swung in. A broken arm and a bruised ego were the consequences.

Meanwhile, the street filled with the curious and the concerned. In an earnest effort to restore some order to chaos, people began to pick up the splintered wood and broken glass, repositioning the tables as if the café might open on schedule in the morning.

Frank suggested ways to secure the front of the building in order to protect what remained undamaged, and two trucks headed for the hardware store to get sheets of plywood.

"Who won the game?" Henry asked amid the debris.

"Carolina," someone said.

"Damn. Wish I could have seen that."

"Who's taping it for Charlie?" Frank asked. "Someone go get the tape."

CHAPTER SIXTEEN

Dusty didn't particularly enjoy mucking out horse barns, but he liked Ben Harper, and when he could, he spent Saturday mornings at his family's farm. Following weekend chores they had a good lunch and either went horseback riding or built something with the tools in the barn. Ben was helping Dusty make a small jewelry box, which he planned to give to his mother for Mother's Day.

"You ever go to church?" Ben asked one morning as they shoveled manure into a wheelbarrow. Ben wielded his shovel with an ease that Dusty admired.

"Nope." Dusty shrugged. "My sister does."

"Yeah? Which one?"

"One about a mile outside of town. She sings with some friends in the choir."

"Oh," Ben said.

"You got a choir at your church?" Dusty asked.

"We don't have any music at our meeting house."

"Really? None?"

"Nope, just silent worship."

"No preacher?"

"No."

"What do you do?" Dusty asked. He was having a hard time picturing a church where nobody spoke.

"We wait." He paused. "And listen."

"What for?"

"My dad says we're giving time for our inner voice to be heard."

"An inner voice?" Dusty said.

"It's sort of like if you've got a problem, or want to figure something out, if you clear your mind and put aside some time to sit quietly, then you can understand things better."

"You think that's God talking?"

"Some people do." Ben stumbled over his words looking for a better explanation. "Sometimes someone in the meeting will stand up and speak. They call that 'being moved to speak.' What they say can relate to something someone else is thinking. So it's not always quiet. A lot of people believe that messages come from God."

"But you don't like music?"

"It's not that we don't like music. Just—it gets in the way. Music makes you think about what's happening outside you instead of searching for the light of God inside you."

A horse's neigh broke their conversation, and Dusty stopped shoveling for a moment to run his hand down Dakota's long chestnut neck.

"He wants a ride," Ben said. "We got to get the hay in first."

They pulled a bale out of the rafters and used pitchforks to spread it out. The sweet smell permeated the barn. Dakota began to prance, and Ben pitched a forkful over into his stall.

"Your mom and dad ever fight?" Dusty asked.

"Sometimes they disagree."

"Like on what?"

"We got an old truck out back my dad's been repairing. He told me once he got it fixed up and when I turned sixteen, I could drive it to school. My mom 'bout had a stroke. She says it's not safe."

"So who won?"

Ben smiled. "Won? Nobody. They're thinking on it, which means I'll be in college before they decide. When they don't agree, it's sort of a standoff. Nothing happens. In the meantime, I'm putting aside my money to buy my own car."

"Which really means your mama won."

"Nope, it just means they're not ready to give me an answer."

Dusty thought of the times his mom and dad had fights. They weren't disagreements; they were knock-down-drag-outs. His dad ruled by force and fist. The only one who ever got a break was Savannah. Maybe that was why she seemed more ready to forgive than he did.

~

Dusty and Ben sat on the far edge of the school cafeteria watching peas periodically sail through the air and stick to the acoustic tiles on the ceiling. A small clique of admirers cheered on Jim Gorman, Greg Russo, and Carl Newcomb as each took one green pea at a time, placed it on the end of his plastic fork, and pulled back the handle in slingshot fashion. About two of every five landed with precision. The other peas either decorated the floor or hit unsuspecting students lunching on pizza and fries.

The lunch monitor, a first-year teacher, chatted with the basket-ball coach, their backs to the room. Before the end of the day, someone would notice the collage on the ceiling and order the janitors up on ladders to clean the mess. The teacher would eventually become more of an enforcer and less of a socialite.

"Idiots," Ben said. "No imagination."

"Chiquita bananas," Dusty added, referring to the way the three would occasionally place Chiquita banana stickers on their fly zippers and walk nonchalantly down the halls, soliciting giggles from the girls and snickers from the boys. "What lame brains."

As Jim, Greg, and Carl rose to leave, several peers gave them a snappy salute. The trio acknowledged their admirers in similar fashion and then flipped the bird at Ben and Dusty on their way out.

"We've got way more imagination," Ben said.

"Yeah." Dusty nodded in agreement.

"I'm ready to show them up."

"Me, too," Dusty said.

"I was watching an old movie with my dad the other night and saw something I think we could pull off. Are you in?"

Dusty had no idea what he was agreeing to, but he was itching to put those guys in their place. "I'm in," he said.

❧

While the high school football team had a dismal year, the basketball team had redeemed their reputation by at least making the semifinals for the eastern conference. The track team and baseball teams now took center stage.

According to custom, the school held a pep rally at the beginning of each grading period to recognize the scholars and athletes from the previous quarter. Ben found the tradition humiliating. Despite the fact that he made the honor roll every six weeks, he would walk across the stage to limited applause and receive nothing more than a paper certificate. In contrast, the coaches called on each athlete one by one to receive sweater letters and trophies followed by a rousing pep rally with cheerleaders twirling in a dizzying array of amazing legs and perky boobs.

Ben's plan involved challenging what he considered a disgraceful celebration of what he called the beauties and the beasts.

❧

Word spread quickly and had been circulating even before Ben and Dusty arrived at school. First one teacher and then another was summoned to the girls' restrooms until one of them solicited the help of the school nurse, Mrs. Frothmeyer. She, in turn, accompanied Adam Hoole into each of the restrooms to confirm that all of the toilet seats were missing.

There followed a great deal of conferencing. The janitors shook their heads and swore each seat had been in place when they finished cleaning the previous afternoon. Girls rolled their eyes, and the boys made stupid wisecracks.

Speculation mounted over who might be the culprits, and several names were raised. There appeared to be a certain amount of admiration attached to the prankster who had managed to remove the seats and make them so handily disappear overnight. Mr. Hoole collected the list of absentees while Ben and Dusty relished the fact that their names remained unmentioned as possible suspects.

A double backdrop curtain in the auditorium allowed for stage props to be conveniently hidden while still maintaining a third curtain to close off the backstage area from viewers. Between these two back curtains Ben and Dusty had lined up the toilet seats the night before and hooked up the riggings. The first piece of their little caper had simply involved tedious work, which they did after hiding in the boys' room until the last employee went home. The next part would require more skulduggery.

Dusty couldn't help but be impressed with Ben's creativity, but after all, this boy could snag a thirty-five-pound turkey in a slipknot, so why not a toilet seat?

"Ben Harper," Principal Seeworth bombed out over the microphone. The speaker squealed and students grimaced as Ben walked on stage for the fifth time in two years to collect another piece of paper that his mother would file in a drawer of keepsakes.

Mr. Seeworth tapped the microphone and shot a sideways glance at Adam, who fidgeted with the speaker system. The principal handed Ben his certificate, shook his hand, and murmured, "Keep up the good work." There was a smattering of applause, and as Ben hoped, no one paid much attention to him. He slipped over to the side exit, stood for a few moments acknowledging the next paper award, and then quietly scooted out of the auditorium and around to the back door. Dusty was already there. The backstage area was completely empty.

"You know what to do?" Ben said to Dusty.

"I just have to pull the curtain, that's all."

"Right, then get out of here as fast as you can, because they'll be scrambling to find out who's back here."

"What if you get caught?" Dusty feared as much for Ben as for himself—not for what the principal would do but what Jim Gorman would do if they actually pulled this off.

"I won't. Don't worry."

Five minutes later the principal completed handing out paper awards, and the program began to move into what most students considered the important stuff—sports. Coach Harris took center stage. Barney, the black-and-white bulldog who was the school's mascot, accompanied him to thunderous applause.

He reviewed the season. "We've got a bunch of young players," he reassured the student body. "They're sophomores and juniors for the most part, and they'll be with us next year and the year after. What that means is we're in for a really good two years. I'm confident these boys are going to carry us all the way."

The cheerleaders could be heard starting a chant from the first row: "Bulldogs, Bulldogs, BULLDOGS." Applause and cheers followed as Coach Harris first called up the captain of the team and then one player at a time and presented them with their letter for the year. Another chant followed the final presentation, and Coach Harris said, "Now, in recognition of what our baseball team is doing and will continue to do, I want to call Coach Smocker."

Smocker had been the only white coach to make the cut after the schools' consolidation. He also taught history classes, but most of his colleagues considered his teaching very much a sideline. A hero among the white male students, Smocker coached the one team that remained predominantly redneck—baseball. Mothers who complained about his habit of teaching and coaching with a wad of chaw tucked into his cheek found their sons warming the benches. Students learned quickly that Coach Smocker's tobacco habits should not be mentioned at home.

Coach Smocker swaggered onto the stage, hiked up his trousers, and ran his tongue across his gums to secure the tobacco chaw. Ben stood behind the back curtain and looked across at Dusty. They locked eyes and waited. God bless him, the coach was so predictable.

"I wanna tell you we got a great team going this year," Smocker said. "These are my boys, and I love 'em, each and every one of them." He picked up a paper cup off the podium and only half pretended to take a sip of water as he spit into it. A Yamaha keyboard grin exposed his stained teeth. "First I wanna call up my captain, Jim Gorman, and his two cocaptains, Greg Russo and Carl Newcomb. You boys come on up."

The clapping started as the three boys climbed the stairs to center stage. Baseball doesn't require as much weight as football or the height of basketball players, but all three boys walked with the self-assurance of Zeus. When the three stood in a row on the stage, Coach Smocker extended his left arm over his head. "These are the boys that make my day." Evidently more than a few in the crowd agreed, as many voiced approval.

Dusty could feel the sweat roll down the back of his neck. This could backfire, backfire badly. He looked over at Ben. Ben nodded. *Steady and ready.*

Jim Gorman raised both of his fists in a victory salute and did a pivot to face both sides of his audience.

Dusty pulled the stage cord as fast as his arms would move. At first he wasn't convinced the back curtain opened. The process felt painfully slow. No one seemed to notice. Then the cheering stopped, and there was a lull. As soon as the curtain cords locked, Dusty turned and bolted out the backstage door. Simultaneously, Ben pulled the cord that he had rigged to each of the toilet seats, and the top lids of the toilets all opened wide, giving, in effect, a twenty-one toilet seat salute. Just in case anyone had missed the gesture, he released the rope, let the seat tops fall with a loud clap, and then saluted one more time before he darted out the opposite door.

As the significance of what happened began to sink in, pandemonium erupted. Coach Smocker looked confused. Coach Harris took the steps two at a time and darted backstage, only to see the outer door swing shut. Ben and Dusty slipped back in on either side of the auditorium and joined the students who were laughing, pointing, and pushing down the aisles toward the stage to get a closer look.

Dusty stuffed his hands into his jean pockets to stop them from shaking. A feeling of total exhilaration swept through him. Across the aisles of students he and Ben exchanged grins. *Chiquita bananas,* Dusty thought. *They're nothing but Chiquita bananas!*

CHAPTER SEVENTEEN

Ray emptied the pockets of his pea-green military jacket, removed it, took off his boots, and glared at the guard who ran a wand up and down his jeans as he stretched his arms out. He objected to this procedure adamantly, but went through the degradation for Hank's sake. He wanted Hank to know that he'd get him out of this hole one way or the other.

Hank waited for him. He looked worse and worse with each visit. His eyes were bloodshot, broken vessels streaking across them in comic book fashion. His hair was pulled back into a slick ponytail.

"Dammit." Hank jerked his hand away from the table as he sat down. "This place is disgusting." A wad of chewing gum still soft enough to stick created twisty fiber strands between his thumb and the metal rim. He picked at his thumb to rid himself of the grime.

The guard let Ray through, and he sat down, pulled his chair as close to the bulletproof glass as he could, and leaned in. He'd been told conversations were not taped, but he remained cautious. "Hang tight, man. A week from today the trial begins, and you're gonna be a free man."

"You sure of that?" Hank said. "I don't have much faith in that crappy lawyer I got."

"They can't prove a thing. The witnesses have all folded."

"All of them?" Hank asked.

Ray tilted his head in the direction of the guard. He didn't want to raise suspicion. He'd made contact with everyone except Laura Attwuld, and he thought any lawyer worth his salt should be able to question her ability to correctly identify a murderer while in shock.

"I really needed that Wiseman lawyer," Hank said with exasperation. "I should have offered Katy a better deal. It's just that she pissed me off."

Ray scratched the corner of his eye, and there was mischievous pleasure in his response. "Katy's making deals herself," he said with some satisfaction. "She's hired Wiseman. Rumor is she's suing the medical practice for a wad of cash."

"You're shittin' me." Hank's jaw tightened, and his face turned a deep shade of red. "She screws the doctor and gets paid for it?"

"Ain't that a bitch? She's a whore, man. Never been good for you."

Hank ground his teeth. His four fingers hammered the table. "I'm gonna even things out once I'm outta here."

"You deserve that money. She cheats on you, and she's out there partying it up on New Year's Eve."

"You know that?"

"I saw her."

Hank's chest heaved, and he snorted.

"Man, she's probably been cheatin' on you for years. Came on to me a few times," Ray egged him on.

Hank locked eyes with him.

"I never did nothin'." Ray held up both hands. "But she was trouble from the very beginning. You just couldn't see it."

"You hear me, Ray. You GOT to get me outta here." Hank raised his voice, his ire building. The guard took a step in his direction.

"Trust me," Ray said, lowering his voice and holding his palms up to calm Hank. "Remember the Mahoney kids—when they keyed your car and we got even? What we did to the inside of their car?" Ray raised one eyebrow.

"Yeah?" Hank looked sideways at his brother, and the flicker of recognition told Ray that he understood.

"If worse comes to worst . . ." He glanced suspiciously at the watching guard and stopped. "Don't worry. I've got it figured out. It'll work."

Ray raised an unlit cigarette high in the air, indicating to the guard that he wanted to pass it to his brother. The guard shook his head and grumbled beneath his breath. Ray shrugged his shoulders in a helpless gesture and smiled in an effort to look inexperienced on jail decorum. "I'll be in the courtroom, sitting as close to you as I can get," he said. "Keep me in your sights."

Chapter Eighteen

The line to enter the Chowan County Courthouse moved slowly. Katy knew that the oldest functioning courthouse in North Carolina held only a few people, and she would have preferred to give her seat to someone else, but the subpoena didn't give her that option.

Joe Wiseman had assured her that she wouldn't be called to testify. If Ray's attorney put her on the stand, the prosecution would take every opportunity to raise the issue of domestic violence. She would come across as a very sympathetic witness. Joe knew that the subpoena was a sign of the defense lawyer's inexperience.

Katy leaned on Sam, grateful for his presence. He had postponed a trip to Colombia to be with her. He kept his arm around her shoulder and guided her toward the far end of a row of folding chairs midway toward the back.

The majestic two-story Georgian building located on East King Street overlooked the bay. Originally, the interior seated only prosecutors and defendants. A jury sat on straight-backed benches facing a large, elevated magistrate chair. Floor-to-ceiling palisade windows in the front half of the courtroom provided ample light and cross ventilation. At a time before air conditioning, the windows proved to be a blessing, and even now on days when the spring air was refreshing, the windows were opened. Additional light from twin windows at the opposite side of the room reflected brightly off the whitewashed walls.

English ballast stones pieced together an uneven floor behind the juror benches. This space was obstructed by four pairs of rounded columns in the back half of the courtroom, necessary to support the second floor. Available standing room allowed for up to fifty spectators—fewer with folding chairs.

The unevenness of the stones made the chairs wobbly, and seated observers tried to stabilize the legs by wedging them into grooves. Sam adjusted their chairs for Katy to sit.

The room filled up quickly. Katy recognized no one. "Who are all these people?" she whispered, hoping they weren't all reporters. Already she could imagine the headlines. The scandal, she knew, would be revisited in detail.

"I'm not sure." Sam eyed the suits. "I don't know why, but I get a feeling there are too many lawyers in the room."

"There's Joe Wiseman." Katy turned in her seat and gestured to a man leaning against a back column. Dressed far more casually than the others, he wore jeans, an open-neck collared shirt, and a sport coat. His lack of formal attire didn't seem to diminish the attention being turned on him.

"This is starting to make me nervous," Sam said.

Katy watched as Harold Miller entered with Laura Attwuld and her sister. He pulled out seats for them on the opposite side of the room in back. Katy recognized them both from the multiple pictures in the newspaper a year ago. Dressed smartly in a three-piece suit with a burgundy tie, Harold seated Laura and then walked over to Joe. They exchanged handshakes and huddled for a few minutes. Two other suits joined them, and the foursome engaged in animated conversation.

The back entrance to the building provided access to the presiding judges, lawyers, the prisoner, and the district attorney. A jail cell built in 1825 and the jailor's house added in 1905 sat directly behind the courthouse, both long since condemned. For lack of a proper holding cell, a guard remained by the prisoner's side at all times.

A rescue squad vehicle could be seen parked to one side of the building, a common practice if any defendants or potential witnesses happened to be in poor health. Given the age and questionable health of the presiding judge, this seemed acceptable. He was known for his strong opinions toward those who entered his courtroom and was prone to argumentative outbursts. Some had suggested that given his age and cantankerous disposition, he might one day die on the bench.

The jury waited in the second-floor west office.

Dressed court appropriately in tan khakis and a white dress shirt, Hank Devine stood by his guard in the hall near the back entrance. He remained handcuffed until just before he entered the courtroom. Obvious efforts had been made to upgrade his appearance. His hair had been trimmed to a respectable Mr. Rogers look. The grease was gone. Although thinner than a year ago, he had more muscle in his biceps and shoulders. The goal, his attorney had advised him, was to come across as so nonthreatening that even the most squeamish of the women on the jury would want to hand him her purse for safekeeping.

Hank stopped and looked around the courtroom. It was small. He seemed pleased. One of his two lawyers walked across the floor to meet him as he entered and ushered him to the defense table. The guard followed. His lawyers sat. Hank remained standing. He eyed the room: the door at the back, the closest windows where guards stood. He saw Ray, one row behind the jury box. He scanned the others until he caught sight of Sam—long legs crossed, the same cowboy look. They visually sparred like two roosters marking their territory. Katy angled her shoulders away from him to avoid eye contact.

One of his lawyers tugged at his coat. "Sit," he said. "Don't intimidate the crowd."

Laura Attwuld followed Hank's gaze and caught sight of Katy.

"Is that her in the navy blue?" she asked her sister, Nita, seated next to her.

"That's her," she confirmed.

"Not what I expected."

"What did you expect?" Nita asked, her bottom already feeling the discomfort of her chair.

"Someone a bit more sophisticated looking, I guess. Who's the man with her?"

"Her brother, I think."

Laura had never met the woman—had seen a couple of photos of her in the newspaper. But the femme fatale who had seduced her husband appeared nonthreatening—insignificant even. She had no reason to care what happened to her. The animosity had waned until Harold told her that Katy Devine had filed a lawsuit against the medical practice. Laura no longer considered Katy a tragic result of poor judgment. She was now a financial menace creating complications.

Laura glowered at Katy and then caught herself. People were watching, trying to catch any exchange between the two women. She didn't wish to reward the photographers.

"Hear ye, hear ye." The bailiff shifted the attention within the courtroom. "The court is now in session. The Honorable Judge Argyle Burgwyn presiding. All rise."

Members of the courtroom rose as a barrel of a man entered from the first-floor west office. A pair of frameless squared-off bifocals was nearly obscured underneath a shaggy crop of gray hair and unruly eyebrows. He mounted the elevated bar with a heave, pulled a large pillow off a nearby chair, and arranged it in meticulous fashion before he sat. After some further adjustments to his comfort, he repositioned the water pitcher and glass on the small table to his right. Only then did he recognize the members of the jury on the straight-backed benches facing him. He offered them a gracious, although not entirely genuine, smile.

Judge Burgwyn was a man known to like the sound of his own voice. In fact, most lawyers joked about his ability to try an entire case without either lawyer being allowed to finish a complete sentence. In addition, he liked to quote Shakespeare; often ad infinitum. District Attorney Toland Vaughan, the prosecutor, swore that he'd listened to enough quotes to memorize at least four of Shakespeare's plays.

"Welcome before the gates of Edenton," the judge began. Vaughan's assistant district attorney jotted down *"King John"* on a sheet of paper. It was his job to recognize every quote and record it or research the source. Toland Vaughan had learned not to be caught unprepared without a quick reply. It had become a kind of parlor game that the judge and Vaughan played, but not in public.

Several people within the courtroom, including some of the jurors, glanced at one another. *Gates of Edenton?* What was he talking about?

The judge silently acknowledged the pillow beneath him. "'Self-love, my liege, is not so vile a sin as self-neglecting.'"

The assistant DA looked at Vaughan, and the prosecutor mouthed, *"Henry the Fifth."* The jurors seemed even more confused.

"Should any of you need additional comfort, I shall not object if you wish to bring your own cushions," Judge Burgwyn offered as an explanation.

Katy recognized none of the jurors. Six men and six women sat in front of her facing the judge. Only two were black—a woman Katy guessed to be a teacher and an elderly man who probably could have opted out of jury duty due to age, but may have enjoyed the temporary prestige or mental challenge of determining right and wrong. The others were in their midthirties and forties, although she guessed one man was in his twenties.

"You have before you a man accused of murder. Let me remind you that according to our legal system he is innocent until proven guilty. 'Give every man thy ear, but few thy voice.'"

The judge loved that quote and used it at the beginning of every trial. The assistant DA saw no need to jot down *"Hamlet."*

Judge Burgwyn now shifted his attention to the district attorney. "Is the prosecution ready to proceed, Mr. Vaughan?"

Toland Vaughan, a distinguished-looking man more than a decade younger than the judge, ran his hand across the side of his impeccably coiffed hair and replied with a nod of his head, "Aye, Your Honor."

Hank Devine rolled his eyes and leaned into his attorney. "What's going on? Are these guys nuts?" Reggie Matthews patted him on the arm and shook his head slightly to quiet him. It would be unwise to get a reprimand from the judge at this point.

This exchange told Katy that the district attorney and judge probably had drinks together on a weekly basis and maybe even included Laura Attwuld in their list of friends. Small towns made social and professional boundaries impossible to separate, unless, of course, the attorney in question was considered an *outsider*. An outsider was generally a female, someone of a different race, a juvenile fresh out of law school, or a carpetbagger. Reggie Matthews, the counsel for the defendant, met the last two criteria.

Matthews specialized in trusts and estate planning. When no other offers came his way after he passed the bar, he had reluctantly accepted a position with Winslow Howland, a fraternity brother who grew up in Edenton. Matthews hoped to gain some experience and then land something with a larger firm in Raleigh or Charlotte before too many years trapped him in a small-time family law practice. The other lawyers in town recognized a wannabe when they saw one, and although they remained polite, they kept their distance.

Howland convinced his new partner to file as a court-appointed attorney until business picked up. Although Matthews was raw and had no experience with murder cases, Howland had the minimum five years' requirement, and with few lawyers to meet the needs of the county, he and Matthews were assigned to represent Hank Devine.

Unprepared to represent anyone on a criminal charge, Matthews had visited Hank as seldom as possible and made a feeble effort to get up to snuff before the trial date. The fact that Hank had languished in jail for a year didn't bother Matthews in the least. Many murder cases stalled for two to three years with the hopes that time would deflate emotional tensions, dull memories, and make witnesses disappear. Matthews believed his client was probably guilty, but he also knew that the truth would put him in jail faster than not saying anything at all. When his client told him he was not guilty, Matthews advised him to stick to his story and let time pass.

"And the defense?" the judge said. "Mr. Matthews, Mr. Howland?"

"Yes, sir, we're ready to proceed."

Judge Burgwyn had a quote from *As You Like It* on the tip of his tongue, but he held back. He glanced over at Vaughan, who had heard him say "the best is yet to come" so many times he was expecting it. The judge didn't give him the pleasure. Better to keep him off guard. He smiled at the jurors and deferred to the prosecutor. It amused him somewhat that people quoted Shakespeare every day and never acknowledged his greatness. Ah, now there was a man who would be worth listening to in a courtroom.

"Would the prosecution like to make an opening statement?" the judge asked.

"I would, Your Honor." The DA rose and buttoned his suit coat. "I'll make it short and to the point." He addressed the judge first and then turned to face the jury. "Your Honor, esteemed jury members, personally I considered this case a waste of your time and taxpayer money. The case is quite simple. The defendant believed his wife to be unfaithful to him, and he took revenge by killing the man he thought to be her lover. We have an eyewitness. The defendant was identified at the scene of the crime. Case closed. His lawyers should have taken a plea bargain a year ago, but here they are, trying to make you believe that what happened didn't really happen. I refuse to insult your intelligence." Vaughan turned with a nod to the judge and took his seat.

Judge Burgwyn smiled appreciatively. His sentiments exactly, although far be it from him to say so. He thought the fact that Vaughan had never mentioned Doc or Laura Attwuld's names showed class. He turned to the defense. "Opening statement?" he asked.

Winslow Howland rose, a bit piqued at what he considered a condescending opening statement by the DA. The implication that he and his partner were either opportunists or amateurs annoyed him to no end. Now more than ever before he wanted to kick ass.

"Your Honor and ladies and gentlemen of the jury. Mr. Vaughan has just insulted your intelligence. He would have you believe that just because he has already assigned guilt, it is a done deed. I'm sure that each of you, should you ever be on trial, would hope to have a lawyer who gave you every opportunity to clear your name. That is what my partner and I have done. We have numerous questions that need to be answered before guilt can be dispensed, for, you see, our client was not the only one who had motive and means to kill. We plan to prove that our client was not even in town at the time of the murder, nor was he aware of what had occurred during his absence. We intend to prove that others had motives and access to the murder weapon, and their whereabouts at the time of the good doctor's death cannot be verified. We believe when we have finished there will be enough doubt in your minds to find our client not guilty."

Judge Burgwyn raised an eyebrow, and as Howland seated himself, he nodded to the district attorney to call his first witness.

The prosecution called the dispatcher who received the 911 call on March 18, 1994. She testified that the call came in at 6:58 p.m. A woman identifying herself as Laura Attwuld, at 218 Riverdale Street in Bixby, reported her husband had been shot. According to her records, police and an ambulance were dispatched within seconds . . . ten, to be exact.

"Had you ever received a 911 call from this address?" Mr. Vaughan asked.

The judge interjected. "'You speak a great deal of nothing,' Mr. Vaughan."

The prosecutor knew when to cut his losses. He recognized the quote from *The Merchant of Venice* and knew from experience not to aggravate the judge this early in the proceedings. It was a sign the judge might be sitting on hemorrhoids. "I have no further questions."

Matthews rose. He had taken note of the unusual number of press people and legal colleagues in the room with more than just a bit of curiosity. For the first time he realized that this might be an opportunity to create an impression on a few out-of-towners as a potential rising star. He buttoned the two lower buttons on his suit jacket and wished that he'd taken his wife's suggestion and bought a new shirt and tie while in Virginia Beach the past week. He felt somewhat shabby compared to the flawlessly dressed prosecutor.

"I just want to verify the time that the call came in. Would you state that again, please?" Matthews asked. He heard the judge groan.

"'Words words more words.' Have you nothing more interesting to add?"

Matthews appeared slightly confused. "I'm just trying to establish the possibility of mistakes," he said.

"No mistakes. They're always right," Judge Burgwyn said with a frown.

"Always, sir?"

"ALWAYS. Have you been in this court longer than I have? 'I wasted time and now doth time waste me.'"

Judge Burgwyn had anticipated this. He knew the process of trying to break in young lawyers not up to snuff in criminal cases. Personally, he objected to such inexperience, but he knew too well the daily dilemma of not having an adequate pool of qualified criminal lawyers in rural areas. He felt obliged to accelerate their education.

Matthews apologized and took his seat. Momentarily subdued, he reevaluated his plan of action. He could acquiesce and come across as docile and inept, or he could remain forceful and gain the respect of the press for being persistent.

Vaughan wrote "hemorrhoids" on a slip of paper and slid it over to his assistant. This trial was going to move along faster than either had anticipated.

The prosecutor called the policeman who arrived on the scene first and asked him to describe what he found when he entered the Attwuld home. "Did Mrs. Attwuld describe the individual who shot her husband?"

"Yes, sir, she did."

"That's all, Your Honor," Vaughan said and quickly sat down.

Matthews rose and approached the witness. "Are you aware that eyewitness identification is frequently inaccurate?"

"I am, of course." The police officer shifted in his chair, ground his teeth, and balled his hands into fists. All he knew about Matthews was that he was new to the area. This had been deemed an open-and-shut case. He didn't like to think that this upstart was going to try to turn it into a case of police incompetence.

"Could Mrs. Attwuld have mistaken a female for a male if the attire was appropriate?"

Judge Burgwyn waved him down with a hand and stared over the rim of his glasses. "Mr. Matthews, Shakespeare's *Julius Caesar.* You should read it sometime."

"Very well, if you say so, sir," Matthews said, somewhat bewildered. "I just wanted to establish—"

"Then you need to call the witness herself and question her. The police officer answered your question."

Matthews returned to his seat and shrugged at his law partner. Hank slumped back in his chair.

Vaughan rose from his table with a look of mild amusement. He had planned to call Rachel Mayfield before he got to Laura Attwuld, but he already knew that Rachel's testimony had been compromised. She now claimed to be unsure of her prior statements, and he didn't want to find himself with a hostile witness on his hands. It was clear that Judge Burgwyn thought this case could be wrapped up quickly. If the judge was ready for Laura Attwuld, he'd put her on the stand.

"I'd like to call Laura Attwuld to the stand," the prosecutor said.

"Your Honor . . ." Matthews hurriedly conferred with his partner. The judge knew what he'd say before he opened his mouth.

"You'll have your chance to call your own witnesses, Mr. Matthews. 'How poor they are that have not patience.'" And in a stern voice he added, *"Othello."*

"Yes, sir. I mean, Your Honor, I'm wondering if I could have some time to confer with my client?" Hank had become increasingly agitated at how unprepared his lawyers appeared and had begun to talk incessantly in Matthews's ear.

More than ready for a break himself, Judge Burgwyn obliged and called an early lunch.

❧

Outside the courtroom a photographer clicked several times as Katy and Sam left. "Back off," Sam warned and stepped between the camera and his sister as he opened the door to his truck. They headed north on Broad Street for several blocks.

"I thought for sure the DA would put Rachael Mayfield on the stand." Katy shook her head. "She kept track of everyone in that trailer park. She heard our fights, and she saw Hank leave the trailer with a gun. She said so in the newspaper."

"Maybe he doesn't need her. All they need is for Laura Attwuld to identify Hank at the scene of the crime."

Sam pulled into a small shopping center where a café named Nothin' Fancy was tucked in between two shops. Larger inside than the exterior suggested, the café quickly filled with lunchtime business. A gift shop occupied the right side of the restaurant with a wrought iron fence separating the two sections. Sam saw one empty table for two situated beside the railing and grabbed the spot. After scanning the menu, Katy ordered their Brunswick stew and corn bread, while Sam ordered meat loaf.

"Sam, what if Laura won't identify him? I'm sure she hates me. I had an affair with her husband and filed a lawsuit against his medical practice." Katy picked at her food. "Maybe she's going to tell them she saw me."

"Stop that," Sam said. "Laura Attwuld won't lie. When she testifies, it's over."

The front door of the restaurant opened, and Katy looked up to see Laura enter with her sister and Harold Miller. A foursome next to Katy and Sam got up to leave, and the waitress immediately came over to clear the table.

"Oh Lord," Katy whispered. "That's Mrs. Attwuld over there. They're going to sit next to us. Let's get out of here."

"It's your call." Sam shrugged his shoulders and looked regretfully at his half-eaten lunch. He tried to get the attention of their waitress for their bill, but it was the peak of lunch hour, and she scurried from one table to another. Dishes banged into a plastic bus tub, and a teenager squirted disinfectant on the adjacent table and flipped down three clean paper mats. The three edged their way between tables before Laura noticed Katy. Laura took the chair with her back to them. Harold glanced in their direction, nodded recognition, sat down, and opened his menu. Nita leaned over and whispered something to her sister.

When their bill arrived, Sam and Katy rose to leave. Sam led the way. Katy started to follow but then stopped. "Mrs. Attwuld," she said in a voice that was barely audible above the restaurant chatter, "I did not murder your husband."

Laura looked up, speechless. Harold Miller rose immediately. "Mrs. Devine, really, you shouldn't be talking to us here . . . now."

Sam turned, took two steps back, slipped his hand under Katy's elbow, and nudged his sister to the door. "What are you doing? No one has accused you."

"She could. She might."

An ash-colored Silverado pulled in at the other end of the parking lot and waited for Sam's truck to pull out. Ray Devine casually walked into the restaurant. He had hoped to catch Laura Attwuld by herself. He watched the threesome across the room until they left. It was more important now than ever that he talk to her. She was the weak link in his plan.

CHAPTER NINETEEN

By 1:30 p.m. people again began to pack the courtroom. Hank appeared nervous when he entered. He scanned the seats and saw Ray in the same spot as before. Ray gave him a reassuring nod.

A few new faces were visible, but in general those who hadn't been admitted for the morning session hadn't tried to come back. Judge Burgwyn appeared unlikely to tolerate any grandstanding. He looked out across the courtroom and shook his head in resignation. *All the world's a stage*, he thought, but didn't say anything.

Toland Vaughan rose and did exactly as the judge had requested. "Your Honor, I'd like to call as my next witness Mrs. Laura Attwuld."

A surge of energy went through the room, and Laura felt her stomach twist into a knot. All morning the thought of having to take the stand had eaten through her like a virus. Months ago she'd been as honest as she could about what she saw, but time had taken its toll, and her confidence in being sure enough to convict a man of murder had faltered. After all, she'd only seen him momentarily. He had worn a hat, and his face was partially concealed. Plus, she deeply resented the lawsuit filed against the medical practice on behalf of Katy Devine. It was hard to mask those feelings. Could it have been a woman with her hair tucked under the hat? Possibly.

Vaughan slipped his left hand into his suit pocket and smiled genuinely. He knew Laura. She knew him. They had socialized as couples. She wondered how much he had known about Doc's philandering.

Laura could feel moisture gathering under her arms. A tremor began in her left hand, and she firmly placed her right over the other to control the shaking. Several cameras clicked, and the sketch artist busied himself with her likeness. "Mrs. Attwuld, would you please explain to the jury how you know me."

Her heart did that little flip and beat erratically. She heard herself reply, "We've been at social events together."

"Oh Lord," Judge Burgwyn groaned. He faced the jury. "It's a small town. We all know each other. Anybody have a problem with that?"

If they did, no member of the jury raised a hand. Hank Devine gave an audible groan, and the judge shot him a warning glare. "If you have a problem, Mr. Devine, please express your objection through your attorney." Hank crossed his arms and stared at the table.

Vaughan ran his hand down the front of his suit coat. "Would you tell us in your own words, Mrs. Attwuld, what happened on the afternoon of March 18, 1994?"

Laura tried to steady her nerves. She crossed her legs and readjusted her posture. The discomfort of the stand's straight wooden back forced her to shift once again. "I was at home. Had played some tennis at the club and came in around four. My sister called about four thirty." She acknowledged her sister, Nita, with a glance and was glad she'd insisted her son, Brett, and daughter, Haley, not come. Despite their objections, they were preparing for final exams, and she didn't want them to be in the middle of this humiliation again.

"She told me she was at the hospital with her son, Todd. He'd fallen and broken his ankle," she finished.

"Did she tell you anything else?"

"She said I should call my husband. There had been some trouble."

"Did she tell you what this trouble was?"

"I don't remember exactly," Laura said. "It involved Lawrence." She looked down at her hands and realized her palms were wet. She rubbed them down the side of her dress.

"What did she say about Lawrence?"

"She said to call his office."

The prosecutor walked over to his table and picked up a few papers. He read silently and then turned back to the witness. He expected Judge Burgwyn to cut him off at any moment. He knew the judge admired Laura Attwuld and wouldn't put up with much more. "Did you call your husband, Mrs. Attwuld?"

"I tried, but his line was busy." Momentarily she closed her eyes. The reporters took notes frantically.

"What did you think might be the problem?" Vaughan asked.

"'Skip hence,'" the judge interrupted. "We don't care."

Actually, those in the courtroom, particularly the newspaper people, cared immensely. This is what they'd been waiting for . . . Laura Attwuld's description of her husband's infidelity. His admission. Her shock. The murder.

Vaughan was tempted to give the judge a Shakespearean retort, but he knew better. He had played this game once before in the courtroom and had only increased the displeasure of the judge. They could play "name that quote" over drinks or at the club, but not in front of an audience.

He cleared his throat. "Mrs. Attwuld, suffice it to say your husband came home. Tell us what happened then?"

She took a deep breath and swallowed hard, as one might before diving off the high dive of a swimming pool.

"Are you all right, Mrs. Attwuld?" Vaughan asked.

She hesitated. She was definitely *not* all right. "This is difficult. I need a minute."

"Of course. Take your time." The prosecutor paused. Concern registered on his face.

Laura lowered her eyes. "He told me he'd had an affair," she said, her voice barely audible. There, she'd said what everyone already knew but still wanted to hear.

A camera flashed. The judge immediately banged his gavel. "'Go, get thee hence,'" he bellowed.

The photographer sat immobile, lowering his camera in hopes of a stay of execution, but the judge was having none of it.

"'Who is so deafe?' You, I meant you." He shook his finger at the photographer. "Out this minute."

The assistant DA looked confused and jotted down the quote. After a long silence and the beady eyes of the judge bearing down on him, the lone photographer slunk to the door while the rest of the media hounds slipped their equipment into their shoulder bags. The sketch artist frantically tried to capture the scene.

The judge turned his attention back to the prosecutor. "Continue."

"And what happened then, Mrs. Attwuld?" Vaughan asked, unsure how all the drama was playing in the eyes of the jury. He wanted Laura Attwuld to be center stage, not Judge Burgwyn. It was hard to compete with him.

"I got up and went to the bathroom. I felt sick . . ."

"I'm sorry, Mrs. Attwuld. I know this is hard for you. Do you need a break?" Vaughan could see that the color was rapidly draining from her face. She was his star witness. He couldn't afford to have her crumble on the stand. The defense might challenge her stability.

Matthews was frantically taking notes at this very minute.

"Just give me a moment, please," Laura said. She picked up the glass of water that had been placed to her right. Her hand shook visibly. She took a sip. Closed her eyes. Breathed slowly in and out.

"Would you describe to the best of your memory what happened next?" Vaughan proceeded cautiously. He was so close to the climax of her testimony that he wanted the intensity of her emotions to reach the jurors.

"I went to the bathroom. I was feeling a bit sick. I heard the doorbell. I thought it was our lawyer, Harold Miller. Then I heard a shot . . . like a firecracker. It took me a minute or so to realize I'd heard a gun. Then a second shot." Laura paused. "I ran to the front door." Laura's voice trembled. She tried to control it, but it was hopeless. "My husband was on the floor, bleeding profusely." Laura dropped her head into her hands, her eyes beginning to water. "I just grabbed something . . . to apply pressure and try to stop the bleeding."

"Did your husband say anything?"

"*Sorry*, I think he tried to say *sorry*." She reached down to find a tissue in her purse. Vaughan produced a clean white handkerchief from his pocket.

"Did you see anyone, Mrs. Attwuld?" he asked.

"Yes, I did." Involuntarily her gaze shifted to Hank Devine . . . then to Katy. Back to one and then the other. "I . . ." She started to say something, but the room started to spin and tilt precariously. She felt herself slide and immediately tried to grab the arms of the chair to steady herself. She swooned. Her eyes rolled back into her head, and she was out cold before she hit the floor.

❧

Shouts echoed through the courtroom, and Ray jerked upright. "Medic, coming through . . . coming through!" he yelled.

Katy sat up straight. "My God, Sam. That's Ray. What's he doing?"

Sam stood to try to see over the commotion. Ray bent over Laura, another medic pushing through the crowd to her side.

"Bloody hell," Judge Burgwyn mumbled.

Ray checked Laura's pulse. "Pulse rapid. Breathing irregular." He ordered, "Let's get her into the ambulance." *What luck*, he thought to himself. He couldn't have planned this any better.

Once Mrs. Attwuld had been carried out of the courtroom and the ambulance departed, Judge Burgwyn called a forty-five-minute recess and asked the presiding lawyers to meet with him upstairs. He would have preferred the comfort of his own office, but not having that available, he waited for the claustrophobic one-man elevator that reminded him of a walk-in casket. After the apparatus had jerked and groaned its way to the second floor, he lumbered into the side room. He dropped onto the Queen Anne chair at the head of the table and beckoned the more athletic lawyers who had taken the stairs to sit.

"Never, Mr. Vaughan, never in my thirty years on the bench has a witness died under questioning. 'Some rise by sin and some by virtue fall.' Ever heard that, Mr. Vaughan?"

"*Measure for Measure*, Your Honor."

"Good man."

"Your Honor . . ." The district attorney appeared conciliatory. "I don't believe Mrs. Attwuld is dying. Having to relive it all in front of everyone . . . the stress, I think."

The judge shook his head and sighed audibly. "This is a dirty business; lovely lady like Laura Attwuld. This sordid affair. It's hard to believe Lawrence used such indiscretion."

The prosecutor grimaced. "The ladies all loved him. That's one of the perils of being a doctor."

"So what do we do now?" the judge asked, not really wanting an answer. He would make the decision.

"I think we should adjourn for the rest of the day." Howland spoke up. He knew recent developments had just given him ammunition to throw this whole case into question. Mrs. Attwuld's performance in the courtroom had proven her fragility. She would have been in no condition to correctly identify anyone. He wanted to research her health records. "My partner and I need some time to review the witness list."

"I have another witness I'm prepared to bring forward today," Vaughan volunteered. "A Mr. JD Green."

Matthews hesitated and glanced at his partner. Both would have to look at their notes. JD Green was not a witness they had expected to take the stand today, if at all. He was a high school kid—probably a character witness for Katy O'Brien. They had previously decided they didn't want her on the stand if possible.

"Your Honor," Howland objected, "the defense would need time to review their notes."

Judge Burgwyn looked at the two young lawyers in hopeless resignation. "You've had a year. That's sufficient time." He turned to Vaughan. "Is Mr. Green in the courtroom?"

"He's standing by. I can have him here in thirty minutes."

"Then we'll reconvene in one hour. Alas, 'give me my robe. Put on my crowns.'" As he passed the assistant DA, his eyes dropped down to the notepad in his hand. *"Antony and Cleopatra,"* he said. "Write it down."

<hr>

At 3:00 p.m. the jury members took their places. Judge Burgwyn entered, looking more tired and less willing to indulge in any courtroom antics. He spent considerable time on the adjustment of his pillow and then nodded to those in attendance. "Ladies and gentlemen, I am relieved to be able to tell you that I have spoken with Harold Miller, and he asks me to convey to you that Mrs. Attwuld will recover and return to court tomorrow," he announced.

"Mrs. Attwuld reminds us that most individuals feel a great deal of stress when they step onto the witness stand," he added. "It is, however, my responsibility to use the time of the court wisely. We will continue. Mr. Vaughan, please call your next witness."

The district attorney rose. "I'd like to call Jonas Daniel Green."

<hr>

JD Green entered between the folding chairs, conservatively dressed in tan khakis and a white collared shirt. Shaneen Towers followed him, rocking her hips. Her gait was exaggerated by silver spike heels that matched a short-sleeve studded silver jacket. She clearly felt the thrill of being center stage in a command performance. Loopy earrings dangled alongside her long hairpiece, and bangles of bracelets jangled around her wrists. A tight, above-the-knee pink skirt showed off her bronze legs. Heads turned. The men on the jury acknowledged her appreciatively. The guards standing at the doors raised their eyebrows and exchanged looks across the room. Even Judge Burgwyn peered over the top of his spectacles and waited while an extra folding chair was brought in for Shaneen. There may have been a Shakespearean verse that came to mind, but for the first time, he kept it to himself.

JD stepped to the witness box and took the oath.

"Mr. Green, for the court record, would you please state your age and occupation."

"I'm nineteen years old and a student at Bixby High School."

"You've been at Bixby High School for how many years?"

"Feels like all my life, sir." A slight chuckle rolled through the courtroom.

"This is your fifth year, correct?"

"Yes, sir."

Toland Vaughan waited for the judge to interrupt with a classical quotation that would cut him off, but none came. For the first time that day, he appeared amused, even interested.

"Is it true that you know how to get into the school at night after it's locked?"

JD didn't say anything for a moment. He looked down at the floor and then back up. "This answer is going to get me into trouble, ain't it?"

"Objection." Mr. Matthews rose. "What is the purpose of this line of questioning?"

"Your Honor, if you'll give me a few minutes."

"Continue, Mr. Vaughan," Judge Burgwyn said. "You've got my attention, but not for long."

JD crossed his arms, straightened his shoulders, and sat back in the chair. "Well, yes, sir. I guess I do."

"For what purpose?"

JD looked over at Shaneen. She squirmed in her seat as she realized her mother might read an account of what JD said in the morning paper. Mama would not be happy.

"Shaneen and me, we go there sometimes, to . . . uh . . . to. . . uh . . . have some fun," JD said. A snicker was heard.

"We could use a little fun in this courtroom," the judge interrupted. "Have you brought us Yorick, Mr. Vaughan, 'a fellow of infinite jest, of most excellent fancy'?"

"No, Your Honor."

"Will you enlighten the court as to why this man is on the stand?"

"'Better three hours too soon than a minute too late,' Your Honor." Mr. Vaughan paused, knowing he had taken a chance, but was rewarded for his ingenuity when Judge Burgwyn smiled and nodded his approval.

"Continue, Counselor."

Matthews stood to object and was hushed with a look and one raised eyebrow. Hank sank lower in his seat and dropped his head into his hand.

"On the night of March 18, 1994, were you in the school gymnasium?" Vaughan asked.

"Yes, sir, we were."

"Why do you remember that specific night?"

"Because that's when Mrs. Devine and Dusty and Savannah showed up. 'Bout near scared the sh—" JD paused and for the first time noticed the one black woman in the jury. He recognized her as his fifth-grade Sunday school teacher, Miss Ronda Chapman. He caught himself. "Scared us silly."

"Would you describe what happened?"

His swagger now turned to humble pie. "Well, me and Shaneen were in the supply room getting ready to pull out a couple of those floor mats, you know, the ones they put on the floor for gymnastic practice?"

Vaughan smiled, and mild laughter rippled through the jury, except for Miss Chapman. She crossed her arms, and her lips froze in a frown. JD stopped. The judge tapped his gavel for order and motioned for Vaughan to continue. His curiosity had been tweaked.

"Go ahead, please," the prosecutor said.

"Well, Shaneen and me was in the supply room about to pull a mat out when we heard someone walking down the hall toward the gym, and then she pushed the gym door open . . . the one on the inside that comes from the school building directly into the gym."

"Did you see who it was?"

"Yes, sir. We could see Mrs. Devine from where we was hiding."

"You would recognize Mrs. Devine, then?"

"Sure, of course. She was the front office secretary. I spent more time in the front office than the classroom. Mrs. Devine and me, we know each other pretty well."

"Your Honor." Matthews was on his feet. "Mrs. Devine has nothing to do with this case. I don't see where this questioning is leading."

"I disagree," the prosecutor protested. "I think Mrs. Devine has a great deal to do with this case. The defense said in his opening statement that he intended to cast doubt by implicating others who could not account for their whereabouts at the time of the murder. I wish to simply eliminate one of those 'others.'"

The judge removed his glasses. He pinched the ridge of his nose between his thumb and forefinger and closed his eyes for a few moments. He exhaled, put his glasses back on, and addressed the prosecutor. "I'm going to allow you to continue, Mr. Vaughan, but don't test my generosity."

"Thank you, sir." Vaughan turned his attention to JD.

"Mr. Green, what did Mrs. Devine do when she entered the gym?"

"She flips on some lights and walks fast over to the outside door in the back of the gym. She opens the door, and in comes Dusty and Savannah."

"You recognized Dusty and Savannah."

"Sure, I know who they are. We don't hang out together or nothin', but I know who they are."

"And then what happened . . . after they came in?"

"Mrs. Devine tells them to get some mats out of the storeroom to sleep on, and Shaneen, she starts wheezing and squirming all around saying 'oh no, oh jeez, oh no' over and over again. The room, see, it's stacked with stuff, not always put away right. There're some portable basketball stands and hoops in the back. We dragged one of the mats over behind them and hunkered under. Was hoping they'd pull out the two or three mats up front, which is what they did."

"And you stayed there all night?"

"No, sir, we wanted to get out, but as long as Dusty and Savannah was there, we were stuck. After a bit, Mrs. Devine left. We heard her say she was going to make a phone call. We saw her give Dusty and Savannah some money for the snack machines, and they headed to the cafeteria."

JD stopped and looked over at the sketch artist. He paused and then asked, "What's that man doing?"

"He's a sketch artist," Vaughan said. "He's sketching your picture."

"Yeah?" JD looked amused. "Can I see it?"

"Mr. Green," Judge Burgwyn interjected. "This is not a portrait studio. The picture is not for your inspection."

"But what if I don't like it?" JD asked.

The jury snickered. The prosecutor grimaced and hurried along in hopes of keeping his witness focused.

"Would you continue to tell us what happened after Dusty, Savannah, and Mrs. Devine all left the gymnasium? Briefly," he added.

"Sure," JD said. "Shaneen and me was headed to go out the gym door when Ms. Devine came back. We ducked under the bleachers and lay flat. She was crying, and Shaneen wanted to go to her, but I held her back. Shaneen—she likes Mrs. Devine a lot. When Dusty and Savannah came back they talked for a while and then went back into the storeroom to look for blankets. That's when Shaneen and me slipped out the back door."

"JD—may I call you JD?" the prosecutor asked.

"Everybody does."

"This is a very important question. Can you tell us what time Mrs. Devine was there?"

"Yes, sir, I can tell you most exactly. There's a big clock in the gymnasium. They lock everything up after basketball practice at five. That's when Shaneen and me slipped in. It was about five twenty when Mrs. Devine shows up."

"Do you remember what the clock said when you left?"

"Yes, sir, it was after seven o'clock. 'Cause I was supposed to meet my uncle to help him close up at the feed store no later than six thirty. He wasn't happy."

A scurry of activity broke out in the back of the courtroom. Harold Miller had returned to court and was standing next to Joe Wiseman. They immediately left with several other lawyers. Judge Burgwyn shot a glance over the heads of the jurors, aware of their exit, and knew that deals were underway. He hadn't been a judge for these many years without understanding that most justice took place out of public view. Who would have thought the testimony of JD would be the key to send the suits to the back rooms?

Hank Devine turned and saw his brother's expression. He could tell immediately that JD's testimony surprised Ray, too. Hank knew Ray would have made contact with all the potential witnesses in ways that encouraged them to have a lapse in memory. But he had worried about Laura Attwuld. After all, she'd seen his face. Then he'd gotten a break. She'd passed out under questioning. He felt sure now she would be too rattled to point the finger at him. So what was the big deal with this kid on the stand? he wondered.

CHAPTER TWENTY

"Here's the deal." Joe Wiseman pushed aside a Coke can and spread out a scrawl of papers on a coffee table in front of Katy. "If you approve, they'll work tonight to get it typed up."

Katy and Sam sat in Joe's private hotel suite. Joe had practically yanked them out of Sam's truck as they left the courthouse and then sent them to dinner while he finished up business. "Don't drive back to Cedar Branch," he insisted. "What happens tonight is crucial."

Katy was emotionally drained. Her back and legs ached. She wanted nothing more than a hot bath and a warm bed. The thought of a two-hour drive to Cedar Branch and turning around in the morning to drive back to Edenton seemed unbearable. Even Sam looked exhausted.

"Go get a steak," Joe had said, handing them two twenties. "Then meet me at the hotel."

"What about the kids?" Katy asked Sam.

"For heaven's sake, they'll be fine. Savannah's a senior in high school. Just give them a call and tell them it may be midnight before we're back."

Two hours later they dragged into Joe's hotel room where the smell of stale cigarette smoke lingered. Half-eaten Subway sandwiches sat strewn in open wrappers with numerous empty soda cans resting on a dinette set. An opened fifth of bourbon stood on a side table.

Rumpled but wired to the point of exuberance, Joe was manic as he explained the deal. "The medical insurance company is willing to settle out of court." He motioned to a floral couch. "Sit. Sit," he insisted as he waved his hand at them.

"The insurance company?" Katy asked. Weren't they in the middle of a murder trial? When did the insurance company come into play?

"They're offering you $350,000 if you take it tonight."

Katy gasped.

"Only if you take it tonight," Joe repeated.

Sam sat back, not yet sure that he understood. "I don't get it. What's happening?"

"No guarantees. Tonight they believe that JD's testimony will hold and that Laura will nail Hank when she returns to the stand. He will be convicted. I've threatened that I'll follow with a suit against the medical practice on your behalf for a million dollars. They're nervous. They're willing to make a deal tonight to avoid that."

"A million dollars . . ." Katy muttered and slumped back in the sofa.

Sam, in contrast, sat upright. He was all ears, the fatigue vanished. "So why take three fifty if there's the possibility of a million?"

"Because that won't happen. It's just bait. I'd start at a million, and by the time the bargaining and appeals are all over, it could even be less than $350,000, depending on the jury and the judge. They'd do their best in court to show that you were not only a willing partner but had intentions of seducing the doctor. It would be an ugly trial, with a lot of character assassination on both sides. I'm good at that sort of thing, but I don't like to play that game if we can avoid it."

"What if she doesn't take the deal tonight but waits to see what happens in court?" Sam asked.

"If the defense lawyer is able to discredit JD Green, and Laura Attwuld's testimony gets fuzzy, Hank's lawyer may be able to create enough doubt in the minds of the jury that Hank could walk away a free man. In that case, the insurance company will hold off to see if you get charged with the crime."

Katy felt as if she'd just been dropped into a time warp. First Joe suggested she might get an exorbitant amount of money, and in the next minute he was talking about murder charges. "Why wouldn't Mrs. Attwuld identify him?" Katy asked. "She was there. She saw him."

"She's so worked up over this testimony she collapsed today in court. Matthews could hammer away at her credibility—whether or not she could clearly remember anything that she saw. He'll need to be careful, though. If the jury starts to feel sorry for her, it could backfire."

Katy took a deep breath. Her mind raced. "What if," she stuttered, "what if they do charge me with murder?"

"Here's how it works," Joe said. "This is an out-of-court settlement. You will sign an agreement not to disclose the amount you have received or to discuss your involvement with Dr. Attwuld with anyone. You forgo the option to sue the medical office, Attwuld's estate, or any of the past or present employees at any time in the future."

"But what if I'm questioned under oath?"

"You won't be," Joe said. "Once you've signed, I will immediately request to speak to the judge to inform him that an out-of-court settlement has been reached. The judge will then disallow either attorney to question you regarding your involvement with Dr. Attwuld. That pretty much blows to pieces Matthews's defense and leaves open the opportunity to bring in domestic abuse if you're called to testify. I promise you, he won't call you."

"You didn't answer the question," Sam pressed. "What if Hank goes free and Katy is accused of murder?"

Joe pulled at one side of his moustache. "Being accused and being convicted are different things, but regardless, you're covered." His eyes sparkled with obvious pride at what he considered the perfect addendum. "If you're charged, the money would be put in a trust for the children's education until after the trail."

"And if she's convicted?" Sam asked. Katy looked at Sam in disbelief. How could he, of all people, be thinking such thoughts?

"If she's convicted," Wiseman continued, "which I don't anticipate, the money still stays in the trust for the children's education and their descendants."

Katy had difficulty keeping up. Were they really discussing the possibility that she might be charged and convicted of Doc's murder?

"What do you get out of this?" Sam focused. He seemed to be following the thread of Joe's presentation better than Katy.

"I get what Katy and I agreed upon when I took her case: thirty percent of the first $250,000 and twenty percent of anything after that. Katy walks away with a check for $255,000."

"Sam," Katy gasped. "How can I possibly say no?"

Sam's eyebrows went up, and he shook his head. "I don't think you can."

Joe smiled and gave them a quick nod. "I'll make the call, and the papers will be ready to sign in the morning. Be back here by eight o'clock."

CHAPTER TWENTY-ONE

Laura Attwuld's recollection of who Ray was confused her. One moment he was a face in the crowd, and the next moment he was leaning over her, his breath so strong that the pungent odor of garlic set her stomach churning. Then she was weightless, on a stretcher, in a moving vehicle, and the motion made the nausea worse. She rolled over and vomited.

She remembered the siren. This man who looked uncomfortably familiar was talking. His words seemed far off, caught in an echo chamber of sorts. He'd encouraged her to rest. Said her memory may be impaired. After she felt herself lifted out of the EMS truck, he disappeared.

The next voice she heard was a reassuring one. "Mrs. Attwuld, I'm Rosemarie. Rosemarie Diggers. I worked with your husband. Remember me? You're going to be all right." Relief washed over her.

Laura Attwuld came into the courtroom the next morning feeling a bit light-headed. The doctor had suggested that she might want to delay her court appearance for a few more days, but she refused, and Harold Miller encouraged her to try. "It's going to work out," he whispered in her ear. "We've got a deal. Just tell the truth. Tell them exactly what you saw."

Before court even began, the prosecuting and defense attorneys plus Joe Wiseman and two insurance attorneys left the room to move upstairs to the west office. Afterward, Judge Burgwyn returned to the bench, adjusted his pillow, and then welcomed the jury. Nothing more was said about the behind-the-door meeting.

Matthews began his cross-examination of JD. "Mr. Green, how can you be sure that the night you saw Mrs. Devine was on March 18 and not maybe March 17 or March 19?"

"Because on March 18 there was a junior varsity basketball game. Both Shaneen and me stayed to watch that and then hid in the equipment room until after everyone left."

"To practice gymnastics?" Matthews's caustic remark came across as just that. Nobody laughed, and JD appeared confused.

"No, sir, we wasn't practicing gymnastics."

"Mr. Matthews." The judge shot a look of disapproval at Matthews. "'Go wisely and slowly.'"

JD seemed to have the sympathy of the jury. Matthews decided to cut his losses and stop. If he had prepared better, perhaps he would have had a quick comeback, but he didn't.

As the next witness, Toland Vaughan called Shaneen. The curvaceous Miss Towers attracted more attention than JD. The sketch artist scribbled off several pictures, and Shaneen kept one eye cocked on him as she straightened her back and readjusted her position to give him a different pose. She let one heel of her strapless spike sandals hang loosely from the tip of her hot-pink toenails. A thread of an ankle bracelet with several gold charms slid up and down as her foot tapped the air. The jurors' eyes scanned the spaces between the railing in front of the witness chair to catch the curve of the calf and the rounded thigh.

Vaughan wasted no time in getting a confirmation of JD's testimony and relinquished the witness to Matthews. He felt Matthews was doing such a superb job of alienating the judge and jury that he would simply step aside and give him as much rope as he'd take.

"Do you frequent the gymnasium after hours on a regular basis?" Matthews asked.

"I go to all the games," she said, twirling that long dark strand from her hairpiece with her fingers.

"And you take gym classes?"

"Yeah."

"Miss Towers, can you tell me how many clocks there are in the gym?"

"Let's see." She twisted her lips from side to side and looked at the ceiling as she did a mental calculation. She stopped and grinned. "Is this a trick question?"

"No, ma'am," Matthews assured her. "I'm just wondering how you keep track of the time."

"Let's see." She gave him a wink.

Judge Burgwyn put his hands together in prayer fashion and rested his nose on the tips of his two index fingers. He should have stopped them, but the entertainment factor had won him over. Shaneen was more enjoyable to watch than any witness he'd seen in recent months.

"There is one behind each goal," she cooed. "One in the coach's office . . ." She leaned down to adjust her ankle chain and let her blouse slip open to expose a breadth of bosom. The anticipation in the courtroom was pronounced. "Three, I guess."

Matthews cleared his throat. "Do you pay much attention to the time when you're in the gym?" Nobody in the courtroom, including the judge, was paying any attention to time at the moment.

"When I have to," she said, fluttering her eyelashes.

"On the night of March 18, 1994, were you in the gym with JD Green?"

Shaneen shot a flirtatious smile at the good-looking security guard in front of the west office door. He responded in kind. "Yes, sir."

"Do you recall the time?"

For someone who had failed algebra and struggled with geometry, Shaneen proved to be very good with numbers. She recited a minute-by-minute account of how she and JD had moved in and out of the equipment room to the bleachers and out the back door. She had been an hour late getting home, and her mother had to call in late for work since no one else could take care of her baby sister. "You can call the Red Apple and check," Shaneen volunteered. "They're real picky about time. One minute and they dock your pay a half hour."

"What do you order to eat when you go to the Red Apple?" Judge Burgwyn jumped in.

Flabbergasted, Matthews looked mystified at the judge. What on earth did that question have to do with Shaneen's testimony?

"Personally, I like their hot dogs," she said, "but you got to be sure to get them before two o'clock, otherwise they've been rotating on that roaster too long and taste like beef jerky. Course, some people like beef jerky."

Judge Burgwyn smiled. "Why don't we break for lunch?"

The following day when Hank entered the courtroom, he appeared dark and dodgy. He hadn't been able to eat. He felt nervous, his stomach twisting inside him. His eyes darted from one side of the courtroom to the other. The case was slipping away, and it didn't appear the testimony was going in his favor. Laura Attwuld could blow it all for him.

Laura returned to the stand looking almost as unsteady as Hank. She turned to retrieve her sweater from the back of her chair and caught a glimpse of Ray. Momentarily she was confused. Who was he?

He smiled and nodded at her recognition.

"Are you feeling well enough to continue with testimony today?" Judge Burgwyn asked in a gentle voice. "The court is aware of how difficult this is, reliving the events surrounding your husband's murder. You will tell us if you need to take a break, won't you?"

"I will, thank you."

The prosecutor approached the witness solicitously. While Laura wasn't the entertainer that Shaneen had been, she was a strategic witness. He wanted the jury to feel the weight of her dignity and character.

"Mrs. Attwuld, yesterday you testified to the events that led up to the point where you discovered your husband shot in the foyer of your home. You testified that you heard two shots."

Upon request, the court stenographer read the last page of Mrs. Attwuld's testimony.

"Did you see anyone when you ran to your husband?"

Laura paused again. She took a breath. She had to do this, get it over. *The person responsible for my husband's murder is the man who pulled the trigger, not the woman who had the affair.* Had it been nothing more than an affair, Doc would still be alive. They might still be together. Her children would still have a father.

The judge asked softly, "Did you hear the question?"

"Yes, I did." She turned and looked at Judge Burgwyn for a moment. Their eyes met. She could see his regret for her having to endure this all again.

"Would you please answer?" the judge gently encouraged her.

Laura raised her head and looked at Toland Vaughan. "Yes, sir, I did see the man who shot my husband."

"Can you identify him?"

"Yes, sir." Laura looked at the defense table and met Hank's stare straight on. She paused and looked back at the prosecutor. "The cap," she said.

"Oh yes." Vaughan pulled out a black NASCAR cap with "3" on the front. "Your Honor, would Mr. Devine please put on this cap?"

"Objection, Your Honor." Matthews and Howland both leaped to their feet.

"Your Honor," Vaughan complained. "Not an unreasonable request."

Murmurs rippled through the courtroom.

The judge gaveled the court to silence. "Attorneys at my bench," he ordered.

After some discussion, during which Matthews and Howland argued fervently, the judge announced, "I'll allow it. Mr. Devine, please put on the cap."

"Again, Mrs. Attwuld," the prosecutor asked, "do you see that man in this courtroom?"

Laura looked at Hank and nodded. "He's thinner now, but yes, sir. It was that man over there."

"Please let the record show that the witness has identified the defendant, Hank Devine."

There was a flurry of activity in the courtroom. Tears streamed down Katy's face. Sam held one arm tightly around her and squeezed her shoulder. Joe Wiseman and two other lawyers left the courtroom. Harold Miller nodded with satisfaction. Several reporters headed for the exit.

The noise escalated. Judge Burgwyn banged his gavel. "Quiet. Quiet in the courtroom."

Hank jerked his head around to look at Ray. Then he jumped to his feet and shouted, "Liar! She's lying!"

Simultaneously, Ray kicked three vials lying under the bench toward his brother and dropped three more under his own feet. He unleashed a round of pepper spray on those sitting closest to him and broke the vials at his feet with the heel of his boot. Screams erupted as noxious fumes swiftly filled the air.

"Gas! Poison gas!" someone yelled. The stampede began.

The guard next to Hank came to life, but before he could draw his gun, Hank administered a painful blow to his shin and crushed the three glass cylinders now within reach of his shoe. Ray leaped forward and managed to release a stream of pepper spray at the guard and Matthews and Howland before they could respond. They crumpled with their hands over their faces.

Pandemonium broke loose. The guards at the main entrance and east door pulled their revolvers, shouting, "Down. Down!" No one paid them any attention. People stormed the two exits as if they were running with the bulls in Pamplona. Folding chairs collapsed. Men and women tripped and fell over one another. Sam grabbed Katy's arm and pulled her toward the east exit.

Judge Burgwyn rapped his gravel twice, but the fumes quickly overwhelmed him. He coughed and then scrambled to find a handkerchief in his pocket to cover his mouth. His personal rage mounted as he watched Ray and Hank leap together out of the window to his right. This was *his* courtroom, by God. How dare they pull this stunt in his courtroom?

Laura Attwuld remained motionless in the witness chair. Holding his breath and making an effort to crouch, the judge lumbered over to her and nudged her. "Out, my dear. We must get out." Then, like a black bear who'd accidently stuck his nose into a hornet's nest, he helped her to the exit, his temper escalating the closer he got to the door.

Outside, people huddled, rubbing their eyes and sputtering. Their eyes burned. They gasped for fresh air. The rescue squad ambulance made its way through the crowd with the siren blaring. Twenty minutes elapsed before the medic on duty reported Ray Devine had taken the vehicle and hadn't turned up at the hospital.

CHAPTER TWENTY-TWO

Sam O'Brien was spitting mad. What he'd smelled in the courtroom wasn't poisonous gas. He knew how to hunt, and he knew skunk oil. He had used it a couple of times to cover up human odor when hunting deer, but if you weren't careful, it left you and everything you touched smelling like skunk all over. Plus, it was hell to get rid of. He had on a new pair of boots and a leather flight jacket that was his second skin, and he was furious at the thought that they might be ruined. He came out of the courtroom cussing, pulling Katy with him and pushing through the crowd that blocked their way. He heard the siren and saw the EMS van take off.

"They were in that ambulance," he said to Katy as the realization hit.

Katy felt the bottom drop out of her stomach. "The kids. He'll go after the kids. Oh my God, Sam. We have to get back to them."

Sam knew she was right. It would be a mistake to get into his truck smelling like they did, but he had no choice. They had to make it to Cedar Branch ahead of Ray and Hank. He found the nearest pay phone and put in a call to the Police Chief. Andy would have someone at the house right away.

Harold Miller and Joe Wiseman, who had been fortunate enough to be outside at the time of the skunk blast, worked the malodorous crowd, trying to caution people. They knew what skunk oil would do to clothes and the interiors of cars.

"The smell attaches to everything it touches, like poison ivy," they warned anyone who would listen. "If you get in your car with those clothes on, the inside of your car is going to stink for months. Best to leave your clothes right here in the courtyard and burn 'em."

Several people looked askance, objected, and drove off. They'd learn the hard truth later. Phones rang across town telling relatives to bring a change of clothes.

Whatever gentle charm Judge Burgwyn had shown toward Laura Attwuld dissipated the moment he stepped outside. His heated exchanges with guards, police, and lawyers nearby escalated into a tirade.

"Find those sons of bitches!" he shouted at one policeman who had the misfortune to be standing nearby. "I'm holding you personally responsible," he said, jabbing his finger in the nose of the officer. "I want those bastards in my courtroom tomorrow morning. I'm going to crucify them both."

The rookie policeman stammered, "Yes, sir," and fled the scene in hopes that the judge hadn't paid attention to his name badge.

Reggie Matthews, who had taken a direct hit from the blast, saw the judge and pulled himself together in an effort to offer assistance. "Can I do something for you, sir? Get you a change of clothes, maybe?"

"Get your own damn change of clothes." The judge turned on him with a vengeance. "You stink, Matthews. Get out of my way." Madder than a grizzly, he lumbered across the parking lot to the back entrance of the Downtown Café and Soda Shoppe.

Jeff McCaffey had been watching the mayhem from the back of his store, and he knew skunk oil when he smelled it, too. He, the judge, and Toland Vaughan all belonged to the same hunting club.

The thought that the judge had been skunked amused Jeff to no end. This was fodder for months of wisecracks.

"Get out of my way, Jeff," the judge said as he approached the door. He saw the twinkle in his hunting buddy's eye and the smirk on his face and wasn't in the mood for any smart remarks.

"Can't let you in," Jeff said with a wide grin.

"I gotta change clothes. Wash up."

"Not here."

"You're telling me I can't come into a public place?"

"You'll kill my business. Place will smell like skunk for weeks. You know that." Jeff shook his head.

The judge growled and tore the black robe off his back. Hurling it to the ground, he swore. "God. Damn. It. There's a murderer on the loose. Wipe that idiotic smile off your face and call Pauline. Tell her I got skunked. She'll know what to do."

Jeff picked up an old egg crate from the side of the building and set it down for the judge to sit on. He felt the judge's angry stare as he slipped back inside.

"He got skunked, Pauline," Jeff told the judge's wife on the phone. "Literally—I'm serious. Someone dropped skunk oil in his courtroom. He's hotter than a firecracker."

⊸≈∽

The courtyard became a rubble of castaway clothing. Mercy arrived swiftly as cars started to circle and friends and acquaintances brought coats and blankets to the outcasts before bundling them up and whisking them away. Some appeared sympathetic. Others teased relentlessly. The main photograph in the *Edenton News* the following day revealed a scene similar to a frat party, with partially clothed individuals peeking out from behind trees and low brick walls. The caption read: *Rapture in the courthouse—clothes left behind.* The photo of Hank and Ray that appeared midway down the page announced, *Brother helps accused murderer escape.*

⊸≈∽

The faded red barn rested in one of the many fields hidden among the fingers of Albemarle Sound. At one time, a home and a garage had stood beside the highway. Pig pens and a chicken coop still shared the space, and cows were fenced in on the back forty. But long ago the other buildings had become vacant and finally collapsed. The land was tilled to make way for cotton and soybeans. The graffiti-laden walls of the old barn had been salvaged to allow storage for an old tractor.

Ray pulled the ambulance into the abandoned building twenty-two miles north of town. A black 1994 Nissan Sentra SE-R that he'd rented in Norfolk three days earlier sat waiting. He had paid for it with a credit card and ID lifted off a drunken sailor who'd been scheduled to ship out the next day.

Hank got out and surveyed the outdated tractor that looked just like the piece of junk Sam's next-door neighbor had. Probably a grandson somewhere had high hopes of restoring it . . . like the car he'd thought about restoring with Dusty.

"Get outta those clothes, man." Ray pulled out a half gallon of cheap whiskey.

Hank stripped and lay down on the mixture of dry straw, dirt, and rubble that made up the rotting floor of the barn. He didn't care. The bare earth felt better than the cement slab of his jail cell. He closed his eyes. His heart pounded. What a rush.

He rubbed the back of his hand across his nose . . . stopped . . . kept his eyes closed for another thirty seconds and then glanced over at Ray. "That wasn't what you promised."

Ray took a swig out of the bottle. "I promised to get you out. You're out, ain't ya?"

Hank took a long, hard swallow. "This ain't exactly free."

Ray spit into the remnants of straw that rotted against a broken stall door. "This isn't the first time I've saved your ass. Don't start telling me what I should've done."

Ray had talked to everyone who claimed to know something about the murder, even gone to that freakin' root doctor. A year had given him a lot of time to make things happen. He had suggested to the folks in the trailer park that they might not remember things so well, and people had recanted their previous statements as he'd hoped they would.

Rachel Mayfield had been more stubborn, and only after he'd commented on his hopes that no harm ever came to her precious cats did she admit she might have been mistaken in what she saw.

What with witnesses folding, no one left to prove that it was Hank they saw, and questions as to Katy's whereabouts at the time of the murder, Ray figured any defense lawyer could shift blame.

Then . . . Mrs. Attwuld clinched it all on her own, without him having to do a thing. She had a history of panic attacks and tachycardia. What luck. She was no longer a reliable witness. There was no way in hell that her testimony would stand up under cross-examination.

Unfortunately, Hank hadn't wanted to give his lawyer one more day. They would've had a chance to discredit Laura Attwuld's testimony. Ray believed they could have done it. But Hank had panicked, and Ray had to bail him out again.

Hank took another swallow from the whiskey bottle. "This place smells like pigs. Where are the other clothes?"

Ray tossed him the keys to the Nissan. "In the trunk."

Hank opened the trunk and pulled out jeans and a black sweatshirt with a large "3" across the front. "Damn it, Ray. You're getting me hanged over that number three. You got a thing with Dale Earnhardt?"

"Hey," Ray barked. "Don't bad-mouth my man. There's other clothes there. I ain't dressing ya."

"We gotta wash," Hank said.

"There's water out back. I checked before I picked this spot. At the edge of the barn."

Hank grabbed a different sweatshirt that had a Panthers logo and started outside before he realized they'd have to wait until nightfall. Not worth taking a chance someone might see them.

Ray pulled out a plastic bag and put both his and Hank's offensive cast-offs inside. He tied it and threw it in the back of the ambulance. "Something to remember us by," he said.

"They're gonna kill us, you know." Hank stood shoulder to shoulder with his brother, both in their skivvies like two jocks about to dive off a cliff. "You're going to die with that stupid buzz cut." He shook his head and turned away. "You should have stayed out of it this time. I deserved what I got. I pulled the trigger. Killed a man. I can't run away from that no matter what."

"Come on, man." Ray went to the ambulance and pulled out a pack of cigarettes. "Don't go pussy on me now. You deserved better. Katy was a little tramp."

Hank shook his head and looked at the floor. "I had other women."

"You're a man—on the road. That's different." Ray lit a cigarette and took a long pull. "She was the one with the kids all week. She set the example. Face it," he said. "You have no idea what went on while you were away."

❧

Pictures of Ray and Hank flashed across the six o'clock evening news with an additional photo of the type of EMS vehicle they had stolen from the courthouse. Olivia Cox, a young and talented news broadcaster out of Raleigh, had been covering the trial and was thrilled to have it jump to the lead story. She'd interviewed everyone who'd stopped and talked to her and then made cuts immediately before the three-minute broadcast.

An alert went out that Ray had worked with emergency medical services for a number of years and might be wearing his EMS jacket. He also had a scanner radio in the ambulance. Hospitals were notified.

The local sheriff, Lloyd Satterfield, reluctantly stepped to the microphone, and cameras whirred. He did not approve of his little town being invaded by murderers or reporters who wished to distort the tourist image that Edenton worked hard to maintain, he said. A rail-thin man with skin the color and texture of sandpaper, he speculated in a monotone that the fugitives had already left the county. "We got roadblocks set up. The US Coast Guard is monitoring Albemarle Sound and the Outer Banks. Just be on alert," he warned the public. "We have reason to believe they may be armed and dangerous."

⌦

Ray and Hank stayed put until after dark.

Ray slept. Hank couldn't. He watched his brother sleep. Ray was right. Ray had always taken care of them. Their early lives had been a daily challenge of avoidance and diversions until finally one night their dad beat Ray so badly that Hank knew his brother would either leave or kill the old man before daybreak. Ray chose the first option and took his younger brother with him. He swore no one would ever lay a hand on either of them again.

They hitchhiked 650 miles south from Hoboken, New Jersey, to Myrtle Beach, South Carolina. Hank was fourteen—Ray two years older. They headed for the ocean . . . someplace where the sound of the waves would wash away childhood memories. Ray found work as a lackey in a small-town auto repair shop and learned some skills. They bunked together in the back of the garage. At eighteen Ray joined the marines and helped Hank forge a fake ID. Hank joined the army.

Two years in the military was enough for Hank. He figured they'd taught him good how to fight. Ray loved it, though. Got promoted to sergeant and was shipped overseas.

Hank bought a motorcycle. Thought he'd check on his mother, but changed his mind. Why revisit a woman who'd never stuck up for him? She'd been nothing more than a doormat in their household. He drove to the mountains instead. On his way back east, he stopped at The Quaker Café in Cedar Branch, a crossroads of a town, and ordered a cheeseburger. Katy walked into his life.

She was about the cutest thing he'd ever seen, like a little doll with that hourglass shape and those dark curls that brushed across her blue eyes. He thought it would be a one-night stand, but he kept coming back for more, and she turned up pregnant before the end of the summer. He thought about running, but where to? He had no home. If he was going to settle down, he'd be damn lucky to have someone as good looking as Katy by his side.

When they told her folks, her brothers stood shoulder to shoulder with nothing but malice in their eyes. Their message was clear. Hank got on his motorcycle and rode away with his prize on the seat behind him.

Ray woke up and turned to see Hank still staring at the roof of the barn. It was after midnight. "Did you get some sleep?"

"Nope."

"Time to get rolling."

CHAPTER TWENTY-THREE

Hank and Ray drank during the day and drove at night in search of the next abandoned barn. Food from a drive-through. A chance for one of them to wash up in the bathroom. Two days max in one place. Ray plotted. Hank swung between periods of remorse and vindictive rants.

Days passed, then weeks. There was speculation that the two men had slipped by the coast guard and were someplace south of Edenton. If a man had access to a boat, there were a lot of inlets and coves to get lost in. Alerts were put out in coastal South Carolina, Georgia, and Florida.

But Ray and Hank had eluded the law. They felt cocky. They'd pick up discarded papers at McDonald's and looked obsessively for news about their escape. As the third, the fourth, and the fifth week dragged into June, the Devine brothers slipped to the back pages. Even Olivia Cox couldn't dig up anything new to report. When she approached Joe Wiseman, he reminded her that his client had signed a confidentiality agreement on the settlement. Katy O'Brien refused any interviews, and patrons of The Quaker Café jumped to her defense. Everything else was speculation.

Laura Attwuld referred any questions to her attorney. Harold Miller was evasive with reporters, but won his appeal with the life insurance company when all charges were dropped by Katy O'Brien. The company would have to pay Doc's life insurance policy since no criminal charges were brought against him.

In May the NC Office of Rural Health found a National Health Service Corps doctor with a four-year service obligation. The practice would survive. Laura would be okay.

⤳

"I can't believe she's going to cash in on this," Hank repeated time and again as he read that an undisclosed settlement had been reached between Katy and the medical practice.

Ray fed his rage. "It's always been about her, what's in it for her."

No details were forthcoming, although one article hinted at rumors of other settlements that Joe Wiseman had brokered being in the millions.

"A million bucks—what'll she do with that?" Hank wondered out loud.

"She'll build a big house; probably get a condo in Florida, vacation in the Caribbean. She'll never have to work another day in her life. And what about you?"

Hank seethed. "She's bettin' I'll rot in jail."

⤳

Hank hoped that Savannah and Dusty would be at the house when he got there. He wanted to see them. He missed them. He cared about them. He wanted them to hear his side of the story . . . to know what a liar and cheat their mother had been. She had pushed him to the breaking point, or so he thought some days. Other days he realized all that he'd lost. They'd loved each other at one time. He knew he'd hurt her, both physically and emotionally.

He and Ray found a dilapidated wooden building back in the woods off the Potecasi Swamp. Once a Quaker meeting house, the structure had endured long after its membership dissolved. With cans of beer, beans, saltines, and Vienna sausages, they camped out for three days, waiting for the moon to wane.

"Man, I gotta have something else to eat besides Vienna sausage," Ray complained late in the afternoon on the second day. "Let's go get us a steak someplace. Cook it over an open fire."

They were in Katy's territory now. The cops would be more vigilant. Hank was itchy to get this over with and get outta there. "Too risky, man."

"We gotta get something to shut up the dogs, anyway," Ray insisted.

"Yeah . . . well." Hank knew he was right. The dogs could be a problem.

They'd seen a dingy country store a mile back propped up beside the road like an invalid on crutches. Broken windows had been reinforced with duct tape, and burglar-proof bars proved the owner had something to worry about. At first, Ray assumed the place was closed, but a car out front was filling up at one of the gas pumps. Ray headed back alone to look for food and some Nyquil to handle the dogs.

❦

Sporting sunglasses and a NC State cap, Ray didn't believe the yahoo behind the dusty counter could possibly recognize him.

In his seventies and wearing overalls with unfastened buttons on either side of what had once been a waistline, Noosh Fellows may have looked one step short of the top stair, but he was no fool. He knew his numbers, he knew his inventory, and he knew his customers: the ones who had cash and the ones who ran a tab and paid it. He also knew strangers came in three varieties: lost, hunters, and thieves.

He watched Ray climb out of his Nissan and walk up to the door. "'Lo there, fellow. Need a fill-up?" he asked.

"Yep, and a little food." Ray tried to be folksy, not something he was good at.

"Lost?"

"Nope. Doin' some huntin'."

Noosh raised any eyebrow. This weren't no hunter. "Staying over at the Lasko place?" Lasko's was an old home with three hundred acres of timberland that the owner rented out to hunters from Raleigh. Could be this fellow was from that group, but he didn't look a banker, lawyer, or doctor neither.

Ray tried to temper the owner's uneasiness. "Yeah, here for the weekend. Not much of a hunter really," he kidded. "Some of the guys talked me into coming."

Noosh relaxed. That made sense. "Hamburger? Steak? I got a couple of steaks and about five pounds of hamburger thawed. Don't want it to sit out much, you know. Got another twenty pounds back in the freezer."

"I'll take the steaks and a couple of pounds of that hamburger."

Two pounds was a right small order when the hunters came in. "You by yourself?"

Ray knew immediately he had made a tactical error. Hunters in this part of the state never hunted alone. The last thing he wanted to do was send up a flare. This guy would probably be on the phone to someone else in town before he cleared the gas pumps. "Naw, me and a couple others tonight. Rest will be coming in tomorrow. Could you have another ten pounds thawed for tomorrow?"

"Sure, I can do that. What about buns? Bread man comes in the morning."

"I'll take a bag tonight and five more when I pick up the meat," Ray said. He pulled out three twenties and put them on the counter. An old state section of the *Raleigh News & Observer* lay open next to the register. A headline halfway down the page caught his attention: "Out-of-Court Settlement Reached in Attwuld Murder. Devine Brothers Still at Large." "Let me go ahead and pay for the extra meat," Ray said.

"Nah, that's not necessary," Noosh said, but Ray insisted.

"Pretty good turkey season?" Ray wanted to keep the focus on hunting.

"Just gettin' started. You're a couple days early, you know?"

Ray didn't know at all, but he fell in line. "Thought we'd put the beer on ice before the others get here. You got any rat poison? A big rat scampered out when we opened the house."

"Them rats, they are a nuisance," Noosh said and pulled a package of d-CON down off the shelf. "Can't hardly control them if you leave a house empty."

"Ain't it the truth?" Ray said. "Wanna pay for some diesel fuel, too." Ray nodded at the pump where he'd already left a gallon can. "Probably going to start a campfire."

Noosh added the amount to the register.

"And how about a Raleigh paper?"

"Only the one here. It's an old one. I always plan to read it and then get busy," Noosh said and rustled the three sections into place. "Still want it?"

"Thanks." Ray flashed a friendly nod and picked up his bag along with the paper.

From the window, Noosh watched him put a gallon of diesel into a gas can. Nice guy. Hadn't ever seen a hunter driving a Nissan Sentra before, though, and funny thing, he didn't turn in the direction to Lasko's.

⚓︎

Ray mixed the rat poison along with some of the Nyquil into the hamburger. He divided it into three portions and put the meat into Styrofoam hamburger boxes on the floorboard of the car. He built a small fire in what remained of the fireplace and cooked the steaks on a piece of foil leftover from a stop at Arby's.

"We're almost there," Ray said as he took a swig from a partial fifth of Wild Turkey. "This time tomorrow we'll be sitting on some beach."

Hank snorted and rubbed the bristle on his chin. He wished he was as confident as his brother. "Nobody gets killed, right?"

"Hey." Ray reared back and stared at his brother. "We take the kids. That was your idea. They go with us while we make a deal with Katy about the money."

The steaks weren't much more than warmed through when he and Hank doused the fire. Didn't want smoke to be seen from the old building. They ate the meat and drank.

"Better get some shut-eye, man," Ray said as he curled up on the wooden floor with a blanket. "Long day ahead of us."

He was like that, Hank thought. Could sleep anyplace, anytime . . . the marine in him. The anticipation of what was to come kept Hank's mind in motion. He couldn't shut off the switch.

His and Katy's personal problems had been smeared across the news for two months now. Made 'em look like a family of crazies. That Rachel Mayfield was talking to every reporter and telling 'bout every fight they ever had. It seemed their escape had liberated her tongue to wag once again. He'd never forgive Katy for what she'd put them all through.

Every family had problems, but theirs had been blown out of proportion. He hadn't been all that bad to the kids. Never hit Savannah. The only reason he came down hard on Dusty was to try to make a man out of him. That's what fathers were supposed to do. He thought of his own father. He wasn't like his own father. *Never*, he reassured himself.

Savannah and Dusty understood. Their mother was like a child. She just couldn't handle things by herself. How many times did he come home to find Savannah doing her mother's work? Katy had been that way since the day he married her. As head of the family, it was his responsibility to set the limits and make sure the rules were followed.

Latisha Anderson pulled herself up on the sheets of her grandmother's bed, crawled under the covers, and rested her head on the generous cushion of Teensy's bosom. "What's the matter, baby?" Teensy said as she wrapped her arm around the six-year-old.

"Scared."

"Ain't nothin' to be scared of," Teensy said, already drifting back to sleep.

The white clapboard house sat off a dirt road three miles outside of Cedar Branch. Teensy and her husband, Lyle, had built it with their own hands forty plus years ago. Building the house had not been the problem. The land was. There wasn't much land being offered up to colored folks back then, but the Bennett family, members of the Quaker community in town, had agreed to sell an acre at the end of their wooded property if Lyle would clear it. Bennett land bordered the Kendalls' cotton field, and with only a pitted dirt road running back through the farms, Lyle and Teensy found themselves living between what God grew and what men harvested.

Latisha listened to her grandfather gasp for air, and Teensy rolled toward her husband. "You okay, honey?" She patted the hospital bed that had been brought in and placed next to her own. She sat up, readjusted the portable ventilator, and rested her hand lightly on his forearm. His breathing evened out.

"He gonna die, Memaw?" Latisha whispered.

"Not tonight, honey. Not tonight," Teensy said and kissed her forehead. She'd grown used to the uneven breathing patterns as the Lou Gehrig's disease progressed. "Why don't you go back in with your sisters? You'll sleep better."

Instead of answering, Latisha nestled in closer and squeezed her eyes shut.

Teensy kissed the top of her head one more time. Ever since Miss Ellie had to close the café in order to repair the hole that Helen Truitt made out front, Teensy had relished the extra time she had with Lyle and the grandkids. She missed the money, but the café would open up again soon, and she could take in laundry until then. Long ago she'd learned how to get by.

She breathed in the lavender scent of the bubble soap that her three granddaughters had bathed in before bedtime. How nice these little ones smelled between evening and daylight, before they had time to walk the dusty One-Mile Road to the bus stop and bring home the smells of the outside world. Tomorrow, she'd cook them something special—banana pudding.

⤚≋⤙

Ray pulled the Nissan off the main road and stopped. With no moon and no streetlamps, Hank could hardly see where the road's edge slipped into the canal that ran alongside.

"Whatcha doing?" Hank asked.

"I got a score to settle first. Won't take a minute." Ray pulled two empty liquor bottles from the trunk along with the kerosene and a can of oil. Mixing the two together, he filled both bottles and stuffed one end of a dirty rag down each neck, letting the other end hang out the top. He got back in the car and handed the bottles to Hank. "Hold these," he said.

"Christ. You making Molotov cocktails?"

"They're a present for a bitch who messed up my truck."

"You're nuts, man. You'll have the cops on us before we get into town," Hank said.

Ray smiled. "I cut the phone line. It'll be morning before she gets word to anyone, and if it's sooner, well, that'll be something else to keep the cops busy."

Ray put the Nissan in gear, cut the headlights, and inched up the road to Teensy's house.

⤚≋⤙

In Teensy's dream she fried chicken in the cast iron frying pan, and as she lifted the hot grease off the stove, the pan got heavier and heavier until she couldn't hold it anymore. She couldn't remember where the children were playing, and when she dropped the frying pan, the room burst into flames. She flinched . . . awoke . . . and sat up straight. It was no dream. Something was burning.

CHAPTER TWENTY-FOUR

They got thirty feet up the lane to Sam's house before the dogs began to bark. Hank had been nervous to start with, and the side diversion to the house on the dirt road upset him. "You planning anything else you ain't told me about?" Hank asked.

Ray didn't answer. He went another ten feet and got out to lay the Styrofoam containers of hamburger on the ground. He got back in the car to wait.

"How long before the Nyquil works, you think?" Hank asked.

"Better give it fifteen or twenty minutes," Ray said.

"You don't think someone's reported that fire by now?"

"You hear any sirens?"

A light flipped on in the kitchen. Sam opened the back door, scanned the yard, and yelled at the dogs, "Quit your yapping." He closed the door, and the light went back off. The barking grew intermittent, less pronounced.

In the house next door there appeared to be some activity. Ray poked Hank with his elbow and motioned in that direction. "Not to worry," Hank said. "Old man. Lives alone. Probably going to take a leak."

Twenty minutes later both dogs staggered and collapsed. Cautiously Ray and Hank opened the car door and got out. Ray approached the first one and gave him a kick. The dog lay rock solid, blood leaking from his eyes and mouth. Hank recoiled. "These dogs are dead."

"And your plan was . . . ?"

"Just knock them out. You had no call to kill 'em," Hank said. He hesitated. Ray wasn't playing by the rules. For a moment he wanted to ditch the whole plan.

"Don't be a pussy," Ray said. "You always was the pussy. You can kill a doctor but not a dog?" Ray turned his back on Hank and headed to the house. "You comin'?"

Everything felt wrong. Hank hesitated. Ray was right. He had been the pussy. If it hadn't been for Ray, he would have been the one getting a beating every night. Ray got him a job and in the army. Ray warned him Katy was trouble long before he saw it.

Years had passed since Hank had been inside the O'Brien home. He still remembered the layout: the one bedroom on the first floor, the three stuffy little bedrooms at the top of the narrow staircase. The windows all around were so worn with age only the layers of paint kept them from falling apart. The back door had always been open. He guessed it might not be now.

The door to the back porch was locked. Ray slit the screen with his pocketknife, reached in, and undid the latch. He wedged a credit card between the door frame and the lock of the laundry room, slid it upward, and, presto, just that easy.

Shame on you, Sam, Hank thought. Unconsciously he winced and let out a soft groan. *This is how you protect my kids?* Now he was angry again. *You deserve what's coming.*

A night-light in the downstairs bathroom and one at the foot of the stairs illuminated the floor enough for Hank and Ray to steal across the kitchen and family room to Sam's bedroom door. Hank gripped the knob and turned it gently. It squeaked once. He drew his gun. For an instant he felt his hand tremble. Hank stopped, but heard no movement inside. Slowly he pushed open the door.

Sam lay sprawled on his stomach across the double bed with his arms stretched out as if he were in flight. A patchwork quilt covered him from the waist down; his upper torso was bare. Ray placed the barrel of his gun to the side of Sam's head and nodded to Hank to flip on the light.

Sam jerked and felt the cold metal. "Steady, cowboy," Ray whispered, a sneer spreading across his mouth. "You get to decide whether Katy lives or dies."

Sam lay perfectly still.

"Thatta boy. Now roll over real slow like, and keep your hands where I can see them. Notice your good buddy, Hank, by the door. Remember him? Your brother-'n-law. You heard tell, he's a murderer."

Sam caught sight of Hank. "Where's your gun?" Hank asked.

"Locked up," Sam said.

"Right," Hank quipped. Ray moved forward and pulled the pillow from under Sam's head. Then he leaned down and checked under the bed. He opened the drawer on the side table, and with a smile he pulled out a Remington six-shooter, rolled the chamber, and saw no bullets. He nodded at Hank.

"Good man," Hank said. "Safety first with kids in the house." He picked up a pair of jeans flung over the chair and threw them at Sam. "Put on your pants, flyboy. We're going for a ride."

Someone moved overhead. Sam's eyes darted to the ceiling, and Hank put a finger to his mouth in warning as Sam pulled up his jeans and slipped on a T-shirt that was lying crumpled on the floor next to the chair. He grabbed his boots. Hank motioned him into the living room.

"Come on," Sam said. "I'll fly you wherever you want to go. Let's go before the others wake up."

Hank wasn't about ready to leave. "Call Katy," he said.

Sam said nothing.

"I'm not playing with you, man. Call her down."

Sam looked from one to the other. He could smell the whiskey. "You've been drinking," he said. "You do that so your kids'll recognize you?"

Ray's boot hit Sam in the small of his back. "Call her," he hissed.

Sam fell forward and caught himself on the couch. He heard the sound of Katy's feet on the stairwell as soon as he knocked the sofa sideways.

"You okay, Sam?" she called. "What happened?" When she stepped off the bottom stair, Hank grabbed her by the arm and yanked her around, pulling her into him. With one arm wrapped around her, he pressed her body to his chest and held a gun to her head.

"You bitch. I see you're gettin' paid for whoring around. I go to jail and you get cash. That ain't quite fair."

Sam was on his feet ready to throw himself at Hank when Ray moved in front of him.

Katy's eyes darted between Sam and Ray. She could feel the barrel of the gun against her head.

"Mama." Savannah's voice came from the top of the stairs. "What's going on?"

"Nothing, honey. Stay upstairs." Katy kept her voice as calm as possible. "What do you want?" she sputtered to Hank. "Money?"

"Yeah, I want money."

"Take it. Just go."

"Right. What you gonna do—write me a check? Maybe me and the kids will go on a vacation together, and when I get what's coming from that slick lawyer of yours, you'll get to see them again."

Katy's jaw tightened. She was amazed at how calm she suddenly felt. So this was how it would end. He'd kill her, but Savannah and Dusty would be okay if Sam was still alive to take care of them. She needed to get Hank and Ray out of the house with her, away from the kids.

"I'll go with you. I'll stay with you until the money comes and then give it to you." Her voice was steady, like a patient telling a doctor to turn off life support. "Then you can shoot me."

Hank seemed amused . . . no begging, no crying. He hated how whiney and mealy-mouthed she used to be—always hiding, slipping around. She'd gotten to be so much like his mother.

A bell clanged in the distance, and Hank and Ray looked at each other. "What the hell was that?" Ray asked.

No one spoke.

"Who's ringing the goddamn bell?" he shouted.

"It's Leland Slade. His animals must be out," Sam said.

They could hear Dusty scrambling upstairs, putting on clothes, talking to Savannah. The two of them hurried down and headed to the door. The sight of their father and Uncle Ray brought them to a halt. One look at their mother and they knew.

"Savannah, Dusty . . ." Hank said. "I've been worried about you." He became aware of how threatening he appeared and let go of Katy. She jerked away, positioning herself between him and the children.

Neither child moved. Hank sniffed. "Your mom and I were just discussing some vacation plans. She thinks you might want to spend a few days with me."

"Like hell," Katy said.

"Shit." Ray shook his head. "What? Are we in divorce court or something? Who's holding the gun? You or her?" Ray swung around and slapped Katy across the face. "Shut up, bitch."

Hank flinched as both of his children shouted "Stop!" in unison. Sam started to lunge at Ray, but Hank fired his gun into the ceiling. Dusty and Savannah screamed.

"Back off!" he yelled. "Everyone."

Tears began to well as Savannah's eyes darted between her father and Uncle Ray.

"I'm okay," Katy said, holding her arms up in surrender. She knew nothing was okay. Not when six people all had their adrenaline pumping like a fire hydrant wide open. She didn't want the kids to get hurt. "I'm okay—really," she tried to reassure them. "We can work something out here."

The phone rang. Everyone paused. Sam's mind was spinning, trying to figure a way out. He knew he needed to get a handle on his own emotions and slow things down before the situation blew up. Everyone was wired to explode.

"Ignore it," Hank said. "Nobody answer."

"It's Leland, needin' help," Sam said.

Hank ground his teeth. "Goddamn."

"He'll have a dozen neighbors here in fifteen minutes," Sam added, hoping the thought might scare them away.

"We gotta go now!" Ray barked, alarmed by the idea. He waved his gun back and forth, motioning them to the back door. "Everyone in the plane."

"I'll take the two of you," Sam said, looking at Hank and Ray and hoping this might be his opportunity to separate them from Katy and the kids.

"We're *all* going," Hank said.

"Take Sam and me," Katy said. "Leave the kids."

"We're all going," Hank repeated louder, "except you, Katy—you're waitin' on a check, remember? Then you can fly down to wherever I tell you and get the kids."

"It won't hold five." Sam shook his head. "It barely gets off the ground with two."

"Figure it out," Hank said. "We ain't playing games here."

Ray pushed Dusty to the door. "I got this kid. You hang on to Savannah," he said to Hank.

"I'm not going." Savannah squirmed away, and Hank grabbed her by her wrist and pulled her back. He wanted to be gentler, but plans had taken an unexpected turn. They would have to talk this through later.

"Look, sweetheart," he said in a weak effort to reassure her, "it's gonna be okay. We're going someplace where nobody knows us. Make a fresh start. Maybe Costa Rica."

"You lied to me," she said, her lip quivering. "I believed you. I believed you both." Savannah practically spit out the word *both* as she shot a hateful look at Ray.

Pounding on the front door stopped them. Adam Hoole called, "Sam, you in there? Leland's animals got out. We need you and the kids."

"Don't answer," Hank said.

"He knows we're here," Sam said.

"Then get rid of him," Ray said, pointing the gun at Dusty.

Savannah looked wide-eyed at her uncle and then at her father.

"Go easy, man." Hank grimaced. "They're kids. That's my boy."

"It's the rest of my life and yours in jail if we don't get out of here in the next five minutes," Ray said. "We're not stopping for family counseling."

"That's MY BOY!" Hank said, louder this time.

Sam went to the door. It was still dark outside . . . a chance to run if they could make a break. He cracked it open. "We're coming," he said.

"Is everything all right?" Adam asked. "Your dogs are flat out down by the road. They look dead."

Sam winced. "Must've got into something. I'll check."

"All right." Adam hesitated again. "Turkeys and pigs. Think some goats, too."

"We'll be there in a minute." Sam closed the door before Adam could say another word.

Leland's farm bell rang again, five times, and then the bell behind Nathan and Euphrasia's home farther down the road rang.

"Let's get out of here." Ray pointed Sam toward the back door, his gun still on Dusty.

Hank wrapped his arm around Savannah's shoulder and pulled her toward him, away from Ray. "We're walking out of here, all of us together. We're walking straight to that plane and getting in. Katy, you make sure the runway is cleared. Any animals in our way get run over when we take off. If that plane doesn't leave the ground, I'm shooting Sam in the head. Swear to God."

"No, I won't let you." Dusty spit his words out. He hadn't said anything up until now. He'd learned how to get quiet and invisible when tempers flared, but the idea that his uncle would seriously talk about shooting Sam and his mother went through him like an electric shock.

Surprised and somewhat pleased by the outburst, Hank smiled. "Whatcha gonna do about it? Let me see those balls, little man." Dusty seethed.

They filed out of the back door of the house toward the Cessna. As they came into the open, Katy caught sight of two cars across the field at Leland's.

Lights were on. It was 5:00 a.m. with the hint of daybreak coming from the east. Vague shadows of animals darted across the newly planted field. Katy thought she saw Leland open the gates to one of the pens. The animals weren't escaping. He was letting them out. He must have seen something, she thought. The dogs, the strange car in the driveway.

Adam ran toward the animals, waving his arms and shouting, "Stop! Stop!" He was literally chasing the animals toward the plane. He called out across the field, "See if you can grab these dang pigs."

Hank gripped Savannah and pushed her forward. "Move faster," he said, squeezing her arm tighter.

Unbeknownst to the passengers, a tom turkey and three hens had hidden themselves under the cockpit of the plane. The sudden invasion of their refuge caused the hens to bolt in fright and the tom to leap to the defense of his harem.

The thirty-pound tom fanned his tail, puffed out his chest, raised himself to a height of almost three feet, and then charged. Hank let go of Savannah, and Dusty seized the moment of surprise. With all the force he could muster, he jammed his boot into his Uncle Ray's kneecap.

"Run!" Sam yelled as loud as he could. Katy and Savannah took off across the field. A gun went off, and the tom turkey flopped down beside the wheels of the plane.

Hank bolted after his daughter.

Ray grabbed Dusty and slapped him across the face. "You sorry little bastard. In the plane," he ordered. You—" He motioned to Sam, who had stopped in his tracks when he realized Ray had Dusty by the arm. "You—drag that dead turkey out of the runway and get in. Ready this plane for takeoff."

Sam did as he was told. At least Katy and Savannah had a chance now. If they got to Leland's barn, Adam and Leland could help. Others were arriving.

Once in the air, Sam hoped he might have more control.

Ray squeezed into the cramped backseat of the plane, his gun pointed at them. Sam knew he wouldn't need much of an excuse to fire another shot, the next one possibly at Dusty. He cranked up the engine and taxied down the dirt runway. Sam looked over at Dusty. Red marks stretched across the side of his face, and he could see the boy was seething with anger.

"Gonna need some help." Sam nodded at Dusty. "Hold it together, kid. Steady and ready."

More farm bells could be heard. "What they doing now?" Ray said more in disgust than ignorance.

"They're calling the Quakers, other town members. An emergency."

Ray groaned.

Headlights appeared on the road ahead. "Get this baby in the air, and I mean in—the—air. No funny business." Ray cocked his gun and leveled it at the base of Dusty's neck. Sam revved up the engine, and the farm animals scattered.

Ray looked down at the growing traffic and across the horizon as the sun began to rise. "Sorry, little brother," he whispered. "I can't help you this time."

CHAPTER TWENTY-FIVE

Behind the Quaker meeting house, Pam Sibley rang the old bell as if the louder the sound, the greater the possibility it might be heard in heaven. It had been years since anyone had used the bells for anything other than a wedding or funeral, and now there was a domino effect as the sounds traveled from Leland's to the Hooles' and now the meeting house. The whole town was waking up in alarm. Something was very wrong.

When Adam drove past the O'Brien home in response to Leland's bell, he'd spotted the Nissan Sentra at the front of the drive. They all knew Katy's story, and while no one spoke of it openly, there had been general concern for her safety and the children's welfare after Hank's much-publicized escape.

Adam found Leland opening the gates for his livestock and shooing them toward the O'Brien house. When they heard gunfire, Adam called his folks and warned them to stay indoors. He told his dad to call the police. No one had heard from Adam since.

A police siren screamed by the meeting house. The Quakers were gathering. Euphrasia and Nathan Hoole entered, followed by Phil and Nanette Harper with their son, Ben. Duncan Howell nodded at Ben and raised his eyes in question to Nanette, wondering why she'd brought the boy. "Dusty and Savannah are his friends," Nanette said.

Henry Bennett walked in minutes later. "Police are converging on Leland's place," he announced. "Someone shot at the police from inside the house when they tried to approach."

"The Devine brothers?" Duncan asked.

"That's probably a safe guess," Henry said.

"Evidently Sam's plane took off," Phil said. "Don't know yet who's in it. Sam's probably flying, but he wouldn't have left Katy unless forced to."

Anna Reed walked through the double doors that led into the thirty-foot-square meeting room lined with rows of small windows set just below the ceiling line. A skylight in the ceiling let the morning light in before it got too hot, and shade from an old sycamore tree blocked the afternoon sun. The walls were decorated only with a coat of white paint. There were no religious objects.

The use of the paint had been controversial. For twenty years the Quakers had considered the possibility that paint could benefit the service by reflecting more light throughout the room. After all, Quakers were all about light . . . seeking the light . . . standing in the light. Gerard Hoffman had considered the addition frivolous and wasteful and had been the one dissenter to stand in the way of consensus. Only after his death was the room painted.

Twenty benches were placed in rows of five in a square so that members faced each other as they worshipped. Leaning heavily on her cane, Anna Reed, one of five elders, walked to the far bench opposite the main door and sat down. Nathan Hoole, Adam's father, followed and sat next to her. They folded their hands, their posture indicating a time for silence.

Following their lead, others moved to the same benches most of them sat on week after week—often the same benches their families had occupied for the past several generations. One by one, members entered the room in silence until their numbers increased to twenty-four: five women, eighteen men, and Ben Harper, a fifteen-year-old worried about his friends.

⚯

At only five feet six inches, what Police Chief Andy Meacham lacked in height, he made up for in character. He exuded the best of the local talents in law enforcement. Despite his youthful appearance, he made good judgment calls and could defuse most situations with time and solicitous nudging. But Cedar Branch had never faced a situation similar to the one at hand.

Chief Meacham entered Sam's house with his deputy. A thorough search revealed no one there, but they found evidence of a struggle. Andy picked up one empty cartridge off the floor. Outside, Leland's animals foraged about in both yards. When Andy approached Leland's house, shots rang out, and he took cover.

"Damn," he cussed to himself. There'd been speculation that Hank and Ray had managed to skip the country and land on some deserted beach in the Bahamas. During the past couple of weeks, he and his deputy had become less vigilant about checking Sam's house.

He radioed Sheriff Howard. "We got a problem in Cedar Branch, Sheriff. I think the Devine brothers have surfaced, and they're in a fightin' mood. It looks to me like they've taken hostages."

❦

Sheriff Howard arrived thirty minutes later. Big and burly, he walked around with a gun strapped to his hip and a second one holstered at his ankle. He had worked his way up through law enforcement from deputy to police chief and, after twenty years, was elected county sheriff. He knew the ins and outs of how each community worked—who had influence and who made trouble. He also knew the Quakers. Leland Slade would not be armed. And given the fact that Leland hardly ever opened his mouth, there didn't appear much of a chance that he'd talk his way out of a bad situation. The Sheriff knew the odds in a hostage situation—fifty-fifty that someone would get killed. The question remained: Who else was in there?

"Anybody notify air traffic control?" Sherriff Howard asked.

"I called the State Bureau of Investigation," Andy said. "And so you know, a call just came in from the dispatcher. There's been a report of a possible fire down One-Mile Road."

"The only house back there is Teensy Anderson's. Check it out," Howard said. His stomach burned.

⸻

A burgundy Land Rover wheeled to a stop in front of the police barricade. Billie McFarland jumped out, dressed for an early morning jog in her pink sweats. Webster barked briefly, then stood alert in anticipation of being lifted from the front seat. Other cars pulled in after Billie's. News traveled like the sound of rain in a drought.

"What's happening?" Billie poked her head into Andy's cruiser. "Is Hank Devine in there?"

"Go on home, Mrs. McFarland. Get off the street," Andy said. This was the biggest problem in small towns, he thought. Each resident felt as if he or she had a right to be personally updated on breaking events.

"It's Hank Devine, isn't it?"

"Don't know yet."

Billie had grown quite fond of Katy. She was her protégée, someone she felt she'd taught how to stand up to adversity. "Has he got Katy and the kids?" Billie asked.

Andy ignored her.

"Everyone knows that Leland's not the one to negotiate, don't they?" Billie wasn't about to let up until she knew the details. Others depended on her to have the most recent information.

"Mrs. McFarland, I can't talk to you now. Please go home."

"You know the Quakers are gathering up at the meeting house," she persisted. "Whatever they're cooking up, you can bet it won't be practical."

⟨≋⟩

Nothing had been said inside the meeting house for more than thirty minutes. Ben found himself almost shaking inside. He didn't know if it was from fear or worry. He just knew he had never felt like this before and that his friends' lives could be in danger. He finally rose to his feet and blurted out, "Aren't we going to do anything? My friends are down there, Savannah and Dusty, maybe Adam and Leland. We can't just sit here."

No one responded. Instead, heads remained bowed. His mother slipped her hand into Ben's, and he sat back down. His eyes searched for some response, any response, from the others.

Five minutes passed before Duncan rose. "Ben's right. This situation could explode into violence with people getting killed. I believe we have a moral obligation to try to intervene."

No one else spoke for several minutes until Chester Messer rose. A man who believed in the biblical basis for his understanding of God, he occasionally found himself at odds with more liberal Quakers. The two beliefs were not exclusive of one another, but they did sometimes delay the decision-making process as consensus became obstructed.

"Is it not our role to trust in the Lord and pray for guidance? We are not the law of the land. We do not govern. We seek spiritual grace and understanding," he said.

Anna Reed stood. "And if people die?" She was deeply conflicted. Just a couple of years before, the Quakers had to confront the fact that had they responded immediately to the atrocity of a lynching many years earlier, they might have changed the course of history within their community. She didn't want them to make the same mistake again. "Will we one day regret that we didn't make an effort to stand for peace at a time fraught with fear and violence?"

Nanette Harper, feeling the need to support her son, rose. "'Where there is discord, may we bring harmony.' I feel that we must turn our beliefs into action."

The quiet but orderly exchange continued for nearly an hour. A plan emerged with only one dissenter, Chester. He conceded. "It is clear to me that I am standing in the way. While I have shared what I think are valid concerns about the actions the meeting is about to take, I will step aside." Having said so, he turned and left the room.

After another period of silence, Anna Reed spoke. "If we now have consensus, I suggest we proceed without further delay."

⤬

Inside Leland Slade's house, Katy and Savannah, Leland and Adam sat on hard-backed benches in the small sitting room off the kitchen. They watched in silence as Hank paced around the room.

"You got a TV someplace?" Hank asked Leland. "I need to know what's going on out there."

Leland shook his head, his eyes following Hank.

"You got whiskey? Beer?"

Leland shook his head again.

Hank looked disgusted. "Coffee at least?" He hadn't had any sleep for over twenty-four hours. He craved caffeine to clear his head.

Leland nodded.

"Get me some."

Leland rose.

"Stay where I can see you. Remember, I've got a gun on these three here."

"You . . ." He pointed his gun at Adam. "Go stand by the window and tell me what you see."

Adam walked to the window facing east and stood directly in the rising sun in hopes that everyone could clearly see him. "There are two patrol cars," he said. "Andy Meacham and his deputy. A number of local people have gathered—ten, twenty. The police are roping off a yellow police barrier in front of the house."

"You see the plane?" Hank asked.

"I'd have to look out the other side of the house," Adam said.

"Go on. I'm watching you. I can see that bedroom window from here."

Adam walked in the room only long enough to confirm what he already knew. "No plane," he said.

Hank thought that he'd heard the engine, but a lot had happened all at once. Savannah and Katy had broken away. A pig ran in front of Savannah and tripped her. Katy had stopped to help Savannah, and together they ran into this sparsely furnished house with Hank only feet behind them. The old man had been standing there. He hadn't spoken. Beside him a much-younger man had moved forward to place himself between Hank and the two women.

Hank had expected a gun to be aimed at him, but no—nothing.

Leland walked back into the sitting room with a mug of hot coffee.

"Put it down. Right there," Hank said, motioning to a three-legged round stool ten feet away. "Don't try to throw anything hot at me."

Adam spoke. "No one here will harm you. We are here to help."

CHAPTER TWENTY-SIX

Sam looked at the fuel gauge and then glanced over his shoulder at the Beretta pointed at Dusty. "We're over Rocky Mount. I've got to look at a map." He tapped on the fuel gauge. "See this, hotshot? I've got forty-five gallons of fuel. We might make it to the gulf. After that, I hope you can swim."

The turmoil and rage had evaporated, and Ray had only threats and a gun. After all his planning, he now straddled the cramped backseat of a single-engine Cessna. He frowned. "Hank said you knew the skies like the back of your hand."

"Sure. Whose cornfield you wanna buzz? I can do that."

"Don't give me that crap. You go to Bogotá every month."

"True, I do . . . on Delta."

Ray floundered for a moment. He knew nothing about the ins and outs of flying a plane and realized that his only leverage was Dusty. If anything happened to Dusty, then it would become a free-for-all between him and Sam. The worst-case scenario was that they'd all three go down. The best-case scenario was that they'd fly into a Latin American country; he could shoot Sam and hold Dusty until Katy appeared with the money.

"I wanna see the map." He talked like he knew what he was looking at. "Show me everything you're doing, and you'd better be straight. No games or the kid gets it."

Sam nodded for Dusty to hand Ray the map. "Show him where Smithfield is," he said, appreciating the few lessons he'd given Dusty on flying. Their time in the air was paying off sooner than he'd anticipated.

Dusty pulled out the aeronautical map, studied it for a minute, and pointed his finger at Smithfield, which was prominent on the flight map. In reality they were skirting the edges of a no-fly zone around Seymour Johnson Air Force Base. Sam bet on the fact that Ray didn't know anything about flight maps, codes, and signals, but he needed to be sure.

※

Police Chief Andy Meacham had never been in the middle of an incident as newsworthy as this standoff with the Devine brothers. After the dramatic courtroom escape in Edenton six weeks earlier, police around the state had set up surveillance teams in numerous places, including Sam O'Brien's house, but recently they had widened their search. Now that both brothers had surfaced in Cedar Branch, Andy felt that he needed to prove himself.

He and Sheriff Howard were discussing their options when they saw the Quakers come across the front yard of Nathan and Euphrasia Hoole. Andy knew they'd want information. Their grandson, Adam, was apparently inside. And Leland was their neighbor. The group approached and then, taking everyone by surprise, walked around the police barrier straight toward Leland's house.

Andy ran to get in front of them. "This is a restricted area. You can't approach this house. It's dangerous," he called out, waving frantically. The Sheriff's officers who had at first been curious now stood at alert waiting for instructions. Sheriff Howard held them off.

The Quakers continued to move closer to the house. "Back away from the house," Sheriff Howard boomed over a bullhorn. "You are in a restricted area."

Andy sputtered and looked around for help. A gunshot rang out from the house. Men came to attention with rifles drawn. The Quakers kept moving forward.

The reporter from the county newspaper arrived, and the sound of a camera clicking was audible. The Sheriff knew it wouldn't be long before Olivia Cox and other state reporters began arriving in droves. Already he thought he heard a helicopter in the distance. He envisioned a horrific image of dead Quakers lying on the front lawn of Leland Slade's home with headlines announcing the slaughter on the front page of papers around the country.

"Stand down!" Howard yelled.

From inside the house, Hank shouted, "Back off!" With his finger on the trigger, he steadied his gun.

Adam scrambled to get in front of Hank's gun. "They're unarmed. Not one of them has a gun. They're Quakers, all Quakers. Look." Adam tried desperately to defuse the situation by talking as fast as he could. "That's Phil Harper standing in front with his son, Ben, and his wife, Nanette. Would a man bring his wife and son with him if he expected a gunfight?"

Frightened and confused, Hank pushed Adam to the door and motioned with his gun. Everything was happening at once. He needed time to think. "Get out there. Tell them to back off or I'll kill someone."

Adam stepped into the frame of the front door and opened it slowly. "Phil, you and the others need to move away from the house. Hank is threatening to kill someone."

Police Chief Meacham tried to gain control. "Tell Hank to come on out, and nobody gets hurt."

Hank bristled. "You said no guns. There's a lawman right there." He cocked his pistol.

"Andy!" Adam shouted. "Andy, please move back. You're carrying a gun, and I told him no one in the group had guns."

Without moving, Phil spoke up. "We've come to offer sanctuary at the meeting house."

"Sanctuary?" Adam repeated.

"We'll walk with him," Phil said. "He can walk in the middle of us. We'll not harm him."

Adam turned and looked over the end of a gun barrel. "They're here to offer you sanctuary at the Quaker meeting house."

"Tell that lawman to get back behind the line or I shoot someone!" Hank screamed.

"Andy," Adam called, "he'll shoot now if you don't move away. Get back."

Andy Meacham found himself in the tenuous position of having to withdraw in front of his colleagues and leaving hostages at risk. He wavered. "One!" Hank yelled out. "Two!" he screamed. Andy withdrew. The Quakers remained in place.

"We're offering sanctuary," Phil repeated. "A safe haven. A place to rest. Time to think."

"What in the hell is a meeting house?" Hank asked.

"A place of worship," Adam said.

"A church?"

"The police consider it a church. The police aren't going to shoot through the windows of a Quaker meeting house."

"And . . . ?" Hank tried to figure out why this would be better than where he was.

"And it would slow things down," Adam said. "Give you more time to consider your options while you wait to hear from your brother. Besides," he added, "there are only two doors, one front door and one back door, and no windows. Here the police have got a lot of ways to come at you."

Hank stared at Adam. He and Ray had planned to be in and out of Sam's house within an hour. By all rights he should be on the plane with his kids headed to the gulf. Everything was going wrong. He and Ray hadn't worked through this possibility, but giving the cops a clear target didn't make any sense either.

"They'll shoot me in my tracks as soon as I walk out of here. No dice," he said.

Adam called back to Phil, "He thinks the police will shoot him if he walks out."

Phil called, "We've got a plan."

Adam turned to Hank. "You better make up your mind. The police aren't going to let that group stay there much longer."

***

"Where are we now?" Ray asked, peering out the window.

"East of Fayetteville," Sam said. "Show him, Dusty. Point it out for him."

Dusty picked up the map and put a finger on a spot east of Fayetteville and knew for a fact that wasn't where they were. Ray looked out the window and seemed satisfied.

***

Greta Isham held the rank of a technical sergeant at Pope Air Force Base. She had just completed her first month with the Ground-Control Intercept and did her best to hide her anxiety. She had bragging rights on being the youngest as well as the only female in the group. When the aircraft showed up on her screen, she attempted to radio for identification. The plane didn't respond. She tried for several minutes and then leaned over to Zeke Walker, who was sitting to her right.

"I've got an unidentified aircraft in restricted airspace," she said. "They're not responding. Do I notify NORAD?" She knew that all unidentified aircraft were supposed to be reported to the North American Aerospace Defense Command, but these incidents were not frequent. She hesitated.

Zeke sniffed and looked at her with an I-can't-believe-you-said-that glare. She was a rookie, he knew. There was a checklist to go through before contacting NORAD. "Have you checked National Guard frequencies?"

"I've done that and others. Their radio must be off."

"Notify the tower. See if he's close enough for them to take a look. Probably some bogey who's flying visual and can't read a map."

Sheriff Howard hated this. He'd have some explaining to do. They had a hostage situation that started with maybe six people inside. Now he had eighteen Quaker men and women standing between the police and the house. One slip and he could have a disaster on his hands.

A white flag appeared at the front door. The Sheriff used the bullhorn and shouted, "Put down your gun and come out. We have the place surrounded." The deputies stood alert behind their cars, guns raised. The persistent gawkers strained to press forward from behind the increasing number of patrol cars.

Who emerged from the house was not one man but a cluster of people cloaked under the semblance of a tent to cover them. Sheets and blankets were draped over bodies with only legs and feet visible. Somewhere in the middle of them was Hank Devine. Phil, Nanette, and Ben Harper remained uncloaked to lead the group down Main Street. With their tented fugitive, they began the half-mile walk to the meeting house.

"Please move back and put down your guns. Only one individual among us is armed. He is very nervous," Phil repeated several times. "We're offering the gunman sanctuary."

"What the f—?" The Sheriff raised his eyebrows and then yelled across the yard to his men, "Stand down."

Andy rushed to Howard's side. "*The* gunman, sir. There's only *one* gunman."

"I heard him," Howard said caustically. "How did this happen? They can't offer him sanctuary."

"I believe they just did."

"Tell the men to give them room. No heroics here. The man is trigger-happy and scared. He might go off on us."

"Yes, sir," Andy said and radioed for three of the patrol cars to clear the road in front of the group and keep people back. Three other cars followed behind. "See if you can get someone into that meeting house ahead of them," the Sheriff said. "Someone who could maybe wrestle the guy down."

Andy raced the short distance down a back street. He saw Anna Reed, leaning on her walking cane, and Nathan Hoole, his shoulders rounded with age. Anna and Nathan watched him as he got out of his patrol car and approached them.

Andy had grown up in Cedar Branch and knew enough about the Quaker tradition to address them by their first names. He spoke with genuine respect for their stature in the community.

"Nathan and Anna, the man you've invited to your meeting house is a criminal. I recognize your good intentions, but the state of North Carolina does not recognize sanctuary. We need you and your members to let us handle the situation."

"How would thee plan to do that?" Nathan asked, using the traditional plain *thee* and *thy* that a few of the older members continued to speak.

Andy hadn't given his actions much thought. He visualized possibilities as he spoke. "I'd like you to allow me into the meeting house in advance of his arrival."

"With thy gun?" Anna glanced down at the weapon on his hip.

"Well—" Andy stumbled over his words. He knew they'd never allow such an option. "I would leave my gun outside."

"And then what?" Nathan asked. "He'll see the uniform immediately."

"I'll talk him down," Andy said.

"We have offered the man a place to think—a place to rest—a place to seek clearness. A policeman in the room planning to *take him down* doesn't sound truthful to me. To you?"

"This man is a murderer," Andy pleaded, knowing that his time to persuade them was limited.

"There is that of God in every man," Anna said.

"He's desperate. This could escalate beyond your worst expectations," Andy said.

"We have faith that we can help find a peaceful resolution," Anna said.

Andy fidgeted, shifting his weight from one foot to the other. In the distance he could see the lights of the police vehicles inching toward them. "I have to try to stop you," he said.

"I don't believe thee can." Anna nodded at a television truck swerving to the side of the road and coming to an abrupt halt in front of them. Olivia Cox emerged with a cameraman scrambling behind her.

Andy turned and barked at them, "Back off! This entire block is restricted."

"Can you tell us what's happening?" Olivia called across the yard.

"Back off, and that's an order!" Andy shouted again.

Olivia and her team obeyed as another police car waved them away.

"I could arrest you for obstructing justice." Andy turned back to Anna and Nathan. He knew he wouldn't.

"Thee could." Anna nodded. "And what then? A shoot-out here in front of our meeting house?" Anna stepped forward and touched his sleeve lightly. "Thee wears a gun. A gun is not the answer. Thee should leave before the group arrives."

Feeling a bit like a child who had just been gently chided by his teacher, Andy withdrew and radioed the two lead patrol cars. "Advance and clear the area around the meeting house."

❧

Sam flew over the east edge of Pope Air Force Base without incident. No Flying Tigers raced into the sky to try to force him down. Ray looked at the map but asked few questions. Sam made a flight adjustment. When the plane veered slightly to the west, Ray looked down at the ground as the plane angled. Sam ran his hand along the side of his seat and switched his squawk code to 7500. Silently, the hijack alert went out.

❧

Hank's finger tightened over the trigger, and he hooked his elbow around Katy's neck to pull her closer. She gasped, and Adam tried to calm him.

"We're where we told you we'd be. No one's out there with guns."

Hank felt the cement steps under his feet and then the wooden porch and finally the carpeted floor inside. "Are we in?" he asked.

"We're in," Phil said.

"I swear if we're not in a church, I'm going to—"

"You're in a place of worship," Phil said. "Stay calm. We'll take the blankets off."

"No funny stuff," Hank warned.

People ducked out from under their tentlike cone. Once free, Hank immediately backed into a corner and pulled Katy with him. He surveyed the room of plain wooden benches facing center. "Jesus," he said. "Now what?"

"Thee are in a safe place," Nathan Hoole said. In his eighties, Nathan stood next to his wife of fifty-three years. "We'll seek clearness together until a way opens."

Nervously Hank looked around. In front of him were now twenty-six people to control instead of just four, but it was just one room. No windows, except for the line of smaller ones under the eaves. Morning was breaking through a skylight overhead. No back rooms or doors to worry about. He was in a church of some kind, but not like one he'd ever seen before. The police would be less likely to shoot at him in here.

He motioned to the left side of the meeting room with his gun, pulling Katy by the arm. "Everyone, sit together over there where I can see you. Savannah, come over here next to me." Savannah hesitated, but followed as Hank pulled her mother with him.

"I'm sorry, baby," he whispered to Savannah." She was stiff, nonresponsive. "Uncle Ray will get us out of here. We just need to wait while he gets it figured out."

"Where's Dusty?" Ben asked as he crossed the room to where he'd been instructed to sit.

Hank looked at the fifteen-year-old, acknowledging him for the first time. "Why are you here, kid?"

"I'm Dusty's friend."

Hank sniffed. "He's okay." Dismissing Ben, he started to count the number of men. If they came at him all at once, they could be a formidable force. "I want the women all on this side of the room sitting on the bench in front of me," he said. "The men across the aisle on that side, just in case anyone has any ideas about rushing me. Katy and Savannah stay here next to me."

Without a murmur of discontent, people moved to accommodate him. Then, one by one, they bowed their heads. Hank sat utterly confused. Light climbed the white walls and illuminated the only decorative ornament in the room—a wooden plaque with the words of John G. Whittier carved thereon:

The Meeting
And so I find it well to come
For deeper rest to this still room.
For here the habit of the soul
Feels less the outer world's control.
The strength of mutual purpose pleads

More earnestly our common needs.
And from the silence multiplied
By these still forms on either side,
The world that time and sense have known
Falls off and leaves us God alone.

Every Quaker in the room knew the words by heart. It would be hours before Hank read them.

CHAPTER TWENTY-SEVEN

By the time Sam breached the restricted airspace of Shaw Air Force Base in Sumter, South Carolina, it was 10:00 a.m. He was crossing his fingers that he wouldn't get blitzed by a Warthog before he saw it coming. By now there should be an emergency signal going out to every air traffic control tower in the Southeast, along with NORAD. He didn't know how they'd respond, but if they hadn't identified him and started tracking by now, the US Air Force was far less adept than he believed them to be.

❧

The caffeine was racing though Hank, and he could sit no longer without relieving his bladder. He calculated where the bathroom might be—behind the door to the right of him. He stood up, grabbed Katy's hair, and pulled. Katy gasped.

"I gotta pee," Hank said. "She's coming with me."

Savannah jerked upright, ready to go after her mother, but a loud tapping on the side of a bench stopped them.

Anna repositioned her cane in front and rose with some effort. "Perhaps thee would let me show the way?"

Who was this woman? Probably twice his weight and twice his age, she was most assuredly someone's grandmother—certainly no one Hank wanted to go with him to the bathroom. He let go of Katy's hair.

"Just point us in the right direction," he said.

"Through the door, to the right," Anna said, tilting her head down to look over her spectacles. "There are extra towels and soap stored under the sink if thee should need them."

Hank looked at Anna, confused by her language, and pulled Katy in front of him. "Nobody move until we get back," he said.

"We won't," Anna said, but remained standing.

Hank pushed Katy in front of him into the bathroom with the one toilet and sink. "Turn around. Face the wall." He unzipped his pants and relieved himself.

She waited until he'd washed his hands and then splashed water on his face. He pulled out several paper towels and scrubbed the back of his neck before she turned. "Are you going to kill me?" she asked him.

"Hell." He looked at her behind him in the mirror. "You made me look like a fool in front of my kids and the whole damn town."

"What I did was wrong," she said, "but it wasn't worth murder. You killed a man."

He faced her. "I loved you once," he said, and there was pain in his voice.

Her voice softened. "And I loved you. We messed up big time, didn't we?"

He looked tired. Whatever liquor had been in him the night before had worn off. If he'd been at home, she knew he would sleep now—sleep until noon.

"Do you think Ray's coming back to get you?" she asked.

"I just got to hold out," he said. "Ray's working on something. Maybe a hostage swap. I got to give him time to get where he's going."

"You always think Ray's got the answer."

"He's the only person who's been there for me from the beginning."

"I'm sorry you never thought me and the kids were there for you, too."

Hank said nothing.

Katy hesitated. "I need to use the toilet, too. Will you turn your back for me?"

Hank turned and faced the wall, the kindest thing he'd done for her in a long time.

When they opened the door to the bathroom, Anna Reed stood quietly leaning on her cane. Startled, Hank pulled his gun and then relaxed. "I told you to stay put."

"I thought since thee were already here, I'd come back. Age has a way of putting more demands on the bladder. Would thee wish to accompany me to the toilet also?"

"No." Hank shook his head. "Just go and come back."

The corner of Katy's mouth curled.

～⚬～

Teensy Anderson hit the turn onto Main Street with her foot to the floor of her 1980 Ford LTD station wagon. If the two police cars hadn't been blocking the middle of the road with their lights rolling, she'd have run the barrier and careened straight into the meeting house.

"Where is he?" She was shaking her fist, eyes spittin' out fire like a sparkler. "I'll take care of him."

Police Chief Meacham came running. "Teensy, Teensy . . . move back. We've got a volatile situation here."

"You bet you got a volatile situation," Teensy said as two deputies jumped to attention to assist, "and you're about to see it explode."

Andy nodded at the deputies to let him handle Teensy. He looked at the smoke smudges across her face and could see the singes on her nightgown underneath the coat. "How are the kids?"

"Scared shitless. How you think?"

"Where are they?"

"At my sister's . . . shaking all over."

"Lyle okay?"

232

"Hell no. Lyle ain't been okay for years. But he's worse now. He's at the hospital in Murphy. I'm going there as soon as I take care of that SOB." She nodded in the direction of the meeting house. "He in there?"

Andy put his hands on Teensy's shoulders and turned her back toward her car. "This isn't a problem you can solve," he said as he slowly prodded her away from the building.

"Them Quakers in there with him? He got Katy?" She wasn't to be turned around easily.

"Go on to Murphy with Lyle. He needs you. We'll handle things here," Andy said.

"Don't look to me like you handling nothin'. You all out here yammering on like nanny goats. That arsonist's sittin' on a bench in the land of nod."

"Teensy . . ." Andy could usually count on his persuasive abilities, but even he was having a difficult time wrapping his brain around the current challenge. "Go on now. Things could get messy."

"You got a madman shacked up with a bunch of crazy Quakers, and you thinkin' things could get messy." Teensy glowered. "If that ain't messy, then I ain't black."

⟡

Hank scanned the room for someone to send out. It was approaching noon, and he hadn't had anything to eat since the night before. Anna Reed and Nathan Hoole appeared old—not probable flight risks but high maintenance. The boy's mother, however—as long as her son was still with him, she would want to protect his safety. He'd learned that much from Katy.

He walked around to the front of the women and pointed his gun at Nanette. "You this boy's mama?" Nanette raised her head and for the first time registered slight alarm. That was a good sign, he thought.

"We need some food. I want food that's prewrapped from a vendor. Bottles of water, cans of soda. Nothings that's been tampered with. You go and bring that back, and your boy will be fine."

Nanette looked across the center aisle at Phil. He hesitated a moment. She would be able to explain to Sheriff Howard what they were doing and perhaps calm everyone outside. Phil squeezed his son's hand and then gave her a nod so slight that only she saw it. Nanette got up. She cautiously opened the front door to the meeting house. The early life of a spring day did little to ease the tension in everyone's eyes. She saw rifles raised and heard cameras click. As she approached the barricade, Sheriff Howard grabbed her and pulled her into his car.

"We need food and water," Nanette said.

"You have no idea how much you've complicated the situation." Sheriff Howard was fuming, with no attempt to hide his anger. "You're providing refuge to a murderer."

"We've offered a man sanctuary."

"How in God's name can you justify that?"

"Because we believe if he is in a safe place with respect for his humanity, he'll give himself up and no one will be hurt."

"Nanette," Sheriff Howard sighed. "You don't know what kind of man you're dealing with. He beats his wife and kids. He killed another man in cold blood."

"We are holding him in the light."

"Jesus." The Sheriff was stymied. He rubbed his forehead. She was living in a fairy tale. "Look," he said. "He's cornered. When people get cornered, they're not rational. You don't know what might set him off. He could start firing on all of you in a split second. Several people could get shot before we get through the door."

"We need food and water," Nanette repeated. She tried not to think about his version of the outcome.

Sheriff Howard tried to control his temper. He didn't know how to explain the cruelty he'd seen inflicted on others, the risk the Quakers inside were taking. He picked up his radio receiver and ordered the food and water. He turned back to Nanette shaking his head. "You are aiding and abetting a criminal. I could have you all thrown in jail."

"You could," Nanette said.

The Sheriff sighed. He saw Andy walking over to his cruiser. It would be one o'clock before they got the food back. The day was slipping away from him. He'd hoped they would end this before noon. With each passing hour the risks got higher.

"Will you tell me exactly who's in there? How many? Where they're sitting?"

"I will," Nanette said.

"Are Sam and Dusty with you?" Howard asked.

"No."

"Ray Devine?"

"All in the plane, we think."

As Nanette spoke, the Sheriff considered who might be the best negotiators among them. Duncan was the most pragmatic of the group. He'd been a college professor for years at Guilford and only recently returned to the area. Adam Hoole, the assistant principal, would be another reasonable man, and his father, Chase Hoole, the pharmacist. If he could get any of them outside, maybe they would see reason and work with him.

"When you return, ask Hank to release the women as a show of good faith," Sheriff Howard said. "Maybe send Duncan or Chase out here to talk with us."

Nanette was slightly offended, although she wasn't sure why. "We're not hostages," she said. "We are there by choice, and unless Hank says differently, you'll be talking to me."

The Sheriff overlooked her last statement. "You may not consider yourself a hostage, but Katy O'Brien and her daughter certainly do. This is the last place on earth the two of them want to be, I promise you."

❦

At noon all eyes in the tower at Robins Air Force Base scanned their screens. In addition to the normal air traffic controllers, the wing commander stood next to a radio transmitter. He was on the phone with NORAD. "Suspect reported in restricted airspace over Robins. No radio contact. Squawking 7500."

"He's got to go down for fuel before long according to our calculations," came the reply. "Hawkinsville or Sylvester, Georgia, maybe. All cars out of sight. Sharpshooters in position."

❦

Ray scanned the landing strip, eyeing the one steel airplane hangar with suspicion. The fuel gauge shuddered over empty. "It better be out of the way," he snapped. "I don't want to see one damn police car or—"

"This is about as out of the way as it gets," Sam said. "No radio contact. Who the hell you think knows we're here?"

"You landed here before?" Ray asked.

"Yeah," Sam lied. "There's usually one person around who keeps the coffee on."

"I need a bathroom," Dusty said. Ray ignored him.

The wheels touched ground, and the plane bumped twice before Sam applied the brakes and made a rolling turn to taxi to the fuel pump at the right of the brick structure. No bigger than a single-story house, this one resembled many of the buildings at the small county airports used by crop dusters and private planes.

With no other planes in sight, Sam tried to figure out how to play this—how to send up a red flag if no help was on the ground.

"Lucky for you," Sam said. "Looks like we're the only customer."

Ray looked right and left and then leveled the gun at Dusty. "Once this baby stops, you get out real slow," he said to Sam. His voice was tense. "I want to see both hands at all times. Dusty, you follow Sam. Don't think for a moment I won't shoot. Any funny stuff and that fellow on call won't be home for supper tonight. Got it?"

"Got it," Sam said as he scanned for anything out of the ordinary. Which direction would they come from? The hangar or the brick building? Inside or outside?

He climbed down from the plane and waited. Dusty followed—his eyes on Sam for any clue as to what to do next. "Steady," Sam said.

"Ready," Dusty mouthed back.

Ray crawled out slowly with the Beretta in his hand, then slipped it into the pocket of his fatigue jacket as his feet hit the ground. He grabbed Dusty's arm and shifted him to his other side, placing himself between the two.

The airport door swung open, and a young man in his midtwenties with shaggy brown bangs and wearing jeans and a sweatshirt jogged out with a wave. "Need gas?" he hollered.

"Fill-up," Sam called back.

"Coffee's fresh. Go on in, and I'll take care of your plane." He slowed to a walk as he got closer, and a big grin crossed his face. "Hey, aren't you Sam O'Brien?"

Their eyes connected. Sam knew at once. "Yeah, Charlie, isn't it? The same guy as the last time I stopped?"

"Right, Charlie Blanchard. You headed down to South America again?"

"I am. You and the girlfriend finally set a date?" Sam noticed Ray shift uneasily. He wouldn't be able to stall with small talk for long.

"I'm going to run on into the bathroom," Dusty said and started to bolt, but Ray reached out and grabbed his arm.

"I'll come along and get some coffee," Ray said.

"Wait," Sam said. "Charlie, meet my boy here. This is Dusty."

Charlie stepped in front of Ray and extended his left arm in Dusty's direction. "Nice to meet you, kid," he said.

Dusty had raised his right arm and then shifted awkwardly. Ray noticed, hesitated, and slipped his hand into his pocket around the Beretta.

Charlie's strong grip had alerted Dusty that this was more than a handshake. In an effort to take Ray by surprise, Charlie suddenly jerked Dusty to the left, out of the way of potential gunfire. Dusty stumbled at first, but righted himself at the same instant he saw Ray pull the Beretta from his jacket pocket. "No!" he screamed, seeing the gun leveled at Sam, and Ray turned. Dusty lunged at Ray. The Beretta fired once. The sharpshooter fired twice. The doors to the hangar swung open, and vehicles burst onto the tarmac. Two bodies lay on the ground.

CHAPTER TWENTY-EIGHT

"So, tell us about the fire," Frank said. "You able to save anything out there?"

Mike Warren sat next to Timmy Bates on the delicate antique chairs at the round parlor table where afternoon sodas and floats had once been part of the pharmacy fare. He drummed his fingers on the tabletop and thought about the breakfast he should be having at The Quaker Café. Being called out at six in the morning to fight a fire was a hard way to start the day.

"Nope," Mike said. "The house is a total loss."

"Everybody got out. Right?"

"Pretty amazing." Mike shook his head and wiped his cheek, leaving soot marks from his hand. "Teensy's adrenaline must have been pumpin' like a locomotive. She dragged Lyle on that monster bed through the door and down the ramp in seconds."

"Wow," Frank said.

Mike kept rethinking every choice they'd made and wondering if they could have done something different. Normally the rest of the volunteer fire crew would all be at the café about now, but with no café . . . well, most went on home. Mike was wired and needed to talk.

"I sure would like a hot breakfast," Mike said.

"Guess we can thank Helen Truitt for that," Frank said. He propped a foot up on one of the chairs.

"Two more weeks," Timmy said. He was crossing off the days on his calendar. "It opens in two more weeks." Timothy hadn't been able to reorient himself since The Quaker Café had closed for repairs. He thrived on routine. Nothing was routine anymore. Nowhere to sell his peanuts. Nowhere to eat.

"I imagine Helen's down at the meeting house by now," Frank said. "If there's a reporter in a two-mile radius, Helen will be there."

"You know," Mike said, "there's only two women I've never wanted to have sex with."

"Oh yeah? Helen and who else?" Frank asked with a smile.

Mike paused. "Actually, haven't met the other one yet."

Frank chuckled. "Billie McFarland would probably fix you breakfast."

"Already thought of that. She's down at the meeting house adding to Andy's worries. As if he doesn't already have his hands full. People are nuts. Don't they know that lunatic may start shootin' the place up any minute?" Mike rose to go.

"You gonna leave me alone?" Frank asked.

"I gotta eat," Mike said. "If you want that café back open on schedule, you better let me get my crew working." He looked through the picture window and saw a small group of people approaching. "Looks like you got more company coming anyway."

Olivia Cox motioned a cameraman and soundman ahead of her. The Reverends Broadnax and Shannon followed. Mike waited and opened the door for them. She was better looking in person than on TV, a bit thinner, perhaps, but still well proportioned and with an ass to die for. She played down the sex thing, though. She was the first African American woman to anchor the evening news on the most widely viewed station in the state, and she had proven herself to be a professional heavyweight.

"Olivia Cox," she said, as if they didn't already know. "WTVD News out of Raleigh. Could we use your store for a live interview for the noon news?"

Frank jumped to attention. "Of course," he said. "You got any updates on what's happening down there?"

She ignored the question. "Just let us rearrange a little furniture," she said, already pulling two small tables together and adding two chairs. "Maybe some water for everyone?" She looked at the soda fountain and assumed it was operational. That was a common mistake. The fountain had been closed for three decades. Frank went to the back of the store and returned with three glasses of water from the tap.

Reverend Broadnax and Reverend Shannon sat down as instructed while the cameraman checked for lighting and the soundman attached a mic to each man's lapel.

The camera whirred on, and Olivia pulled the large WTVD mic to her mouth. "We're here at Hoole's Pharmacy in Cedar Branch following the events of the hostages being held in the Cedar Branch Quaker Meeting House. I have with me Reverend Melvin Broadnax, pastor at the Jerusalem Baptist Church, and Reverend Richard Shannon of the First Methodist Church." She turned to face them. "You both have worked with the Quakers in this community. What can you tell us about them?"

Reverend Broadnax spoke in a deep, commanding voice. "They are good people; persistent and patient. They're willing to take whatever time is necessary to help find common ground."

"So you think they'll be able to resolve the situation peaceably?"

"Nonviolence is a major component of their faith. They practice what they call a peace testimony—a belief in the ability to resolve conflict without violence," said Reverend Shannon.

Olivia raised an eyebrow. "Are you suggesting they expect the gunman to walk out of there with his hands up?"

"I don't know what they expect," Reverend Broadnax said. "*Expect* isn't really the right word. They will wait in silent prayer until a way opens."

Olivia looked confused. "Way opens? What does that mean?"

"It means, given time, prayer, and thoughtful introspection, the gathering of individuals will reach consensus on a path to follow."

"So they might decide the best option is to take the man down?"

"Hardly." Reverend Shannon smiled. "I don't think you'll find any true Quaker *taking anyone down*."

"Here's the problem," Olivia said, now with less amusement. "In reality, they've upped the ante. They've placed more people in harm's way, haven't they? They've made the task for the police force much more difficult."

"The Quakers would probably rephrase that statement. You see, they're showing the gunman that the resolution for conflict is never with guns. The alternative that awaits him on the other side of the door is only guns."

"You realize there's a fifty percent chance that someone will be killed in a hostage situation," Olivia pressed.

"Then there's a fifty percent chance that no one will be killed," Reverend Shannon said.

Olivia arched her eyebrows. "But, Reverend Shannon, they're protecting a man who beat his wife and is now accused of murder. How can they justify such a thing?" This was a debate she knew would play well on the news.

"Most faiths believe that every individual can find forgiveness. Every person can be reborn. Surely Hank Devine deserves the same opportunity," Reverend Broadnax said.

"Are you saying the law should forgive Hank Devine for his crime?"

"Certainly not." Reverend Broadnax paused and took a sip of water. "The man is alleged to have taken another man's life. If he is guilty, he has a debt he must pay to the victim's family and society. That does not exclude him from receiving the grace of God."

"Should that debt to society include the death sentence?" Olivia asked.

Both ministers frowned. They knew the question would draw criticism no matter what they said. "I can tell you that the Quakers would say no," Reverend Shannon said. "They strongly oppose the death penalty."

"Reverend." Olivia Cox became more direct. "It appears that Mr. Devine didn't find it within himself to give Dr. Attwuld a second chance. It doesn't appear that he's offering his wife a second chance. Personally, I find this Quaker approach a bit disturbing. Would your church members respond in the same manner?"

Reverend Shannon didn't answer. He knew in his heart they would not, and he wasn't sure that he'd ever encourage such action. This was not a good precedence to be setting . . . for churches to take the law into their own hands.

Reverend Broadnax interrupted. "I don't know that any of us knows what we will do until we're confronted with a challenge. I like to believe in moments of crisis that the best in each of us will surface. There are times I've been disappointed, but it doesn't discourage me from hoping and believing in the power of the Lord."

Reverend Shannon added, "If the police will give the Quakers time, I think they can end this peacefully."

Olivia Cox looked at Reverend Shannon in disbelief. "Do you really believe that? This could be a disaster, and we'll all be talking about what the police did wrong this time tomorrow. How much longer do you think the police should wait?"

Reverend Broadnax smiled. "I think the Quakers hope they will wait until they find resolution."

"You think the Quakers can last that long?"

"Oh, I know the Quakers can. The question is, will the police?"

◈

By two o'clock, the media had inundated the little town of Cedar Branch like locusts. TV personalities attracted a crowd of publicity seekers, many vying for an interview that might appear on the evening news.

"I'm a county commissioner, and I know quite a bit about Katy O'Brien," Helen Truitt volunteered in a voice calculated to attract further interest. She was dressed in her Sunday suit and low-heel pumps, with her left arm still in a cast—a reminder that she was the reason The Quaker Café was closed. Still, she elaborated with the omnipotence of a politician. "I have a responsibility to my cónstituency to warn them of potential problems. I knew Katy O'Brien was trouble from the day she arrived."

Helen began to recount Katy O'Brien Devine's history as reporters scribbled frantically. "Now look at what's happened." She waved her arm at the meeting house and added peppered sighs. "This is what you can expect from certain elements." She raised her eyebrows. "Our community is reeling—simply reeling—from the effects."

Billie McFarland had seized the initiative to bring a large thermos of coffee from home and ingratiated herself to reporters who welcomed the refills with genuine appreciation. She had changed into burgundy slacks and a pink cashmere turtleneck sweater and moved among the journalists, responding with concern at any camera pointed in her direction. More affable than Helen, she wooed reporters with her hospitality.

"Entire families are in there now," Billie explained. "The Harpers and their son. The elders, Nathan and Euphrasia, their son, Chase, our town pharmacist, and one of Chase's sons, Adam. He works at the high school. Better people you could not meet."

"Do you know Katy O'Brien?" Olivia Cox asked, sticking a microphone closer as Billie spoke.

"Know her well," Billie said. "She's a hard worker, an asset to the community. Born and raised here. Moved back home to get out of an abusive relationship. Her husband is the man holding everyone hostage. Well, of course you know that. Her brother-in-law has stalked her since she left Bixby. A most undesirable character."

Billie twitched her hips and turned slightly for the cameraman closing in behind her. "You've heard about the fire, haven't you? The house belonged to the cook at The Quaker Café. She and Katy's brother-in-law had a what-to outside the café several weeks ago."

❧

The 7-Eleven and Quik Stop had been emptied of vending machine sandwiches, and the Cedar Branch Grocery called their suppliers begging for more deliveries of bags of chips and bottled water. Nanette did exactly as she'd been told and carried the boxes inside the meeting house one by one. She'd worked on a farm her entire life and had the muscles to prove it.

"You all eat first." Hank indicated to Nanette that he wanted her to distribute the food. He'd eat last just in case they'd put a sedative in it. He popped open a soda and pulled two bennies out of his pocket. He was in the habit of taking uppers on long hauls to stay awake, but these were his last two.

Nanette picked up a sandwich and handed one to her husband and son. She approached Hank. "They're asking you to release some of the hostages as a show of good faith."

"Go on, give everyone food," Hank said. Nanette nodded and began to distribute what was there. Hank watched her out of the corner of his eye. She was direct, without being condescending or demanding. He might be able to trust her.

Both Savannah and Katy took sandwiches and began to eat.

Pam Sibley rose to her feet. A woman in her early sixties, she wore a headband to hold back her tangled shoulder-length curls. She pulled a hand-knitted shawl around her loose-fitting gray dress. She bowed her head.

Hank hesitated, confused.

"We are grateful for the food we're about to receive. We are grateful for those who have prepared it and for those who have delivered it to us. For many this would be a Thanksgiving feast, and we remind ourselves to keep the needs of others foremost in our hearts. Bless this food to the nourishment of our bodies as it strengthens us for service to all." She paused and then added, "And keep us safe, each and every one. Amen."

A slight rustling of plastic wrappers could be heard, but only a few ate.

Hank looked around the room, wondering who was going to do what next. He had too many people to keep an eye on. This wasn't good.

Hank motioned to the elders: Nathan and Euphrasia Hoole, Leland Slade, and Anna Reed. "You four, you can leave."

No one moved.

"I said *go* . . . leave."

Still no one moved.

"I'm letting you go."

Nathan Hoole laid his unwrapped sandwich on the bench next to him. "I choose to stay," he said.

Hank scrunched his eyes. "Don't you understand? I'm giving you your freedom."

Nathan paused in thoughtful reflection. "I've always had my freedom. I walked in here voluntarily to be by thy side, and I choose to stay by thy side."

"For Christ's sake," Hank said.

Hank looked over at Anna. "You go on. You and those other old women."

Anna raised both eyebrows at the reference to her age. A slight chuckle slipped from Euphrasia's lips because she knew, as did all of the Quakers, that the weightiest Quaker in the room was Anna Reed, and any implication that she was either old or weak was misguided. Anna would be challenged to hold her tongue.

After due consideration, Anna spoke. "I thank thee for the kind consideration of the limitations of my age, but I also choose to stay."

"What the—?" Hank stopped short and dropped the expletive. For the first time he felt an unfamiliar need to couch his foul language. What was this *thee* and *thy* stuff? Who were these people?

"Why?" he asked.

"Thee may need some help in a few hours," Anna answered matter-of-factly.

"And you think you can help me?" Hank scoffed.

"Yes," Anna said.

~≋~

Sheriff Howard eyed the sycamore that grew at the side of the meeting house for the second time. The trunk looked to be about six feet in diameter and split into twin shafts approximately eight feet off the ground. He predicted the wide, five-point maplelike leaves had bloomed enough to create cover for anyone who might climb it.

"Andy," he called to the Police Chief. "I want to get a camera in that tree so we can see inside those rectangular windows below the eaves."

"That could be tricky to do without him seeing us." Andy hesitated. "But there's a skylight on the roof, too, you know."

The Sheriff raised his eyebrows. "Really?"

"That would be even harder—although if it's dark, maybe we could pull it off."

"We'll need equipment," Sheriff Howard said. "Call the State Bureau of Investigation. I want to light up this place if they're still in there come nightfall. I want floodlights and cameras. Anyone in town been on that roof?"

"Mike Warren installed the skylight, as I recall."

"The Dickel and Dew man?"

Chief Meacham smiled at Mike's reputation. "Yep. Took the Quakers fifteen years to reach consensus and Mike fifteen hours to get it installed."

"I wish it had taken them the same amount of time to decide to invite that son of a bitch into their meeting house." The Sheriff shook his head in disgust. "I want to talk to Mike. Get him here."

༄

As late afternoon approached, tall, dark clouds could be seen building across the sky. Rolling thunder echoed from thirty miles west near I-95. With the thunder, most of the townsfolk headed home. The reporters retreated to prepare for the six o'clock news. The radio call came at the same time the first hard drops began to land with singular thuds on Sheriff Howard's windshield.

"Agent Marty Martin here. FBI. We're calling to give you a heads-up that the Cessna is down in Sylvester, Georgia. Ray Devine is dead."

"God." Howard ran his fingers through the thin strands that remained on top of his head. Given the way things were going, the rest of his hair would fall out before this ordeal ended. "Anyone else hurt?" he asked.

"Unfortunately the boy's in surgery—Phoebe Putney Memorial Hospital. Caught some cross fire from Devine's gun. His uncle's with him."

"Is it bad?"

"It's serious. One collapsed lung."

"Has the media gotten hold of it yet?"

"We're keeping them at bay. Trying not to jeopardize your operation up there."

"Thanks. Keep me posted, will you?"

"You got it. Need more help? We can send some men."

"Thanks. I'll let you know," Howard said and put down the receiver. His stomach churned. The hot dog from the 7-Eleven he'd wolfed down an hour ago was playing havoc with his ulcer. He knew better.

He turned to the deputy who sat next to him. "Got an antacid? Pepto or something?"

The deputy started to rummage through the glove compartment.

The rain pelted harder against his window, almost sounding like hail instead of water drops. The remaining crowd dispersed, and the other officers climbed into lookout positions from inside their patrol cars and hunkered down. They were in for a long night.

Leland Slade had always found a great deal of peace in the sound of the rain. The water nourished crops, filled the wells, calmed the livestock, cooled the air. Void of lightning and thunder, the sound rocked him to sleep and relaxed his aching muscles. In biblical terms, it quenched one's thirst, washed away sin, and provided a rebirth, a baptism, a renewal. In Quaker terms, this sacrament was not administered symbolically by the church, but he felt it within.

Gradually his heart began to quicken. Leland remained seated. He almost never rose to speak in Quaker meetings, and he above all knew the importance of the silence over the spoken word. Now there was thudding in his heart, overpowering the sound of the rain. He tried to make it go away, but it pounded even more persistently. He shifted his posture—pulled his shoulders back, arched his chin to the ceiling, eyes still closed. Was he being called upon to speak? He resisted.

Then, without making a conscious effort to stand, he stood.

"I had an older brother, Griffin," Leland said in a voice so rarely heard that even the Quakers raised their bowed heads.

Hank snapped back to attention. He tightened his grip on his gun. What was this?

Leland continued, eyes still closed. "Griffin was fascinated by tractors and loved the farm even more than I." The brightness from a flash of lightning cut through the skylight and momentarily reflected off the top of his head. He stopped, waited, and then spoke again.

"I followed him around from chore to chore, and he taught me how to gather eggs without letting the hens peck at my hands and how to lure the pigs back home when they slipped under their pens. He became the center of my world. He brought laughter to a house where work and prayer were the sole components of each day."

A long period of silence followed. Hank wondered if that was it. Was that what Quakers did—just stood and said something meaningless from time to time? The big man needed to sit. Hank felt somewhat threatened, although he wasn't sure why.

Leland continued, "The year I was eight, my brother nine, our father bought a new tractor. He was so proud of that machine, and I was just itching to climb aboard and ride with him, but he'd have none of it.

"One day our father left the tractor in the shade of a tree at the top of the hill behind our house. Griffin and I toyed with the idea that we might climb aboard without him seeing us. We did just that. What we didn't know was that the brakes weren't on, and when Griffin pretended to shift gears, the tractor went into neutral and started to roll."

Leland's face twisted in grief, and his voice dropped to a whisper. "I jumped off the back and cleared the tire. Griffin jumped off the side and went under." His voice cracked. He stopped. He steadied his hands on the back of the bench in front of him. "No one could bear the pain to talk about what we had lost, so no one spoke at all."

Leland stopped—stood still.

Hank heard the rustle of pockets as several women searched for handkerchiefs. Anna Reed blew her nose. Savannah, who had been lying with her head in her mother's lap, slowly sat up. Young Ben Harper stared at Leland as if he was looking at this man for the first time.

"I have been led to rise to my feet to tell you how much joy the O'Brien family brought to me with the sound of their laughter. As families will do, the boys and Katy grew up and left home, and the house next door again became silent. Then last year, I heard Dusty, Ben, Savannah, and her friends." He paused and bent his head.

"Dear Lord, I now pray that Dusty will return to us safely so that I can again know the pleasure that he and Savannah have brought to a solitary old man. A selfish prayer, I know, but an honest one."

Chapter Twenty-Nine

Hours passed. By five o'clock, the thunder and lightning had subsided, but a ground-soaking rain continued to fall as Nanette Harper reappeared on the porch steps of the meeting house and walked toward the barricade. Police Chief Meacham and Sheriff Howard climbed out of their car and hurried toward her. Andy wrapped a black slicker around her shoulders that matched his own. Holding an umbrella over her head, he escorted her to the car. Nanette knew they wanted to hear about progress inside.

In the passenger seat sat a rather unassuming older man in rimmed glasses and salt-and-pepper hair. The inside of the car felt humid and sticky. The smell of hot dogs and crumpled bags of Lay's potato chips left no doubt as to what had been their last meal.

Sheriff Howard climbed into the driver's seat as Nanette and Andy got in the back. "Nanette, this is Morgan Sidwell." Howard's tone was instructive and businesslike. "Sidwell has the authority to negotiate with Hank. We need Hank to let him inside. We need to end this thing."

Nanette glanced at the slightly built man next to the Sheriff and nodded. He appeared nonthreatening, rather pedagogical—sort of like one's college history professor. "I don't think he's ready to negotiate yet," she said. "I just came out to see if we can get some more water and a little food for dinner."

"Hank didn't respond to our request to release hostages. Ask him again before we bring more food," the Sheriff said.

"He did tell the elders they could leave," Nanette said. "They chose not to."

"Dear God." Sheriff Howard exhaled and grimaced. "Help us out here, won't you? You're making my job harder. If he's willing to let people leave—then leave!"

"He wants to know if his brother is out of the country," Nanette said.

Howard locked eyes with Chief Meacham, and his face gave everything up.

Nanette picked up on their exchange immediately. "What's happened?"

"The plane's down."

"Where?"

"In Georgia."

"And?"

"And it's over," Andy broke in. He knew the Harpers on a personal level, and if it had been his call, he wasn't sure he would have told Nanette as much as she now knew. She'd feel compelled to tell Hank the truth, and at this point in time honesty might not provoke the best response.

"Look," Sheriff Howard said. "We'll get the food ready. Tell Hank we have news about his brother and want to send someone in to talk to him. And Nanette, if he'll let some of you go, come out this time. Get as many people out as possible. He's not going to like the news."

Nanette pulled on the car door handle with a feeling of foreboding. She climbed out into the rain and left the slicker on a bench on the front porch before going back inside.

"What do you think she'll tell him?" Howard asked.

"She'll tell him exactly what you told her," Andy said.

"And then what does he do?" The Sheriff turned to Sidwell.

"He'll want a phone to speak to his brother," Sidwell said.

"Damn, you're right." Howard groaned. He rubbed his chin and looked out through the raindrops slamming into the windshield. "I want Mike Warren on the roof with those cameras as soon as it gets dark enough."

"It's pouring," Andy said.

Sheriff Howard looked at him in disgust. "I know it's pouring. I don't give a rat's ass. I want cameras on that roof tonight, and I want a sharpshooter in the tree before this nut finds out his brother is dead."

❧

Inside, Nanette approached Hank. Fatigue had created lines on his face. It had been thirty-six hours since he'd had any sleep, and he watched without seeming to care as individuals occasionally rose to use the bathroom.

"The plane is down in Georgia," Nanette said softly. Katy, who had been watching her intently for any news, stiffened. As Katy shifted upright, Savannah readjusted her head in her mother's lap.

"What did they say?" Hank asked, suddenly more focused.

"The plane is down. They want you to let everyone go," Nanette said.

"What about my brother?"

"You need sleep." Nanette avoided the question.

"My brother? Is he okay?" He raised his voice.

"I don't know. They didn't say. They want to send someone in to talk with you . . . a negotiator. He's authorized to make a deal." She added, "He's a small man."

"NO!" Hank shouted. He was on his feet. Savannah sat up straight, looking at her mother and trying to decipher what had just happened. "No one else comes in here. Tell me everything they told you."

Nanette searched for the right words. She lowered her head, seeking guidance, but nothing more profound than the truth came to mind. "The plane is down. It's over. That's all they said," she said softly.

Katy gasped and blurted out, "Dusty and Sam? What's happened to Dusty and Sam?"

"I don't know. They didn't say," Nanette said truthfully, but she knew that Katy, like her, was assuming the worst.

"It's over. What the . . ." Again Hank couched his words. "What does that mean? Did the plane crash? Are they dead?"

With the gun in his right hand, Hank flailed widely and began storming around the room. "You get back out there right now and tell those sons of bitches to get my brother on one of their fancy cell phones and get it in here to me. I want to talk to him in the next thirty minutes or else!"

Or else, he thought to himself. *Or else what?*

What would he do? He could go out in a blaze of glory or just put the gun in his mouth and end it all. He was so tired. If he had some time to sleep, maybe he could think more clearly.

It's over. What the hell does that mean? Ray's dead, been captured? Then his mind slowed and clicked. They were bluffing. This was a tactic to get him to give up.

There was movement now within the meeting house. No one spoke, but several people shifted simultaneously. Under any other situation, the individual adjustments in posture would have been muted. At this particular time, with the pelting rain on the skylight and Hank's outburst, the sound seemed deafening. Hank covered his ears in an attempt to block out the confusion in his head.

Ben Harper had trouble keeping still. He couldn't help but watch Savannah as she shifted her eyes from one person to another in a frantic effort to get information. In a way, Ben resented the Quakers' pacifism. He felt like someone should be trying to talk to Hank, trying to get him to give up. Why wasn't anyone saying anything?

Phil Harper squeezed his son's hand. At this moment Phil was questioning his own decision to allow his wife and Ben to come with him to the meeting house. What had he been thinking? He must have been mad to allow them to put themselves in harm's way. Ben had been so insistent, and it was clear that if he and Ben came, Nanette would be beside them. He began to calculate how best to protect them if Hank actually pulled his gun and started shooting.

A painting came to mind, the one by J. Doyle Penrose that hung in the children's first day school. In the painting, Indians armed with bows and arrows had walked in on a meeting of Quakers in the midst of their silent worship. As the story goes, the Quakers did not break their silence but remained in worship, and the Indians, sensing no threat, chose not to harm anyone and left peacefully. Phil focused on the image, trying to remain calm.

Phil watched Nanette as she walked back to the door. He was so proud of her. She appeared focused and unafraid. *This man is scared. If we treat him with humanity, he will treat us likewise,* Phil told himself. *Surely his life is as important in the eyes of the Lord as any other within this room.* Phil closed his eyes and visualized the painting again.

The fact that Nanette reappeared so soon told Police Chief Meacham what he already feared. "He wants to talk to his brother," she said as she approached.

Sheriff Howard looked at his watch and the sky. In another forty-five minutes dark would begin to descend. Mercifully, the rain would mask the sounds of an effort to install a camera, but the rain was a problem in other ways. It would be harder to install electrical equipment and guarantee that it would work properly, and he still needed another hour before he tried to put anyone on the roof.

"Will he let Sidwell in?" he asked hopefully.

"No. He says he doesn't trust anyone the police send in."

"Go tell him we'll see what we can do," Sheriff Howard said.

He turned back to Sidwell. When Nanette was out of hearing, he said, "Stall for time. I don't want him going berserk on us and opening fire on everyone. We need to get our man in place. We need to be able to see what he's doing."

With a bullhorn in hand, Sidwell waited ten minutes before he called out, "Mr. Devine, we're trying to get in touch with your brother. The weather is interfering with reception. We have to install a phone line. That will take some time." There was a pause to let that sink in. "Let me come in, Mr. Devine. I have the authority to negotiate with you."

Hank frowned. The creases around his eyes had deepened, and splotches of pink seeped into the whites of his eyes. "Tell them I won't talk to anybody except my brother," he ordered Nanette. By default it appeared that Nanette had become the negotiator.

"Ask them about Dusty. I have to know if Dusty is okay," Katy blurted out.

"Shut up!" Hank snapped at her. "Everybody just shut up," he repeated as if anyone other than him and Katy were talking. He needed Ray to help him figure out what to do next. If he could just talk to Ray. Surely Ray was working on a deal.

"Dusty," Savannah called out to Nanette. She was finding her voice. The past few hours had left her confused, hurt, and speechless. She had believed, honestly believed, what Uncle Ray had told her. She had believed her father when he said he loved her and wanted his family back more than anything. But now she no longer recognized the man she called "Daddy." The only one he seemed to care about was Uncle Ray. What about Dusty and her?

"Find out about my brother, please . . . and Uncle Sam," Savannah called after Nanette.

"I said shut up," Hank said with more animosity than he had intended. He was tired. So very tired. He'd never meant for anything bad to happen to Dusty. His thoughts turned to Dusty. He was a good kid. Deserved a better father than the one he got.

Nanette nodded and looked from one to the other. She felt her burden become heavier. She had thought this would all work out. It had seemed so logical when they discussed it among the Friends in the early hours of the day. They'd believed that with adequate time and respect for one another, Hank could still find the love in his heart that he once felt for his family. Surely he still loved Savannah and Dusty. She was beginning to fear that fatigue and despair might trump clear thinking.

She walked outside. There were more trucks now . . . linemen, equipment, ladders, and massive searchlights being hauled off the back of a flatbed. An alarm went off inside her. "What's going on?" she asked.

"We can't let it get dark without lighting up the building," Andy Meacham tried to reassure her. "We have to take precautions, Nanette."

"He only wants to talk to his brother."

"We're probably going to have to put in a line," Sheriff Howard said. "We're not getting through on the cell phone. Storms over the Southeast. It'll take more than thirty minutes. Tell him that."

"Katy wants to know about Dusty and Sam. Don't you know anything?" Nanette asked.

"The plane's down. That's all we know for sure." The Sheriff turned to Andy with a look that told him not to say anything more on the subject. He knew she trusted Andy.

"Nanette," Andy said. "Take the food and water inside. He's got to give us more time. We've got to get a lineman on the building to install a direct line. Convince him that if he wants to talk to his brother, that's the only way we can do it before the sky clears."

Nanette returned inside. She explained the situation as she'd been told. Katy dropped her face into her hands. Savannah bowed her head and began to whisper a prayer. Hank fidgeted, squirmed, got up—sat down—looked over at his daughter and moved closer to her. He reached out to put his arm around her. "He'll be okay. Dusty's tough."

She jerked away.

He was surprised—hurt. He recoiled, then instinctively started to slap her, but stopped himself. What was he doing? Completely alienating everyone who had been good to him? Momentarily confused, he mumbled, "I'm sorry. I never intended to hurt you . . . honest."

Savannah didn't respond but dropped her head into her hands. He thought he heard a sob. When she looked at him again, her cheeks were wet, but her eyes had hardened. Hank rose and found an empty corner of the meeting room away from her. He'd respect her wishes to be left alone. He sank onto the bench. The room felt heavy and damp, as if a miasma hung over them. The rules had changed. Hank had set a deadline. He had to decide what to do. He had to maintain control.

Without permission, Ben stood and moved to sit next to Savannah. "I really think Dusty is all right. He's really smart. Your Uncle Sam, too," he whispered. He watched Hank as he spoke, but Hank didn't seem to care.

A voice over a bullhorn caused everyone to jump. "Hank, we can't get through to Ray. We're going to install a landline into the meeting house. You're going to hear some noise. It's only the linemen. You're going to see a lineman go past the window on the top left of the building."

Hank riveted his attention to the top windows. It was getting hard to focus. With his gun, Hank motioned to Katy and Savannah. "You two—back over here by me."

Katy didn't move. She didn't yell. She didn't beg. She only questioned. "What are you going to do? Shoot us, Hank? Shoot me and your daughter? Shoot everyone in the room because it's raining and they can't get your brother on the phone?"

Anna Reed rose. She nodded gently to Katy, then balanced herself by putting a hand on the end of each pew as she made her way toward Hank.

He looked at Anna with apprehension. This barrel of a woman left him completely at a loss as to what to say or do. She was like a mama bear plodding toward him with her cane in hand.

"I will sit by thee," Anna said.

Nathan and Euphrasia Hoole rose, as did Leland Slade. They joined Anna. "We'll be thy shield," Nathan said. "No one will harm thee while we are by thy side."

Hank's body ached. He wanted to sleep. He needed alcohol—anything to help numb his pain.

Leland, Nathan, and Euphrasia settled into the seats in front of Hank. A brief period of silence followed. Pam Sibley rose and said softly,

"One of my favorite poems comes to mind. It was written by John Whittier:

> *"Drop thy still dews of quietness*
> *Till all our strivings cease:*
> *Take from our souls the strain and stress,*
> *And let our ordered lives confess*
> *The beauty of thy peace.*
> *Breathe through the hearts of our desire*
> *Thy coolness and thy balm,*
> *Let sense be dumb, let flesh retire;*
> *Speak through the earthquake,*
> *Wind, and fire,*
> *O still, small voice of calm."*

Hank was asleep.

❧

"Go," Pam whispered to Katy, and all eyes were upon her. "Take Savannah and slip out."

Katy nervously looked at Hank and back at Pam and shook her head. What would he do to the others when he awoke and she was gone?

"Go," Pam mouthed again, encouraging her with a slight flick of her hand to leave.

Quietly Katy took Savannah's hand, and they stood.

The thud of a ladder hitting the side of the building caused Hank to jerk upright.

Katy and Savannah quickly sat back down.

CHAPTER THIRTY

Dr. Booth walked into the waiting room and spotted Sam immediately. A police officer and FBI agent had been speaking with him, but all three rose quickly when they saw the surgeon.

The smile helped relieve some of the anxiety as the doctor extended his hand. "I'm sorry it took so long," he said. "We had to stop the bleeding and do a little repair work. The bullet punctured the lung, but no other organs were damaged. The fact that an ambulance was at the scene helped a lot. He's a lucky boy."

"The heart?" Sam asked.

"The heart's just fine. Not a scratch. Any word from his mother?"

Sam grimaced. "Not yet. I'm still trying."

The doctor nodded. "It always helps to have mama here when they wake up. Makes things less frightening."

"I understand," Sam said.

⬱

The rain was not helping Mike with his installation attempt. While he strained to get a wire to hold next to the skylight, Sheriff Howard sat inside his car talking into the microphone that fed his voice to the ear of the sharpshooter. It would be dark enough within the next ten minutes for him to get into position in the tree and see if he could get a sight on Hank.

Morgan Sidwell spoke into the bullhorn again. "We're working on it, Hank. Just about got a line for you. Give us another fifteen minutes."

Hank was awake.

Mike's first test showed only static in the first camera, but the second one seemed to rotate fine and provide a clear picture. Still, without the first camera, there was a corner of the room just below that he couldn't get. He needed more time.

"I've got a call coming through from Sam O'Brien in the car," Chief Meacham said. "He wants Katy on the phone. It's about Dusty."

"Shit," Sheriff Howard said for the third time that day. He looked at the top of the roof.

"He's says it's an emergency," Andy said.

Howard waved Sidwell over toward him. "Got Katy's brother on the phone. He wants to talk to her. Says it's about Dusty."

Sheriff Howard picked up the phone. "Sam, how's Dusty?"

"He's just come out of surgery. Pretty serious. We need to get Katy down here."

"That's a problem," the Sheriff said.

"Dusty is Hank's son, too. He's got to care about that." Sam's voice was tense.

"He doesn't know Ray's dead yet."

There was a groan on the other end of the line.

Mike descended from the roof. "I'm not making great progress," he said to Sheriff Howard, talking into the other ear. The rain had slowed him down, and the fact that he was on the tail end of a rather long and challenging day had put a cramp in his pride. "I've got a hookup on one, but there's a jacket tear in the other line. I'll need to get a replacement."

The Sheriff raised his hand to get him to wait. "Hold on, Sam," he said. He was listening to his earpiece.

The sharpshooter in the tree was in position on the other side of the building and had a scope on Hank. "It's not a clear shot," he said over his wire. "There are two older men and a woman sitting in front of him. Their heads are in the way. A second woman is next to him in the back."

"His wife?" Howard asked.

"No sir, a big woman . . . old."

Sheriff Howard rubbed under his eye with the tips of his fingers. He furrowed his brow and turned to Sidwell. "Whatcha think?"

"Let Sam tell him about his son. That way he'll know Dusty's alive."

"He doesn't like Sam very much," Howard said.

"I don't guess he likes anyone much at the moment," Sidwell said.

Howard looked up in the tree at the shooter. Without turning his head he said to Sidwell, "Is that man a good shot?"

"The best."

Sidwell studied the video feed from the working camera and felt reassured that they had a good-enough picture of the inside. He stood in front of the meeting house and picked up the bullhorn. "Hank. I'm at the front steps. I have a phone for you to talk. Would you let me in?"

Hank straightened. The sharpshooter raised his rifle. "I have a clean shot," he said into his mic.

Sheriff Howard grimaced. The thought of shooting into the Quakers' meeting made him queasy. Whichever decision he made could require his resignation in the morning.

"Is it my brother?" Hank rose to his feet and moved out in front of everyone, providing the gunman with an even better shot.

"Wide open," the gunman said.

The Sheriff hesitated—too long. Hank moved out of range behind Nanette.

"Get the phone," Hank ordered.

Nanette turned to look at him but saw instead the Quakers still seated in silence behind him. In contrast, Savannah's eyes were bulging and Katy had risen to her feet. Amid the tension, Phil stood and walked quietly over to Ben and Savannah and sat back down. Nanette knew why. He was preparing for the worst. The elders appeared to be in prayer. But Duncan Howell and Adam Hoole were following Hank with their eyes. What might they do if things suddenly went terribly wrong?

Nanette opened the door and stepped out. Camera crews were emerging from their vehicles, alert to the fact that some sort of shift was taking place. "Is it Ray?" she whispered.

"Sam," Sidwell said. "He wants to talk to Katy."

She retrieved the phone and looked around. The friction in the air snapped like an electric shock. Spotlights on the top of news vans blinded her, and on either side of the meeting house commercial flood-lights were manned, awaiting orders to be switched on.

"What are you doing?" she whispered. Fear, an emotion she rarely put any trust in, had started to challenge her better senses.

"We're ready to go in, Nanette," Sidwell said. "Stay down. Warn people to stay down."

"No," she objected. "We need more time."

"It doesn't look to us like he's calming down, Nanette. We don't like what we see."

"He's coming around." She tried to sound positive.

"We don't think so."

She glanced to her right and left. They didn't have a clue what was happening inside. How could they know? She took the phone and stead-ied herself and went back in.

Hank was waiting for her behind the door. She handed him the phone. "Why don't you sit down?" she said. He ignored her. Nanette looked over at her husband. He searched for any clue as to what was happening. Her eyes darted to the skylight first and then to the narrow windows below the roofline. If they could see inside, it would have to come from one of those angles. She stayed close to Hank. If they had a gun aimed at him, they wouldn't take a shot if she was in the way.

He blurted into the receiver. "Ray? Ray? Is that you?"

"Hank, this is Sam. I need to talk to Katy."

Hank stiffened. His mind went into overdrive. Suddenly the outside noises escalated; the rain pounded on the skylight, and he heard the sounds of motors and engines and saw the light . . . a flash of light.

Hank's voice echoed as he screamed into the phone, "I want to talk to Ray, not you!"

"Maybe you should be more concerned about your son," Sam said.

"Something happened to Dusty? Where's Dusty?"

"The plane went down in Georgia," Sam said. "The police were waiting for us. Ray pulled a gun. His bullet caught Dusty."

"Ray shot Dusty? What the hell are you saying?" As the words escaped his lips, Katy jumped to her feet. Savannah let out a wail.

"He was a hero, Hank. He saved my life. Your son took a bullet meant for me."

Hank said nothing.

"He's coming out of surgery. The doctors want Katy here as soon as possible," Sam said. "The doctors say he needs to see her when he wakes up. It'll help."

Hank's hand began to tremble. Nanette watched the barrel of the gun shake. She thought she might try to take it from him but didn't want to risk him pulling the trigger—intentionally or unintentionally. There were too many people he might hit.

"Where's Ray?" Hank asked.

Sam tried to keep his voice calm. He remembered when he received the news of his brother's motorcycle accident . . . at first the disbelief, and then the anger, and then the grief. "He got hit. He didn't make it."

An agonizing cry escaped as Hank crumpled onto the bench and hurled the phone across the room. Nanette immediately sat down beside him in order to provide cover if there was a gunman somewhere outside the overhead skylight. Her eyes scanned the windows above.

The sharpshooter cocked his gun. Too many heads in front of him again.

Katy was on her feet instantly. She ignored Hank and fled to where the phone had landed and picked it up. "Sam, is that you?"

"Katy, are you all right?"

"What's happened to Dusty?" she blurted.

"He's just come out of surgery."

"Oh my God. How bad is it?"

"He took a bullet in his left lung. The lung collapsed. The good news is that the paramedics were there on the spot to help with his breathing and get him on an IV on the way to the hospital. He'll be on a ventilator for a while, but the doctor thinks he'll pull through without problems."

Katy turned pale. Savannah was standing next to her, tears running down her cheeks as she watched her mother's reaction.

Sam could hear her sobs. "He's a tough kid, Savannah," Sam called out over the phone to reassure them both. "He'll be all right, Katy, but he needs you here."

"I'm coming," she said. "I'm coming." Katy looked across the room at Hank. With his face buried in his hands, he looked broken. She suddenly felt sorry for him. She had loved him once. Why had she not been stronger and stood up to him when things began to go terribly wrong? There was a time he might have chosen her and his kids over Ray.

"Hank, listen to me," she said, putting down the phone. She wiped her cheeks and took a deep breath to steady herself. "Dusty is hurt. *Your son* is hurt. He needs us. Savannah and I are going to walk out of here and go to him." She paused. "You now have the chance to do more for Dusty than your father ever did for you. I'm begging you to make the right decision." Katy took Savannah's hand and placed her daughter squarely in front of her. "We're leaving to go to Dusty . . . right now," she said softly in Savannah's ear.

Savannah looked at her father. "Daddy . . ." she said, but Katy stopped her, turned her toward the door, and pushed her gently forward.

Together they walked from the front of the meeting house past the pews to the entrance door. Katy braced herself, expecting at any moment an explosion to the back of her head or a blow between the shoulder blades. Nothing.

Ben started to rise and follow Savannah, but his father squeezed his hand in a motion that told Ben to stay.

Duncan Howell considered rising also and walking out behind Katy to protect her back. He wasn't the only person in the meeting house who had the same thought. It was as if there was a collective mind within the group that weighed the importance of allowing Katy to stand by herself. This was their test. They had to believe enough in Hank's humanity and goodness to trust that he would make the right decision.

The sharpshooter looked down his scope and adjusted the rifle. Lights snapped on around the outside, sending a flash of artificial daylight through the windows at the top. Nanette looked up and saw the silver shaft of a rifle protruding through the cover of the leaves. She stood . . . angled herself in front of Hank and whispered, "Let her go, Hank. For your son's sake, let her go."

CHAPTER THIRTY-ONE

Once outside on the porch and down the steps, Katy buckled to her knees like a doe spent after a long chase. Chills ran through Savannah. She started to shake uncontrollably.

Andy Meacham and several medics rushed to their sides with umbrellas, blankets, and raincoats. Reporters pushed past the police barriers in attempts to get closer and were ordered back. Cameras recorded every moment.

"I've got to get to Dusty," Katy pleaded.

"Take the King Air the FBI sent me in," Sidwell said. "I'll radio them now."

As the police bundled Katy and Savannah into the car and it sped off for the landing strip, Sheriff Howard and Sidwell crouched around the wire, trying to figure what might happen next. "They're out of my sights," the sharpshooter spoke into his mic. "The entire group is shifting to the opposite side of the room. I can't see them from this angle."

From Sidwell's experience, the threat had either decreased dramatically with Katy's release or things would suddenly spin out of control. His biggest concerns were that Hank might decide to end his own life and take others with him, or rush from the meeting house, gun drawn, in a kamikaze suicide.

"Get those people back," Sheriff Howard yelled into his walkie-talkie. "Back—back—back." Lord, he was tired. He knew his men were exhausted, which made everything that much more unpredictable. Already eight o'clock and his men had been on duty since six that morning. He needed a second shift of men, as if small towns provided such a luxury.

"How much longer do you think Hank can hold out?" he asked Sidwell.

"His emotions are probably all over the place by now," Sidwell said. "Hard to tell, depending on when he last slept and if he's taking uppers. But if it's longer than thirty-six hours, I'm guessing he'll either start to become despondent or irrational. Either way could be a problem."

The Sheriff spoke into his mic. "Have we got any visuals off the camera?"

"No, sir," reported the shooter. "Not on him. He appears to be back in the corner out of range. We can see a few people, but not all."

"Do they appear threatened?" the Sheriff asked.

"Doesn't look like it."

"How can you tell?"

"They're starting to reseat themselves in that one corner of the room. They don't appear afraid. We can't see the fugitive. Some of them have their eyes closed. Praying, maybe?"

"We better all start praying," Sheriff Howard said, "and hope God stays up late tonight."

～≈～

Nanette remained next to Hank. She hadn't pointed out the sharpshooter to Hank, but she had quietly told him that she thought a camera had been installed and that he'd be safer out of its viewing range. He was more compliant than she'd expected. He seemed weary, demoralized.

Despite the gun in Hank's hand, several of the men in the room together could have taken him down at that moment. They didn't. They believed whatever decision Hank made had to be his own, not theirs.

But redemption and God did not play into Hank's thoughts. A heavy sense of despair and darkness weighed on him as if the top of a casket was being closed. He had been left alone—deserted by his parents, his wife, his brother, his daughter, and his son. They'd all abandoned him. What was the point?

He was vaguely aware of someone's hand on his shoulder . . . a gentle hand. Yet he felt empty. The best he could hope for would be to sleep and never wake up. He was so very tired.

When he didn't flinch, Nanette ran her hand down his arm and wove her fingers through his. He sensed the warmth. Her thumb rested on his wrist. He felt the rhythm of a pulse—his or hers? He wasn't sure. Unconsciously, he started to count the beats.

Nathan Hoole bent forward in an effort to rise. A bone in his knee cracked, causing him to lower himself back into his seat. But he spoke regardless. "I believe," he said in the voice of someone who had also shared a troubled past, a voice that had known pain and regret, "I believe that God is present even in the midst of turmoil and grief. I believe that there are no hopeless situations, only men and women who become hopeless. I believe there is a light within each of us that will show us the way."

Shoulders relaxed. Breathing slowed and seemed to find a unified rhythm among the members. What Quakers call *a gathered meeting* intensified. A sense grew among them, not spoken but felt by everyone there, that the threat had passed. They needed only to wait on the light.

A small woman, Dana Everett, broke the silence. "As many of you know, my husband, Martin, and I abandoned our oldest son at a time in his life when he needed us the most. He struggled with drugs. My husband saw his addiction as a sign of weakness that shamed the family. He banished our son from our home, and I was not able to find the strength to defy his judgment. Many a night I have wept over what I failed to do for my son. It took years before I sought to heal the wounds we inflicted on a child we deeply loved. Unfortunately, Martin died before he and our son ever reconciled." She stopped, lowered her head. "By the grace of God, I have been given the additional years and the will to rebuild the relationship we once destroyed. I'm grateful God gave me a second chance. I have learned that God is always willing to give us another opportunity to put our life in order."

A ringing broke the meditation. Phil Harper was the closest to the phone. Hank sat unresponsive. Phil picked it up, glanced at Hank, but received no acknowledgment from him. "Hello."

"Is that you, Phil?" Andy Meacham asked. "Is everyone all right?"

"We're all right," Phil said.

"What's happening?" Andy asked.

"Let it be," Phil said.

"The Sheriff needs something more specific than that," Andy said, almost as an apology. "We can't get Hank in our camera."

Phil glanced at the skylight. "That's all I can tell him. We're fine. God's at work in here."

Andy turned to the Sheriff. "He said to leave them be, God is at work."

"Christ," Sheriff Howard said.

"No, sir, not Christ. He said God."

❧

Teensy combed the few curly knots of hair left on the sides of Lyle's head and brushed them back with her free hand. It was hard to see that her attention to his appearance made any difference, but she repeated the gesture several more times. The breathing apparatus had been disconnected. A nurse stood at the door.

"Is there anything we can get you, Mrs. Anderson?" the nurse asked.

"Can't bring no Sunday clothes. They all burnt," she said to no one in particular.

"I'm sure the funeral home will make arrangements," the nurse said.

"He was one fine man," Teensy said, still staring at his face and working the brush.

"I'm sure he was, ma'am."

"Wish you could of knowed him in his prime. He was something."

The nurse waited before backing away from the door. "I'll be at the nurses' station. You take all the time you want."

Thirty minutes later, the nurse poked her head in to check. Teensy was gone.

~❦~

At midnight, cruisers surrounded the meeting house at every angle. Floodlights destroyed the darkness so completely that not even shadows were able to hide. Two hours passed before there was any more contact. Cameras revealed only slight periods of movement or sounds from inside. Then without warning the door to the meeting house opened, and Phil Harper emerged.

"He wants Joe Wiseman. He says when Joe Wiseman gets here, he'll give up."

Sheriff Howard turned to a deputy. "Find Joe Wiseman. Get him out of bed and here as soon as possible. If they need to send a helicopter or private plane, I don't care."

Most of the media were sleeping in their vans, but a few saw Phil appear and then retreat back into the meeting house. The immediate activity that followed led them to believe that a deal was underway. Reporters began to resurface in hopes of breaking news for the early morning radio and television networks.

Sheriff Howard scanned the growing number of newshounds and avoided comment to any reporters. He knew that regardless if this went down easy or not, the whole damn world would be watching. He braced for the unexpected.

~❦~

The rain continued falling, although the thunder and lightning had stopped four hours earlier. Joe Wiseman arrived with a police escort that had cleared his way for the two-hour drive. Sensing some impending breakthrough, reporters began to rouse themselves, take swigs from their cold coffee cups, and don their rain attire.

Olivia Cox had returned to Raleigh to do the evening news. The story in Cedar Branch was breaking minute by minute, and so far she'd been the reporter with the best coverage. Now she had to make an important decision. She contacted a former boyfriend at the control tower in Raleigh to see if she could get the flight plan for the King Air that had flown out of Cedar Branch. It didn't take much sweet talk to get him to tell her the destination was Albany, Georgia.

She was torn. Should she head back to Cedar Branch or set out for Albany? Which would be the bigger story? At the moment, she believed she was the only reporter who knew where to find Sam, Dusty, Savannah, and Katy. Every other television station in four states had reporters in Cedar Branch at the moment, and her man was on the ground to get footage. To her knowledge, no one else knew what had happened to the Cessna hostages. She could tie into the footage from Cedar Branch and top it off with an even bigger story from Albany, Georgia.

⁓

Joe Wiseman got out of the patrol car, slammed his door, pulled the hood of his parka over his head, and started to push past the reporters. He brushed by Teensy Anderson, who stood next to one of the big news vans with a large umbrella at her side, the rain drenching her from head to toe. He nodded but didn't speak.

Sheriff Howard, Police Chief Meacham, and the FBI agent, Morgan Sidwell, huddled in front of the meeting house nursing their two-way radios. They shook hands with Joe and then updated him.

"Hank Devine says he's ready to come out. Wants you to be by his side when we take him in."

Joe nodded. "I'm here."

"The plan is for Hank to walk out of there in the middle of those Quakers who've been with him all night. At some point we have to make the transition from the Quakers to the police officers. If you would stand next to Hank, it might steady him," Howard said. "He's exhausted and unpredictable. Knows his brother's dead and his son injured."

"And Katy and Savannah?" Joe had been briefed by the police on the way down.

"They should be in Albany by now. Dusty is stable. Sam's with him."

"That's good," Joe said.

"Hank may panic at the last minute," Howard warned. "We're not sure what to expect."

Joe looked back at the cameras rolling and the reporters pushing at the barricade. "Any way to thin the crowd, just in case?"

"We've gotten everyone off the streets we possibly could. Can't ban the media, but they can't come any closer," Andy said.

"We're asking Hank to hand over his gun before he comes out. We think he's only got one gun, but we're not absolutely sure," Sidwell added. "Just so you know."

Joe smirked. "Oh yeah, I'm the guy who cut the deal for his wife. He might want to settle that score."

"We thought of that." He handed Joe a bulletproof vest. "Put it on, just in case."

Howard motioned Mike over. "Mike has a feed for us so we can see some of what's inside. You can take a look if you like. Things have been unusually calm. Although we can't see him clearly, no one appears frightened."

"Then let's do it," Joe said.

Sidwell picked up the phone and dialed in. Phil answered. "Joe Wiseman is here. We want Nanette to bring the gun out first. Nobody will come in, and no one else is to come out. Once we have the gun in hand, you and the Quakers can walk out however Hank feels safest. Joe will meet him."

Everyone waited. Cameras rolled. Newspaper and radio reporters talked into phones. Television reporters held microphones and spoke directly into cameras. Mike Warren watched what he could see on his video feed. He saw Nanette's figure emerge from the corner, and it appeared she had a gun in her hand. Andy Meacham stood behind Mike. "She's coming out," Mike said. Andy waved at the Sheriff and gave him a roll with his fist to indicate things were moving.

The door opened. Nanette stepped out onto the porch. The blare of the lights hit her full force, and she blinked, unable to see beyond them. She raised one arm to cover her eyes.

"No, no, Nanette," the Sheriff barked at her. "Keep your arm down. Put the gun down first. Put the gun down on the porch, Nanette, and step away from it." The Sheriff turned and frowned at the man behind the floodlights. The man angled the light slightly down. They both knew that glare could be effective in blinding a shooter, but Nanette was not their target.

The gun. The gun. Nanette felt the weight of it in her hand. *If there had never been a gun, would there have been a murder?* A buzzing sound distracted her. *The cameras. So many lights and cameras.* She refocused and held the gun in front of her like the decaying corpse of a rotting animal. Carefully she laid it down at her feet and stepped away.

A policeman wearing plastic gloves raced in, picked up the gun, and emptied the chambers. He immediately deposited the evidence in a sterile bag. Sheriff Howard approached Nanette and slipped his arm in hers as he stepped with her off the porch. "Is he ready?" he asked.

"He's ready," she said. "He wants to know about his son. Do you have an update?"

"We'll get one for him as soon as he's in cuffs. Is everyone coming out together?" he asked.

"Yes," she replied. "I told him that I'd be at the jail tomorrow to see him. Will that be possible?"

"Talk to me tomorrow." The Sheriff's attention was riveted to the door. "No other guns or weapons you know about?"

"Not to our knowledge."

The Sheriff looked over at Mike and Andy, who were watching the feed as the Quakers made a circle around Hank inside the meeting house. Andy said, "Our man is coming out in the middle. He's surrounded on all sides by civilians." Both nodded an okay to the Sheriff.

"Okay," Sidwell said into the phone. "However you want to do this. You come out peacefully, and Joe Wiseman is here waiting."

Something had been gnawing at Joe the entire time, and he couldn't quite put his finger on it. At the moment the Quaker meeting house door opened, it suddenly struck him. Why was Teensy Anderson, of all people, standing in the area of the media trucks? And why hadn't she been holding her umbrella over her head?

"Oh Jesus," he said and frantically motioned to Andy Meacham.

Andy's nerves were wearing thin. *What? What now? No mistakes. We can't make any mistakes now.*

"Teensy Anderson's by one of the media trucks. I'm betting she's got a rifle or gun with her inside her umbrella."

Andy turned, sharply surveying the crowd. He didn't see her.

Nathan and Euphrasia Hoole stepped from the meeting house first, with Anna Reed and Dana Everett on either side of them. Then Leland Slade, Phil Harper, Chase Hoole, and Adam Hoole. Hank followed with Pam Sibley and Ben Harper by his side and the rest of the Quakers behind him.

Andy jerked on Mike's arm as he rushed by him. "Look for Teensy. She's over with the press corps. She may have a gun."

The reporters had all rushed in front of Teensy to get closer for the best photo ops, leaving their vans unattended. She opened the side door of one and braced the rifle on the hinge. Too many people in the way. They blocked her view. She needed to get higher off the ground.

The man she wanted was nested in the middle of the Quakers. *What a snake belly coward.* She turned and saw the ladder attached to the side of the van. A large antennae and satellite dish sat on top. The first step up would be tough. She was heavy and not used to lifting her leg two feet off the ground. She braced the rifle on the side of the truck, and with both hands gripping the sides of the ladder, she heaved herself onto the first step. She stopped. Her knees were weak. She steadied herself. That had been the hardest part. She waited a minute for her heart to slow.

"Teensy, whatcha doing up there—climbing Jacob's ladder?" Mike Warren stood just below her with her rifle in his hand.

"Don't sass me," she said. "Give me my gun."

"Who's gonna cook me biscuits and eggs when they throw you in jail?"

"You see that man over there?" She nodded in the direction of the Quakers huddled around Hank Devine. "That man needs killin'."

"I don't know, Teensy. You that good? There's a lot of folks you could hit."

"I'm that good," she said, her lips puffed out in defiance.

Andy had spotted Mike leaning against the side of the van and did a U-turn toward him. When he saw the two of them, he stopped. "Lord, Teensy. We're out here breaking our balls all night trying to prevent a killin', and you're aimin' to blow the man's head off. You don't know how much you're gonna piss off Sheriff Howard if he finds you out here with a gun. He's gonna slap you in jail faster than you can wring a chicken's neck."

Teensy bristled. "You don't know how much those good-for-nothing Devine brothers pissed me off. They burned my house down. Lyle's dead. My baby girls will be havin' nightmares for years. My husband . . ." She stopped and turned her head to the sky, making it hard to tell whether it was the rain or tears streaming down her cheeks. "Lyle, you up there, baby?" she whispered into the sky. "I'm doing this for you."

Both Andy and Mike bowed their heads. "We're so sorry," Andy said. "We didn't know."

"Come on down here, honey," Mike said and reached up to help brace her. "Lyle wouldn't want you hurting yourself." Together Andy and Mike helped her back to the ground.

"Lyle's finally at peace," Andy said with his arm around Teensy. "Standing beside Saint Peter right now . . . looking down . . . wanting more than anything for you to be there for those pretty little girls."

"Let me take you home," Mike said as he took her arm.

"I ain't got no home," she said, wiping her nose with the side of her hand.

"Well, you got plenty of friends, and we gonna fix that for you," Mike said.

"You and who else?" she snorted.

"Don't you worry, I can twist a few arms. You'd be surprised." He gave her a squeeze and kissed her on the cheek. "You smell kind of musty. We better get you some dry clothes."

Teensy pushed him away. "Don't you go sniffin' on me. You get me to my sister's, and we'll see what's coming out of your mouth tomorrow." She turned to see Hank Devine getting into the backseat of a patrol car. "That man yonder gonna meet his maker one of these days."

CHAPTER THIRTY-TWO

Dr. Booth sat down next to Sam and gently touched his shoulder. "Mr. O'Brien." Sam awoke with a jerk out of disjointed dreams of his plane going down in a blaze of fire.

"I wanted to let you know that we're moving Dusty into the intensive care unit. We allow one family member at a time in there, if you'd like to sit with him."

Sam looked at his watch. It was after nine o'clock.

"Is Dusty's mother coming?" the doctor asked.

"She is," Sam said. "They phoned to tell me she's on the way."

"Good, that's good." How many times had he treated a gunshot wound and then been forced to tell a mother that her child had died before she even got there? At least this shooting would have a happy ending. He placed his hand on Sam's shoulder. "Let me tell you what to expect. Dusty's going to look like he got dragged behind a team of horses when you see him, but he's stable. He's on a ventilator and an IV. There are a couple of tubes in him for drainage. He's coming to, but he's groggy. His body has been through a lot in the last eight hours."

"Can I talk to him?" Sam asked.

"Certainly. He won't be able to talk to you, though, with the ventilator down his throat, but we'll try to get that out tomorrow sometime. Reassure him, whatever you say. He may be confused. Some patients don't always remember what happened at first. The anesthesia does that."

⚬

"Hey, kid." Sam sat on the side of the bed in ICU, grateful that he'd been forewarned of what to expect. Dusty opened his eyes and appeared confused. A nurse busied herself checking the IV sack, straightened the sheets, and then left.

"It's me, Uncle Sam." He watched and waited as Dusty tried to focus. "Doc says you're going to be okay. Of course you look pretty silly right now, tubes and needles sticking out, but that all plays well with the girls. They'll be crawling all over you when you get back to school."

Dusty stared blankly.

"There are easier ways to pick up girls, you know?" Sam made an effort to try to sound upbeat although the sight of Dusty ate at his guts. God, he shouldn't have let this happen. He should have done something more to protect the kid.

Dusty didn't respond.

"Can you hear me?" Sam asked.

A cough.

"Hey, yeah. You've got a tube in your throat. It's going to leave you with a sore throat. The doctor said they'd get it out tomorrow, but for right now you're stuck just having to listen to me."

Dusty's eyes searched Sam's. His brows wrinkled.

"Your mom and Savannah are on their way," Sam said, trying to reassure him. "They're okay. They'll be here in a few hours." Sam saw immediate relief on Dusty's face.

"You understood that, didn't you?"

Dusty gave a slight nod.

Sam closed his eyes and lowered his head. "I'm so sorry, buddy. I should have done something more to protect you."

Sam felt something on his thigh. He looked down to see an IV inserted into the vein on the top of Dusty's hand with several strips of tape across it. Dusty patted Sam's leg twice, and for a minute Sam thought he, tough-talking, mean-walking, hard-hearted Sam O'Brien, would burst into tears.

"Hey now." Sam stood and cleared his throat. "Before your mom gets here, I need to give you a lecture on the dos and don'ts of pretending to be Superman. I don't want to hear any mouth from you, and given the fact the doc's fixed it so you can't talk back, this is probably a good time."

Dusty lay still.

"Number one, Mr. Superman," Sam said. "When you get an urge to fly, always use an airplane." He paused. "You did good on that one. You were a great copilot, and I won't forget it. Whoever taught you did a good job." Sam smiled and saw a twinkle in Dusty's eyes.

"Number two," he continued. "When you get out of the airplane and have to pee, run like hell, particularly if there is a son of a bitch with a gun in his pocket standing next to you. Got it?"

One side of Dusty's lip curled, and he gave a slight nod and a wink. This worked better for Sam. He wanted to keep it light, avoid too much emotion.

"Now, number three, and this is maybe the most important of them all. When the Lone Ranger pulls you out of the way of gunfire . . . " Sam stopped in order to emphasize the next words: "STAY . . . OUT . . . OF . . . THE . . . WAY . . . OF . . . THE . . . GUNFIRE. Better yet, start running like you gotta pee."

Dusty coughed a bit. Sam couldn't tell whether Dusty was trying to laugh or not, but he feared he might be choking. He started to push the call button for a nurse, but Dusty settled and the coughing stopped. "You okay?" he asked. Dusty nodded.

Sam pulled the one chair up close to the bed and sat on the arm. Looking Dusty in the eye, he said, "Let me get to the most important rule of all, number four. This is the one you need some more practice on. If you decide that you really are willing to be Superman for the day—I mean really are absolutely sure that you've *got* to be Superman that day—then it's extremely important that you put on your bulletproof outfit. You see, when you jump in front of a bullet, especially one that's meant for someone else, then you've got to know that either that bullet can't hurt you or that someone else is worth more to you than your own life." Sam stopped. He blinked and looked up at the ceiling in order to control his voice. Damn it. He didn't want to cry.

Sam had hoped to sound upbeat and funny, but his heart was in his throat. How do you thank someone for saving your life, for caring about you so much that they're willing to throw themselves in front of a loaded gun? He stood up, bent toward Dusty, and said softly, "I don't know what I ever did to make you risk your life for me. That's the bravest thing I've ever seen anyone do."

❧

Sam felt as if Katy and Savannah would never get there. Dusty drifted in and out of sleep. Sam started to doze, but every footstep in the hall caused him to sit up and listen. Just before one in the morning, a nurse walked in. "We've received a call. Dusty's mother and sister have arrived at the airport. They're on their way now."

Sam waited for Katy and Savannah in the deserted lobby until the police car pulled up in front of the hospital. He couldn't remember when he'd wanted to hold two people any tighter. "Oh my God," he said as he embraced them both. "Are you okay? Did he hurt either of you?"

"I'm fine. We're fine," Katy said, obviously more concerned about Dusty than herself. "Where is he? Have you seen him?"

"I've been with him since he came out of surgery. He's sleeping now, but he knows you're coming. You should have seen his eyes light up when I told him."

"He's conscious, then? He recognized you?"

"He's going to be back to normal in no time," Sam assured her as they followed him up to the room. He turned to Savannah. "I'll bet you've been praying. I think it worked."

Savannah nodded. "Still praying," she said. "We left Daddy and a lot of incredibly brave people behind us. It's not over yet."

"Well, it's over for us," Sam said as he rounded the corner to the nurses' station. He looked at the nurse and the sign that limited visitors into the ICU. "All three of us together with him for just a few minutes. Would that be okay?"

The nurse acquiesced. "A few minutes, and then we'll have to follow the rules."

Katy led the way followed by Savannah and Sam. As if he could feel the energy of their presence, Dusty opened his eyes to see the three of them beside his bed. He tried to smile.

"Oh baby." Katy leaned down and kissed his forehead.

"Hey, hotshot," Savannah said as she swallowed the lump in her throat. "Did I ever tell you how much I love you?"

Dusty raised his free hand to take hers. He now had all the reasons he needed to return to Cedar Branch.

Olivia Cox arrived in the lobby of the hospital with a cameraman at 4:00 a.m. She had been on the phone with her reporter in Cedar Branch since Joe Wiseman arrived. Her colleague had already sent the footage to the Raleigh station. She remained committed to breaking the story that morning with an interview with Sam or Katy.

This story was a gold mine . . . so many questions to be answered that the public would clamor to get. She saw weeks of a leading story, maybe even a documentary.

The public still knew nothing about the hijacking of Sam O'Brien's plane and what happened on that flight. How the Devine brothers evaded capture for six weeks remained a mystery, and ultimately there would be the upcoming trial of Hank Devine with the distinct possibility that Joe Wiseman would be his new lawyer. She got goose bumps just thinking about it. This could go on for months. There might be an award attached for investigative reporting.

A security guard had spotted Olivia in the lobby. He recognized her immediately. Her face on the nightly news was unmistakable, as were her knockout good looks. "Miss Cox, I'm sorry. You're not allowed past the first floor."

"Are you telling me I can't be in the hospital?" Olivia bristled.

"No, ma'am, I'm simply saying you can't go on any of the patient floors. That restricts you to the first floor and the cafeteria. Perhaps you'd join me on my break for a cup of coffee?"

Olivia smiled and returned to the main lounge with her cameraman. At 6:00 a.m. the morning shift was changing over and the cafeteria had opened for breakfast. Sam appeared, poured himself a cup of coffee, and picked up a sweet roll. "Mr. O'Brien." Olivia had been watching the elevator and immediately crossed the room. She still had time before the seven o'clock morning news.

"Could I have a moment of your time, Mr. O'Brien?" she asked, microphone in hand.

Sam stepped back. He knew what she wanted before she opened her mouth. He just couldn't figure out how she'd found them so fast.

"Just one question, Mr. O'Brien." Olivia held the mic in front of him. "The whole state wants to know if Katy and her son and daughter are together at this moment?"

"They are," he said, nodding. "Can you tell me what's happening in Cedar Branch?"

Olivia looks surprised. Of course, how would he know? "It's all over," she said. "The hostages were all released. Hank Devine is in custody. It'll be on the morning news."

"Thanks. I'll watch," Sam said.

"I hope Dusty is doing okay." She was fishing, trying to get a confirmation or clarification out of Sam. She knew Katy and Savannah had walked away and Sam was standing in front of her. That left Dusty, and here they were in a hospital.

"He's doing fine," Sam said.

"You know, people around the country have been very concerned about your well-being and that of your sister and her family. Could I ask you about your flight from Cedar Branch to Sylvester?"

"Not now. I need to get back upstairs." Sam wrapped a napkin around his roll and walked over to the cashier to pay. Olivia followed him. "What happened, Mr. O'Brien? Would you give us some of the details?" she asked.

"Miss Cox," Sam said as he headed out of the cafeteria, "my sister is grateful to be with her two children at this moment. The police have already asked me not to talk to the press pending their investigations. That's really all I can say."

"Are you satisfied that the police did all they could do to protect your sister and her children?"

Sam picked up his pace and entered the main lobby.

Olivia tried to keep up. Sam stepped into the elevator.

"Just one more question. There's speculation that the court will appoint Joe Wiseman to be Hank Devine's new attorney. Mr. Wiseman is known for his ability to get reduced sentences for his clients. Do you think Hank Devine deserves a deal?"

Sam paused and stared at her for an uncomfortable minute. He grimaced, reached across to the panel, and punched the button for ICU. Olivia waited, her cameraman recording the moment in hopes of a reply. In the silence of the vacant hallway, the elevator doors closed.

QUESTIONS FOR DISCUSSION

1. Toward the end of the book, Nanette wonders, "Without the gun, would there have been the murder?" We can take this question back several layers. If not the violent childhood, would there have been the domestic abuse? If not the abuse, would there have been the affair? If not the affair, would there have been the murder? If not the murder, would there have been the lawsuit? If not the settlement, would there have been the kidnapping? If not the kidnapping, would there have been the standoff? Without the standoff, would there have been the shooting? Are these societal, judicial, or personal flaws?

2. Should Katy have resigned from her job? How do you think the school board should have responded to the knowledge of her affair? Should that response be applied equally to other employees? What are the laws in your state?

3. Teensy intervenes on Katy's behalf to send Ray on his way in a most combative manner. In doing so, she escalates the tension between Katy, herself, and Ray. Were her actions justified?

4. Katy receives an out-of-court settlement based on the affair that she had with Laura Attwuld's husband. Meanwhile, Laura Attwuld is threatened with a lawsuit that could potentially ruin her financially while she did nothing wrong. In your opinion, was the lawsuit justified?

5. Savannah longs to have a normal family. In hopes that her prayers might lead her parents to find redemption and forgiveness, she disobeys her mother, continues to meet with her Uncle Ray, and even skips school to visit her father in jail. Did she make the right choices?

6. Root doctors are fairly common in the Southeast, although they are not readily recognized by the general public. Some of their medicines are gathered from local herbs and roots to create tinctures similar to commercial items sold in stores. Others practice more traditional methods to confront the spirits that inflict pain and suffering. Are you aware of root doctors in your community? How would you know?

7. In an attempt to de-escalate a volatile situation, the Quakers decide to intervene by placing themselves between Hank and the law. In addition to putting more people in harm's way, they created a tremendous strain on law enforcement. Was this choice justified? Do you feel religious institutions have an obligation or right to place their moral convictions above the law? What alternatives might be used?

8. Could Sam have done more to protect Dusty? What?

9. Do you think law enforcement was at fault when Ray was killed and Dusty was caught in the cross fire?

10. Do you think Hank will get "a deal"? Does he deserve one? What would be fair in your opinion?

ACKNOWLEDGMENTS

I am extremely grateful to the Camden, South Carolina, critique group, which has coached me through two novels, three anthologies, and a memoir over the past seven years. These people deserve mention: Douglas Wyant, Jayne Bowers, Martha Greenway, Ari Dickinson, Mindy Blakely, Nick West, Sandy Richardson, Myra Yeatts, Bobbi Adams, and Paddy Bell. In particular, I wish to thank Kathryn Etters Lovatt, who has taken much of her personal time and used her professional skills to do a complete edit of my manuscript from beginning to end more than once. Her sharp mind catches inconsistencies in character development and plotline.

The following people have contributed information and insight into several aspects of my story, ranging from airplanes, turkeys, and guns to the insides of courthouses and jails: Nicholas Remmes, Jeff Feinstein, Bill Jones, Pat Lampe, Ross Rusch, Sergio Sanchez, Dick Dabbs, George McFaddin, Jack Warmack, and Charles Slade. I am grateful to Gene Bennett for the afternoon on his farm in North Carolina and to Amanda and Joe Jones for the tour of Doko Farms in South Carolina. I also spent a delightful morning with Jim and EveVonne Muff and Rolly Laubscher around a very large breakfast table with other farmers in Arion, Iowa. They entertained me with enough stories for more novels to come, but I won't turn down another opportunity for a meal if I'm ever invited again.

I wish to thank Vernie Davis, a retired professor in the Conflict Analysis Department at Guilford College in Greensboro, NC, who discussed hostage negotiations with me. He has not yet read what I wrote, and I admit that I strayed somewhat from his recommendations. If you need a hostage mediator at any time, I recommend you call Vernie, not me.

To my husband, Bill Remmes, my mother, Louise Bevan, and my very good friend Pam Slade, I appreciate your never-ending editing and support. They keep me strong. I feel very fortunate to have Catherine Drayton at Inkwell Management as my agent. She reads every word that I send her and gives me honest and straightforward feedback on my strengths and weaknesses. I would be lost without her.

To Jenna Free, who compared herself to a dental hygienist when it comes to editing manuscripts, I appreciate the good cleaning job. To the mysterious copy editors, Renee and Kirsten, who have obviously memorized the *Chicago Manual of Style*, 16th edition (CMS), I stand in awe. I am indebted to my editor, Danielle Marshall at Lake Union Publishing, and her author team. I mention Gabriella Van den Heuvel, Thom Kephart, and Jessica Poore, knowing that there are undoubtedly countless others working behind the scene whom I don't know. They have been enthusiastic in promoting my work from the beginning. I am most grateful. I feel in very good hands. Thank you all.

ABOUT THE AUTHOR

Brenda Bevan Remmes has spent her career in health care education as adjunct faculty with the medical schools at the University of North Carolina–Chapel Hill and the University of South Carolina–Columbia. Her stories and articles have appeared in *Newsweek* and Southern publications and journals, and her first novel, *The Quaker Café*, was published in 2014. Remmes is a longtime member of the Religious Society of Friends (Conservative) of North Carolina. She lives with her husband near the Black River Swamp in South Carolina.